er family on a fa...
...eighbo... ...n all directions are members of a
... When she's not homeschooling
...ssons, or tending to a menagerie
..., chickens, ducks, rabbits, dogs,
...g up her next romantic novel.
...readers.

...annhopkinsfiction.com

...om/karenannhopkins
...k.com/temptationbook
...am.com/karenannhopkins

Y0353

D1485307

WILLOW CREEK

KAREN ANN HOPKINS

One More Chapter
a division of HarperCollins*Publishers* Ltd
1 London Bridge Street
London SE1 9GF
www.harpercollins.co.uk

This paperback edition 2020
First published in Great Britain in ebook format
by HarperCollins*Publishers* 2020

A catalogue record of this book is available from the British Library

ISBN: 978-0-00-843185-3

Printed and bound in Great Britain by
CPI Group (UK) Ltd, Croydon CR0 4YY

Dedicated in memory of my mother.

You were my number one advocate, loved me unconditionally, and were my best friend. You were a beautiful woman, inside and out, a wonderful mother, and the best grandma ever. You're reunited with Dad, and that makes me happy. I will think of you every day until we meet again.

Marilyn Norma Lanzalaco
11/13/1937 ~ 12/17/19

Prologue

October 2014

Willow Creek Amish Settlement, Indiana

Katie dodged the sheets of pouring rain, her boots splashing with each stride she took. A dazzling claw of lightning streaked across the sky as she grabbed for Dusty's reins. The strawberry roan mare jumped sideways just as the crack of thunder rolled across the wet field. Katie's fingers closed tightly around the reins. Though snapped upright and dragged a dozen feet, she didn't dare let go.

"Shh, girl. It's all right. Just a silly storm. No need to pitch a fit," Katie murmured through trembling lips. Her hip and thigh throbbed with pain, and a glance downward confirmed her entire right side was plastered with mud.

Dusty threw her head up higher and when the sky lit up again, her eyes widened in fear, exposing their whites. Katie held on, moving with the horse the best she could and trying hard not to lose her own footing. The countryside was a glistening, fuzzy picture of tall grass, trees, and dark, angry clouds. She could barely see through the splattering raindrops pelting her face and stinging her eyes. Even though her sight was compromised and the storm raged in her ears, she still managed to catch a glimpse of an approaching horse.

Katie grunted in surprise. *Of all the people in the world, it had to be him*, she thought in surprised disgust. She dropped her head to avoid looking directly at the boy as he jumped down from his bay horse.

"Are you hurt?" Rowan shouted above the wind, his voice concerned as his gaze skimmed over her.

Before Katie had a chance to reply, the boy tossed his horse's reins to her and grabbed onto Dusty's.

"Whoa, girl, whoa," Rowan cooed to the frightened horse. He was a few inches taller than Katie, and even though he had a slim, wiry build, he was still stronger than she was. Between his coaxing voice and steady hands, the horse settled into a quivering standstill. "Go on and ride Scout back to the barn. I'll take the mare."

The downpour subsided, leaving only spattering

raindrops in its wake. Katie's cheeks flamed hot and she narrowed her gaze at Rowan. "I don't think that's a good idea. Dusty started bucking when the storm hit. It's not safe to ride her."

The corner of Rowan's mouth twitched, then lifted a little. His usually stoic dark eyes twinkled, as if he'd just heard something funny, but was trying hard not to laugh out loud. He didn't seem to notice the flashes of light or the battering wind. He stared back at Katie with the challenging look of an arrogant boy.

Katie's mouth dropped open and bubbles rose in her chest. At that moment, she both hated Rowan Coblentz and admired him greatly.

A jagged finger of lightning hit the ground not far away, splitting the air with a deafening crack. Hot tingles ran up through the girl's boots, along her body, and straight into her hair. Scout took a step back, but remained calm. Before Dusty could bolt, Rowan swung into the saddle. He was one with the horse when she crow-hopped, kicking out. The confident grin didn't leave his face as he expertly moved with Dusty, guiding her into a sideways trot.

"Come on! We don't want to get struck by lightning," Rowan urged, losing some of his annoying smile. His brows lifted questioningly when Katie didn't immediately move.

Katie was certain he'd wait there all day in the raging

storm, just to prove the point that he wasn't afraid. She wiped the water from her eyes with her arm and lifted her foot to the stirrup. She flung her leg over and grasped the horse's sides with her legs. She dug in her heels and hung on, leaving Rowan behind without even bothering to look back.

Dusty's heavy breathing reached Katie's ears and she glanced over her shoulder to see the roan horse galloping a few lengths behind her.

They raced through the grass and didn't slow when they turned onto the narrow path that went through the woods. Katie leaned forward as the fallen log came into view. Scout jumped the obstacle without losing stride. Katie pulled back on the reins just enough to watch Dusty also glide over the log. She had to admit that Rowan was an excellent rider, but only grudgingly so. Her evil side still wished Rowan would get tossed into the mud the same way she had.

By the time they slid to a stop in front of the training barn, the wind had died down to a stiff breeze and the rain had all but stopped. A shard of sunlight broke through the clouds as the storm moved away to the west.

Katie lowered herself slowly from Scout's back, bracing her muscles as she gingerly stepped down onto her sore leg. She glanced sideways, watching Rowan dismount effortlessly. His dark brown hair was a little too long in front and he shook the wet locks to clear his vision. The suspenders over his shoulders drew her eyes, reminding her that he was her Amish neighbor – a boy who had been working at the ranch for almost a year, but who had only spoken to her a handful of times. Her father had hired him to exercise the horses and clean out the stalls. The kid took his job very seriously and didn't make time for small talk with Katie. Today was probably the most he'd ever said to her at one time.

Rowan's sudden loosening up intrigued Katie. They were both sixteen years old. *Why shouldn't we be friends?* Fixing her gaze on him, she noticed his high cheekbones and full lips. His nose curved ever so slightly and his brown eyes were wide and curious. He pinned her with a steady gaze and one cocked brow. She answered her own question. *Because he's gorgeous and my knees go weak when he looks at me.*

"How did you know I fell off?" she asked pointedly, looking past him and hoping he didn't notice the slight tremor that shook her. She handed Rowan Scout's reins and took Dusty's from him.

His cheeks darkened a shade and he sniffed, shifting his weight between his feet. It struck Katie as odd that he wasn't as bold on the ground as he was when sitting on the back of a horse.

He drew in a sharp breath. "I didn't, but I noticed how high stepping Dusty was when you left the barn with her. She sensed the coming storm, and so did I."

5

Katie squinted at Rowan's face. "So you came to my rescue?"

Rowan's blush deepened and he dug the toe of his boot into a clump of mud. "You're a good rider and all"—he shrugged—"but no match for that mare on a day like this."

Katie's mouth gaped open. She wanted to knock the smug look off his cute face. She raised her hand, pointing at Rowan's chest, but before she could set him straight, he reached for her elbow and said, "You're bleeding."

Distracted by his touch and the worried look on his face, Katie followed his gaze. Rowan was right. Blood dribbled from an inch-long gash on her arm.

"Does it hurt?" Rowan asked.

Until he pointed it out, she hadn't felt any pain. Now, as she watched the dark liquid pool in the wound, it began to throb. A rush of dizziness hit Katie like a wall, and she wobbled on suddenly jelly-like legs.

Rowan's arm snaked out and firmly grasped her side. With his free hand, he quickly looped Scout's reins around the hitching rail, and then tied Dusty the same efficient way. Katie let Rowan slip his arm around her waist without argument and guide her out of the brisk air and into the dim, quiet stable.

She worked up a weak smile. "I don't know what's wrong with me. Blood never bothered me before."

Rowan helped her onto the nearest bale of hay and

stepped back, appraising her with a cocked head and a frown. "You came off your horse in the middle of a downpour, jumped back on Scout, and galloped home." He lifted his brow and Katie saw admiration shine in his eyes. "It took a toll on you." His mouth lifted into a grin. "Or maybe it's the sight of blood that got you. I remember when my sister, Rebecca, fainted the first time she helped me and Da butcher a steer."

Katie swallowed down the acid that burned her throat as the image of the poor cow appeared in her mind.

"Don't talk."

She shook her head.

Rowan spun on his heels and sprinted down the aisle, and Katie's head snapped back up to watch him go. Several stalled horses shied back when he rushed by. He turned into the tack room, disappearing for less than a minute. When he emerged, he held the first-aid kit in his hands. He jogged back at a slower pace than he'd left and Katie reclined against the wall, considering him.

When Katie had first laid eyes on Rowan the previous year, she'd immediately developed a secret crush. She appreciated his serious demeanor, and he brought that same quiet reserve into the saddle when he rode the horses. Over time, his aloofness had annoyed her. He'd move about the barn silently, and she was never successful at luring him into conversation or any kind of playful banter. He'd all but ignored her for months, and she'd finally given up hope of any kind of relationship with Rowan Coblentz.

Katie's stomach clenched with discomfort that she'd been stupid enough to be smitten with someone who usually didn't even acknowledge her existence. She snorted. "Now you're a doctor?"

Rowan ignored her, opening the kit and pulling out a wad of gauze and the medical tape. "Not much different than bandaging a horse, I reckon." He glanced up and there was a brightness in the brown depths Katie had never seen before. "Not that I'm comparing you to a horse or anything."

She smiled reluctantly and held out her arm like a dutiful patient. It was an awkward place for Katie to bandage herself, she reasoned in her mind – and if she pulled her brand-new hoodie on to keep from shivering, she'd get it all bloody. She didn't want that to happen, either.

Rowan's questioning gaze met hers. When Katie nodded once with her lips tightly pressed together, a soft flicker of surprise lit his face. He quickly recovered and went straight to work on her elbow. He applied the antiseptic wipe, dabbing the cut carefully. Then he squeezed some antibiotic ointment onto the bandage and covered the wound.

He sat back, balancing on the balls of his feet. "How's that feel?"

Katie gingerly pressed the bandage with her fingertips and then flexed her elbow. She found the confidence to look up and saw him waiting. His lips turned down slightly and his anxious expression caused a million needle pricks in Katie's belly.

"You did a good job." She swallowed, forcing her eyes to meet his. "I guess all your practice on the horses has given you some people-doctoring skills, too."

He broke out in a grin. "You're my first patient."

His smile was contagious and Katie finally relaxed. She liked his warm brown eyes, and his lips were curved and playful. Rowan was awfully close – maybe too close. She caught the scent of horse hair, leather, and sweet hay and breathed in deeply, swaying slightly closer. Her cheeks warmed and she exhaled.

Something changed in him at that moment. His brow crinkled and his eyes widened for a second, and then the moment of confusion was gone. It was replaced by the hungry look of anticipation.

It happened so quickly, Katie didn't have a chance to pull back when Rowan's lips carefully touched hers. Her mind froze in shock, but also pleasure. The last thing she expected was to be kissed, but even though she should have been offended by his presumption that she wanted to be kissed, she wasn't. He was the first boy who had even tried. Most of her friends had gotten their first kisses out of the way by the time they were fourteen, and here Katie was, a sixteen-year-old who'd not only never had a boyfriend, but who had never been kissed. Up until now, she hadn't really fretted about it. But the thrill of having it over with, coupled with the fact that the boy kissing her was a real cutie, made her sag against Rowan and open her mouth wider to allow his tongue access.

Thoughts slipped away. A small groan escaped his lips and she sighed into his mouth. Her knees dropped to his sides and Rowan took advantage of the opening to slide in closer. His arms encircled her and his fingers dug into the small of her back. Katie could feel the heat seeping through her bones and the weight of his arms around her shoulders was already familiar.

Suddenly, he broke from the kiss, pulling back a few inches. His eyes were wild.

"I like you, Katie. I've liked you for a long time," he said with a rasp.

Rowan's change of behavior was startling, but Katie wasn't disappointed by his unexpected display of affection. As a matter of fact, she welcomed it. The reality that he was Amish and she wasn't was only a tiny pestering jolt at the back of her mind.

Fearing that she might say something stupid, she ignored his words altogether. She slipped her hand behind his head, spread her fingers into his thick hair, and pulled his face back to hers.

Their mouths had barely touched when a voice boomed, "What's going on here?"

Rowan jumped away from Katie as if he'd been stunned with a cattle prod. His back snapped straight and he faced her father.

"I'm sorry, sir, it's not what it appears to be—"

Charlie Porter was a large man. He wore his usual button-down flannel shirt, blue jeans, and a ball cap. His blue eyes flashed as he strode forward and loomed over Rowan. "I wasn't born yesterday, boy. It is what it is."

His steady, calm voice didn't deceive his daughter. Anger practically puffed off her dad, causing Katie to jump to her feet and take the two steps to Rowan's side. "It's nothing, Daddy. Rowan bandaged my arm." She lifted her injured elbow and waved it back and forth. "See? I fell off Dusty and gouged it. Rowan was just helping me take care of the wound. That's all."

Her dad's gaze rested on Katie for only a few seconds. She thought she saw a glimmer of sadness in his eyes before he returned them to Rowan. His voice was still under simmering control when he spoke.

"I hired you with reservations. I thought having a teenage boy around here would be trouble, but I owed your father a favor and took you on with strong misgivings. I see I was right to worry." He jabbed his finger at Rowan and she honestly feared for the boy. "I warned you to stay away from my daughter. Simple thing to do, and you promised you would."

"I'm sorry—" Rowan rushed the words out. He tried to say more, but her dad interrupted him again.

"How long has this been going on?" Charlie glanced between Katie and Rowan.

"Today was the first time, Daddy. It's not a big a deal, really—"

"Go to the house, Katie." His mouth was drawn into a tight line and his cheeks were flushed with anger.

She opened her mouth to protest and her dad bellowed, "Now!"

Charlie was a temperamental man. His shout sent shivers shooting down her spine, and she glanced sideways to find that Rowan wasn't looking at her. His chin was raised defiantly at her dad and his eyes were stony.

Almost as if Katie had been physically pushed, she stepped away. Tears blurred her vision. She hardly knew Rowan, and the kisses they'd just shared were probably insignificant to most people. Whatever connection had sprung sweetly to life only moments before snapped, leaving Katie feeling sick.

She jogged through the doorway and stopped, hesitating. Cool wind dried her cheeks and she strained to listen.

"Don't come back here ever again, Rowan. You can tell your father whatever you want, but I don't want to hear from him either. Do you understand?"

"Yes, sir. I won't be back."

The finality of Rowan's words caused Katie's insides to twist in knots. She whirled around and sprinted toward the house.

With a sinking feeling, Katie slowed and turned to look back at the barn. *Daddy ordered Rowan not to talk to me a long time ago. It all finally makes sense...*

Rowan untied Scout from the hitching rail and mounted swiftly. Without looking in Katie's direction, he kicked his horse into a canter. There was only the sound of hoofbeats striking the driveway as he rode away.

Katie's mind was fuzzy for a moment. When her vision cleared, she was crying.

She sucked in a quivering breath, and vowed that she didn't care if her dad ever changed his mind about Rowan. Katie never wanted to see the Amish boy again.

ONE

Katie

October 2020

Willow Creek Amish Settlement, Indiana

My sight blurred as I stared at the ledger. I finally lifted my gaze to the open window, watching the gold and red leaves sprinkling down from the old maple tree in front of the house. After rubbing my eyes, I thumped my coffee mug on the table.

"Stop it, Katie. Your fidgeting is going to be the death of me." Momma's voice wavered from behind the mug of steaming liquid held to her lips.

"It's hopeless." I slouched, dropping my head back with a grunt. "The money coming in doesn't equal the money going out."

"So what's your answer, then? Sell the ranch?" Momma said it in a casual way, but I wasn't fooled. The color had drained from her tanned face and her lips thinned.

A horse whinnied and my gaze was drawn back out the window. The countryside was awash in fall splendor, but there was a hint of chill in the air that hadn't been there the day before. I breathed in the crisp breeze fluttering the gingham curtain. It carried with it the scent of rotting foliage and damp dirt. Winter was on its way. We had thirty-eight horses and nearly one hundred head of cattle to feed.

"I can train the two-year-olds and have them ready to go by the December sale."

Momma blasted out a loud snort. "How can you do that with your arm in a sling?" She leaned back, shaking her head. "Better to cut our losses and sell them now, while they're still fat and looking good. In a few months we won't be able to feed them. It's the right thing to do."

I rubbed my face and pain throbbed in my forehead. I knew my eyes were bloodshot from too little sleep the night before. "If we don't make some decent money on those horses, we won't be able to pay the mortgage." I regretted raising my voice when I saw Momma flinch.

"I was such a fool. I trusted your father to take care of things." She rose from the table, knocking the chair backwards with her sudden movement. "But he was squandering our hard-earned money on that"—she took a gulp and my heart burst for her—"that woman. Now he's gone because of her."

I slid around the table and grabbed hold of Momma with my good arm without remembering the action to get there. Momma's gentle sobs rocked against me. "It's all right. I'll figure it out. Why don't you go lie down? You should rest."

Momma pulled back, wiping her eyes and sucking in wet breaths. "You're only twenty-two. This responsibility shouldn't fall on you. I need to be stronger."

I gave her a pat on the shoulder. "You've been through so much. It's okay to take it easy for a few days and catch your breath. We have until the end of the month to come up with a plan. I can take on more hours at the restaurant, and—"

She raised her hand to silence me. "You're already working seven days a week as it is." Her eyes watered and she swallowed hard, softening her voice. "You must prepare yourself, Katie. We're going to lose the ranch." Her features hardened and she drew herself up taller. A wisp of faded red hair, streaked with gray, fell over her eye and she brushed it aside. She was in her late fifties, but her skin was still smooth, the only wrinkles on her face being at the corners of her eyes from smiling all the time. Momma was a beautiful, vibrant woman. It made it even more difficult to understand why Daddy had done what he had.

"I'm not giving up hope." Mom's brows shot up and I quickly added, "At least not until the end of the month. Give me a few weeks to fix this." Stupid tears filled my eyes and I blinked them away. "This is our home. There has to be a way to stop the foreclosure."

"Unless we have some rich relative that I don't know about who's going to pay the back payments and taxes, I don't see a way out of this mess. But I won't keep you from trying, my girl. You're a stubborn one, and it will eat you alive if you don't at least give it your best shot." She reached out and cupped my cheek. "Just don't be too hard on yourself. This isn't your fault. It's *his*." She hissed the last word out and turned away. She walked slowly, slouched over, to the doorway. "I'm going to take your advice and close my eyes for a little while. Wake me if you need anything." She glanced over her shoulder. "Do whatever you think is best, Katie. I'm leaving the decision-making up to you. I'm in no state of mind to run things at the moment."

She disappeared into the hallway and I sagged into the nearest chair. Lady pushed her nose into my leg and I reached down to rub the dog's shaggy black head. Her little whine made my heartrate speed up. It wasn't just Momma and me losing our home; our horses and the rest of the animals would be homeless too.

Life had changed so much in the six days since the accident. A week ago, I had no idea that we were four months behind on the mortgage payments, and also owed the IRS last year's taxes. I was blissfully unaware that my daddy was having an affair, and that he was secretly blowing all his income on a woman who wasn't much older than me.

My stomach rolled and the inside of my mouth became thick and dry at the sick visions that rose up before me. The images had pestered me for days, and I inhaled deeply and exhaled slowly in an attempt to cleanse my mind. Momma's health was nagging me, too. She had multiple sclerosis and the stress of all this could definitely bring on a relapse.

Drastic times called for drastic measures.

I reached across the table and snatched my cellphone up. Before I could change my mind, I searched for the number and hit the call icon.

Sitting back into the chair, I closed my eyes and said a silent prayer that I was doing the right thing.

TWO

Rowan

I pushed the hat back and ran my fingers through my sweaty hair, staring at Scout's forelock. There were gray hairs mixed in with the brown ones, and it struck me for the first time that the gelding was getting old. I frowned at the horse, trying my best not to look at my sister, who was sitting on the bale of straw in front of Scout's stall. She cradled her head in her hands and occasionally she sniffed or mumbled something.

I closed my eyes, remembering happier times. When we were little kids, Rebecca would ride her pony beside me, her chin held high and her eyes laughing. Back then she was my shadow, following me around like an eager puppy. Sometime between then and the past few years, she'd changed. Her carefree spirit had darkened and her laughter had stopped. She never smiled anymore and most of the time she sulked about, quietly murmuring to herself. Occasionally Rebecca's eyes cleared and a small light sparked in those pale depths. Those times were the worst. That was when she became jittery and defiant; that was when she'd fight with Father and Mother.

I dropped onto the straw beside her and thudded my head back against the wooden boards. "Why do you do this to yourself?" I asked, unable to keep the annoyance from my voice. I had worked all day with the building crew and now there were four horses waiting to be shod. The sun had dipped beyond the horizon and the air was still and hazy. It would be a miracle if I finished all the horses before darkness fell. And without lights in the barn, that meant an extra early morning the following day.

Rebecca sat up. She dabbed at her eyes with a handkerchief and then stared back at me with a furrowed brow. Her skin was drawn tightly over her face, and it suddenly occurred to me that she'd lost weight. Her eyes and cheeks were hollow and she was rail thin. In recent days her mood swings had become more severe, and I'd tried avoiding her. It was just too difficult to see my sister withering away and losing her mind at the same time.

The doe-eyed look she shot at me created a sinking feeling in my heart. I rubbed my hands together. "I'm not being mean. Mother and Father just want what's best for you. You should listen to them and take their counsel," I urged.

Rebecca's eyes narrowed and she leaned in. "They're wrong, Rowan. They think they know what's best for me but they don't. They're selfish and want to make me like them. I'm not the same." Her voice came out in a wet whistling sound.

I licked my lips. "Of course, you are. You and I are Amish, just like our parents and everyone else in the community. You're going through a rough patch. It will pass in time, and you'll see the light."

Rebecca's eyes widened to saucer size and the side of her mouth rose into a sharp smirk. "That's what you all wish, but it's not going to happen. I have a sinful heart, brother, and you know it. I can't follow the rules anymore. I don't even believe in the minister's teachings. I can't pretend any longer to be something I'm not."

I swiveled my head, scanning the barn's hallway warily. When I saw that the coast was clear, I lowered my voice to an urgent whisper. "Don't say such crazy things. You don't have anywhere to go. You'd never survive as an Englisher."

"How do you know that? I couldn't be much worse off than I am right now." She adjusted her white cap, pressing a pin down sharply on her head. I winced; it looked painful. "Jessica said there's medications available that would help me feel better and you know that's not an option if I stay here."

I shook my head. "Jessica is just a driver. What makes her an expert on such things?"

Rebecca let out a small grunt. "Her sister suffers from depression and some other things. She thinks I might have the same problems."

"You shouldn't listen to her. She's just trying to corrupt you into running away." I looked around again to make sure no one had snuck up on us. When I returned my attention to Rebecca, she was staring straight ahead with pursed lips. "Don't you remember what happened to Lucinda when she went English?" Rebecca took a shallow breath but otherwise didn't respond, so I plowed on. "She got mixed up with a man who did drugs and he got her hooked on them too. She was pregnant and homeless within a few months."

"She killed herself. Tied a couple of sheets together and hanged herself off the back porch of the rundown rental she was living in." Rebecca's tone was lifeless, as if she was reading from a boring book. She continued to stare straight ahead.

My chest constricted painfully. Before I had a chance to chastise her callous words, she turned and sputtered, "It didn't have to be that way for Lucinda. If her family had supported her, she might have gotten the aid she needed..." Rebecca trailed off and began quietly humming. She pushed the dirt around with her black tennis shoe as what she had said settled on the quiet, dusty air.

Did my younger sister think she would end up like poor Lucinda? Was she threatening to run away or maybe even kill herself? Was she crying out for help and no one was listening?

I swallowed down the uncomfortable knot growing in my throat. It wasn't easy being Amish. Temptations from the outside world were always present. Things like driving cars, going to the movies, listening to music, and even wearing modern clothes, were off limits to us. It was worse when we were teenagers. When the English kids were learning to drive and hanging out unchaperoned, we were sneaking out behind the barn after our parents were in bed to play games and listen to music on our secretly purchased cellphones. The lack of freedom caused many of us to rebel against the elders in even more serious ways. Some kids fancied the English ways and fell in with the wrong kinds of people. They drank alcohol, did drugs, and other things that were strictly forbidden for our people. Sometimes they were discovered and punished severely or even shunned by the community for an extended period of time. Other times they escaped that reckless time without anyone being the wiser.

Our community was even tougher than some others when it came to the number of rules we had to abide by. Our teenagers didn't get the opportunity to experience Rumspringa, either. The short period of relative freedom that some communities let their young people celebrate helped many decide which way they wanted to go – Amish or English. The Willow Creek settlement had decided long ago that allowing their teenagers to run amuck was a recipe for disaster and a threat to growing the population of the community. Sure, back in those days even I resented the harsh rules we lived by, but over time my restless heart had steadied and I had realized there were good reasons for the authority. For me, it all became shockingly clear when one of my closest childhood friends, Abe Schrock, snuck out one night with an English girl he was sweet on. She picked him up in her dented little red car and they went somewhere to fool around and drink beer. The girl was drunk when she drove Abe back to his farm. It had been raining all day and she slid off a slick road into a telephone pole. The car had been traveling at a very high speed – at least that's what the police officer told the bishop the next morning. The officer also said that both teenagers had probably died instantly. It wasn't long afterwards that word reached the community that Lucinda had committed suicide. Both incidents had dulled my desire to leave the Amish and most of the other kids my age felt the same way. The outside world was a dangerous place. I was content to farm the land, just like Da, and live a simpler life.

Rebecca was a few years younger than me. She hadn't experienced the jolt of losing a friend to bad judgment. Lucinda's death was only a hazy, dreamlike event to my little sister. Rebecca seemed more intent on idolizing the troubled young woman for having had the courage to leave, rather than actually pondering what had really happened to her out in the world.

Glancing down at Rebecca's head, I forced myself to really look at her. She bobbed up and down nervously and her sniffs were the only sounds in the ever-darkening barn. Rebecca's body was wasting away, and her soul was lost and lonely.

"Ma and Da are coming ... and the bishop is with them!"

Our heads snapped up in the direction of the fearful voice. Nathaniel stood in the doorway. He was out of breath and his cheeks were red. Our little brother was only fourteen, but he was already tall for his age. People said he favored me with his dark hair and eyes, but he was a dreamy kid, like our sister. I was more likely to find him reading a book under the willow tree than doing his chores. He was trustworthy though, and the warning look on his face made me jump to my feet.

Rebecca didn't move; she simply clasped her arms around her frail body and rocked back and forth.

"Nathaniel, take the trash down to the road," Father bellowed when he came around the corner. Nathaniel didn't move quickly enough and Father swiped the air in between them for emphasis, getting my brother's legs moving in a hurry.

I strode after Nathaniel but Father grasped my arm. "You can stay, Rowan. You're a man now. This is community business and you need to learn the way things work."

Anger flared within me. "I thought it was a family matter." I glanced at Ma but saw no support in her pinched face.

Bishop Elijah Graber stepped forward. He glanced between me and my sister. He was shorter than me and thickly built. His beard was as rough-looking as his hair. Elijah's round face was always ruddy and his eyes were unfailingly alert. As a child, he had reminded me of a plump fox, and now that I was an adult, I still found it to be a good comparison. The bishop wasn't an imposing man, but somehow he managed to intimidate people with his quick and cunning mind. The fact that he was taking an interest in my sister's problems was a real concern – and I had no doubt it *was* Rebecca he had come to see.

Bishop Graber smoothed his black beard down. It was

largely peppered with gray hairs, matching his bushy eyebrows. "When our young people rebel, it becomes community business," he said softly and very matter-of-factly.

I saw emotion flare in Rebecca's face and then settle as her features slowly became expressionless. Anger bubbled to the surface as I turned back to the bishop. "My sister's issues are not rebellion." I glanced at Ma. "Please explain her situation to Elijah," I begged.

Ma's face twitched in disapproval. "Your father and I asked Elijah to come. As our bishop and an elder in our church, Rebecca needs his guidance."

I rolled my eyes and looked away when I caught the bishop's gaze narrow at me. I didn't want his attention.

"What do you want of me?" Rebecca's quiet question turned all our heads.

The bishop took the few steps needed to face Rebecca. He tilted his head as Rebecca looked up. "You'll meet with me and the other ministers on Wednesday afternoons. We'll read the Bible together and discuss how you can fit into the community better by making friends and becoming more involved in the women's activities."

Rebecca nodded passively. She stood and forced a smile, saying, "Thank you for thinking of me. I look forward to our meetings." She searched our parents' faces as they stood stoically, side by side. "If you'll excuse me, I'll go close up the chicken coop."

Father raised his gaze to the bishop and received a curt nod in return. "You may go."

Rebecca scurried out of the barn, shooting me a quick look as she passed by. The sour expression on her pale face caused a lump to form again in my throat.

When Rebecca was gone, Ma turned back to the bishop. "Thank you for doing this, Elijah. I only hope your guidance will put that girl on the right path."

The bishop tipped his hat at me and then strode for the doorway. "Only time will tell. Some young'uns need a little coaxing, while others are impossible to reform. I'd hate for you to lose your daughter if it turns out she's the latter."

Mother and Father hurried after the bishop into the darkness without giving me another glance. A bird made a shrill call as it settled down for the night in a nearby tree and a cow bellowed in the lower field. I removed my hat, wiping the sweat from my brow. Cool wind brushed my face when I leaned against the doorframe, watching the bishop untie his horse and climb into his buggy. The sound of my parents' goodbyes were muffled, and I ignored their voices and the *clip clops* of the hooves on the driveway. The memory of Rebecca's bewildered face hammered a place in my head. A sort of foreboding chill raced up my spine and I grunted.

My parents were trying to do what they thought was best for Rebecca, but they were mistaken to think Bible classes with the ministers and lecturing from the bishop would make any difference whatsoever. Rebecca couldn't be fixed in the way they wished. As much as I hated to admit it, even to myself, she had serious problems that required a professional's help – and she would never get that kind of aid if she stayed with the Amish.

Somehow, I had to get her out. But how? It would require a decent amount of money to spirit her away to one of our distant English relatives in Pennsylvania. I had some savings, but I gave much of my earnings back to Father to help pay for the farm expenses. Father had promised to deed me the bottom land acres along the river if I contributed my income for another year, but that left me short on money most days. Now I was twenty-two, Mother was pushing me to begin seriously courting, and she even had a girl or two in mind. I could hardly argue with her on that matter. I felt the itch to settle down on my own land and start a family with a good woman. Unfortunately, up until now, none of the girls had struck my fancy – at least no one in the community. There had only been one girl who had quickened my heart, but she was English, and that was a very long time ago.

Still, more often than I liked, a certain face came to mind. I shut my eyes and let the memory flood in.

It was an overcast, rainy day, and the girl's blue eyes shone brightly from her round, fresh face. Wisps of red hair escaped her ponytail and she kept pushing her hair back behind her ears in annoyed movements. A light smattering of freckles splashed her straight nose and over her pink cheeks. She walked with confident, ground-covering strides that reminded me of a prancing filly on a springtime pasture. This special girl liked to talk about horses and the books she was reading, and often there was a thoughtful, far-off look on her face.

I opened my eyes, shaking the memory away. That was six years ago, and the girl was a grown woman now. I had only caught glimpses of her here and there in all these years, but still, she was never far from my mind. I resented the strange, invisible hold she had on me. We'd kissed a couple times in the span of a few minutes, and that was all. It was the most exciting thing that ever happened to me, but if I was going to be a good husband, I had to let go of the dreams I had for a woman I could never have.

The simple truth was, thoughts about the English girl made me happy. How I had wanted that girl – and I still did.

For now, my main concern was figuring out a way to raise some extra money to save my sister. I scratched my chin, staring up at the stars that began appearing in the dark sky.

"Please, Lord, provide me with the means to take Rebecca to the English world, if it be your will," I whispered.

The telephone rang and the loud bell made me jump. I ran across the barnyard to the shed where the phone was kept, searching down the lane to see if anyone else was coming. I was alone when I threw open the door and grabbed the receiver off the hook.

"Hello," I said into the phone.

There was a long pause, and I repeated myself.

"Is this Rowan Coblentz?" a female asked.

I held my breath. Something about the pensive voice made my heart pound.

"Yes, yes, it is. May I ask who's calling?"

There were a few more seconds of silence. Just when I was about to speak, she finally answered.

"It's Katie Porter. You probably don't remember me. I live up here at Diamond E. You worked at the ranch some years ago. Would you be interested in breaking a string of colts for us?"

Her words were rushed and anxious but they were music to my ears. I couldn't keep the grin from my face when I glanced up at the stars and mouthed a thank you to the Lord for answering my prayer so quickly – and in more ways than one.

I cleared my throat and worked hard to keep the excitement from my voice. I hesitated, gripping the receiver tightly. "What about your father? Is he all right with me lending a hand? The last time I spoke with him, he made it quite clear he didn't want me around anymore."

I couldn't stop myself from heating uncomfortably. Thoughts that I'd tried to keep bottled up, and which had kept me up many nights, came flooding back in. I remembered Katie's plump lips moving against mine, and the warm, vanilla scent of her skin.

"Daddy's dead. Momma and I are running things now," Katie said bluntly.

I stood up straighter and my mind cleared as if it had been slapped. "I hadn't heard. I'm so sorry—"

"Don't be," she snapped. "Can you break the colts or not?"

Her tone was unmistakably hostile, and as the shock settled in the pit of my stomach, I quickly responded, "Of course. I can be there tomorrow evening if that works for you."

"It does. Meet me in the training barn at seven o'clock," she instructed and then she was gone.

We hadn't even discussed payment, but I didn't care. I hung up the telephone and replaced my hat.

Any extra money at all would help Rebecca and I'd finally get to talk to Katie Porter again. Maybe she was nothing like I remembered and had grown into a nasty shrew but I doubted it. I guessed she'd blossomed from a pretty teenager into a beautiful young woman.

The girl who'd been nothing but a fantasy in my

mind for so long was about to become reality. That realization both terrified and excited me in ways I should have been ashamed of.

As I walked toward the house, I whistled an unnamed tune, thinking, *God has one hell of a sense of humor.*

THREE

Katie

The bay horse tied to the hitching rail swung his head my way and nickered. I instantly recognized the white star in the center of his forehead and the bushy black mane and tail. It was Scout – the same gelding that had carried me back to the barn that stormy day six years ago. I reached out and touched the gelding's velvety nose and murmured, "Hello, handsome." I didn't linger at the rail. My heart jumped and my legs felt weak. I tightened my ponytail with a tug and let out a breath as I stepped into the dim interior of the training barn. My eyes adjusted and I quickly found who I was looking for.

Rowan Coblentz stood a few stalls down the hallway, petting Remington, a two-year-old palomino stud colt. I wasn't surprised that Rowan had honed in on that particular horse. The tall, golden-colored colt was stunning with heavy muscling in just the right places, a refined head, and intelligent eyes. Remington was also pawing at the ground and flipping his pretty head from side to side. With his good looks and breeding, he'd do well in the sale ring, but the horse had a mean streak that made him impossible to work with safely.

"He's Daredevil's colt out of Dixie Belle," I said when I stepped up behind Rowan.

He didn't even startle, which disappointed me a little. When he turned around, I struggled to keep my expression neutral, but it was difficult. Rowan had grown several inches taller since I'd last seen him, and now he towered over my five foot five inches. Still lean but with broad shoulders, his arms now bulged with muscles. The boyish fullness of his sixteen-year-old face had been replaced with sharp, strong lines. His dark brown hair was as thick and messy as it used to be and his eyes still held that wolfish intensity that I remembered so well. My first glimpse of Rowan confirmed one thing: The attraction I used to feel for the Amish horseman hadn't diminished one bit in the years we'd spent apart.

Rowan tilted his head and leaned against the stall door in a very relaxed way. Remington's ears went back and I thought the colt was going to strike at Rowan with his teeth, but he ended up only shaking his head, dropping it out the stall door opening beside the man's shoulder. Rowan ignored the ornery horse completely. His gaze locked on me, causing me to fold my arms over my chest and stare back.

Unhurried, Rowan's eyes lowered to my boots and then back up to my face again just as slowly. The leisurely appraisal made my belly tighten into a fiery ball that flushed my face. Irritation filled my insides, and I was just about to tell him how rude I thought he was when he decided to talk.

"It's good to see you, Katie," he drawled.

I opened my mouth and then closed it. Rowan's voice was husky and smooth at the same time, and the way he said my name sent a sprinkle of tingles over my skin.

When we were teens, I had been bothered by Rowan's inattention. He'd all but ignored me when I worked here and when I'd found out it was all because Dad had ordered him to stay away from me, his unfriendliness had at last made sense. Now, with his hot gaze drilling into me and making my stomach do flip-flops, I almost longed for the days when he wouldn't even look at me.

I was determined to not to offend the only man I knew who could train the colts, including the fiery-tempered Remington, in such a short time period. Momma and I needed to sell them for enough profit to pay the bills and save the ranch from foreclosure. I'd given myself quite the pep talk the night before as I'd lain awake in bed, imagining this encounter, and I wasn't about to let Rowan rattle me.

"Nice to see you, too." I gestured to Remington. "Do you think you can get him working well under saddle in six weeks for the McGovern horse sale?"

The corners of his mouth lifted slightly. He dropped his eyes and when he raised his head again, the wispy look of amusement had vanished. He was a patient man; that was one of the reasons the horses liked him. He thought about things before he said them and rarely did anything impulsively. I was the complete opposite, and his overly laidback demeanor was beginning to fray my last nerve.

"What happened to your arm?" he asked pleasantly.

My brows shot up and the all-night pep talk went straight out the window. I was exhausted and stressed about everything from the farm bills to my mom's health. I'd lost my dad on the same day I'd discovered he was a cheating piece of crap. Yeah, I was done with niceties.

"Why don't you just answer my question? This isn't a game. Momma and I are going to lose the ranch if I can't get these horses ready for the sale," I spat.

Rowan wasn't relaxed anymore. He rose to his full height and hot energy pulsed tightly from his athletic frame. His brown eyes were troubled.

"I'm sorry if you took my response as rude." He shrugged and the tightness faded from his face. "I thought you were a friend who I hadn't seen in a while. I apologize for making assumptions about our relationship," he said gently and motioned at the horses. "I can get your horses fit and ready in time for the sale, even that belligerent one." He pointed at Remington. "If this is just business as usual, we'll need to discuss my payment."

Dammit. I'd shot myself in the foot. Instead of being sweet and flirty, like a woman in need of some cheap labor, I had attacked the man with the force of a dragon.

Rowan's jaw became firmly set and his brows arched. I took a breath and, for once, gathered the words in my head before I spoke. "I was thinking we could pay you a set amount per horse after they sell. What do you think?"

He pursed his lips, continuing to stare at me with those probing eyes. Rubbing the side of Remington's face, he replied, "I'd like ten percent of the sale price per horse."

I quickly calculated average selling amounts at ten percent in my head. It was a fair fee and also encouraged the man to train up the horses to their very best, as his fee would be directly dependent on how much each horse sold for.

I exhaled. "Done. When can you begin?"

A smile appeared on his serious face. "Right now."

I hated that my eyes bulged and my heart raced. This

was business, nothing more. "Perfect," I managed to say with some constraint.

"I do have a question, though."

I nodded for him to continue.

"When did your father pass away?"

The warm breeze sweeping through the barn hallway caught my hair and lifted it away from my face. Scents of horse manure and the hay in the loft mingled. I breathed in the familiar smells with a sigh.

"A week ago tomorrow."

"If you don't mind me asking, what happened?"

I studied the Amish man's rigid features. Curiosity oozed off him, but his voice was tentative, almost as if he was holding his breath. He recognized my hesitation and quickly added, "I caught a glimpse of him a couple of months back at the Willoby stock sale in Ohio. He looked pretty healthy at that time."

Something about the way he said the word *healthy*, with too much emphasis and hidden meaning, made me incline my head. "It was a car accident. Happened in Ohio."

Rowan nodded slowly and didn't look away. I shivered and blinked, forcing my legs into motion. I brushed past him and snatched Remington's halter from the peg, holding it out to him.

His face became guarded as he took the halter. "I guess we don't have time for small talk."

"Only six weeks to get all these horses ready; there won't be much time for anything else." I regretted the words as soon as they left my mouth.

"Got it." He slipped the halter over Remington's golden head and then spared a glance for me. "Are you going to watch the first lesson?"

As I cradled my hurt arm, which still throbbed and was itchy, I couldn't help smiling back at Rowan. "I wouldn't miss it."

FOUR

Rowan

I slipped the halter over Remington's chiseled head and led him out of the stall. The colt leaned heavily on my shoulder and I stopped, wagging the reins to force him to take a step backwards. He snorted and flashed a wide-eyed look around the aisle. "You aren't going to push me around, boy. I'm the leader and you're the follower." I tilted my head. "You'll have some manners soon enough."

After tying the large colt in the cross ties, I took the brush Katie handed me. She avoided my gaze as she moved to the bale of hay and plopped down on it. Stretching her legs out in front of her, she crossed her arms and studied Remington, refusing to grace me with even a glimpse of those pretty blue eyes.

I turned back to the colt and groomed his golden coat

until it shone. A dry breeze stirred the dust in the barn. I exhaled and wiped my brow, considering the English woman who seemed intent on ignoring me. She was even more beautiful than I'd remembered. But that carefree quality she'd once possessed appeared to have gone – or was hidden deep down – replaced with anxiousness and anger. There seemed to be a lot more to her father's passing than she was willing to talk about. The mere fact that she wouldn't answer my simple question about his death struck a nerve with me. She was hiding something – something that had upset her greatly. It pained me to think that the sweet girl I'd stolen a couple of kisses from in this very same barn was having troubles. I wanted to ask her what I could do to help, but feared she'd shoot down my offer quicker than I could blink an eye.

I was being overly presumptuous anyway. Katie Porter was nothing more to me than an employer. My obsession with her as a teenager was just a crush and maybe even my own form of quiet rebellion. I was Amish, and Katie wasn't. It was for the best for both of us that her father had warned me away. She had probably only kissed me in a moment of boredom or experimentation. By now, she had surely learned the ways of the world and had her own man to kiss.

I shook my head at the uneasy thought, chastising myself for being a fool. I couldn't help it that the now-grown woman still got under my skin. It wasn't right that I should feel any kind of jealousy toward any man who might be her beau, though. It had been six years without us having any real contact, and it wasn't like we were ever a couple or anything like that. Katie was entitled to her own happiness. With her beauty and intelligence, I wouldn't be surprised if there was more than one man seeking her attention.

Besides, I was Amish and she wasn't. Anything more than a friendly business relationship was impossible. I was a fool to let so many thoughts about an English woman fill my head.

The colt relaxed under the gentle strokes of the brush. A swath of late evening sunlight covered Remington's face and he closed his eyes. His breathing steadied to a calm rhythm as I glided my hand down his leg, leaning into his forearm until he picked up his hoof. I murmured a few words of encouragement and used the pick to loosen the packed dirt out of the hoof quickly, setting it back down smoothly. I moved around the horse silently, repeating the act with his other three hooves.

Katie didn't say a word but I could hear the shuffling sound of her shifting weight on the bale and I caught the whiff of her vanilla scent whenever I inhaled. The aroma bothered me. It was familiar, the way a memory jerked at your senses. I purposely took shallower breaths, beginning to believe that Katie was purposely trying to bewitch me.

As if on cue, she spoke, breaking the humming sound of Remington's breathing. I paused working and glanced over my shoulders.

"How's your family?" Katie asked. Her voice was brisk yet a little looser than it had been earlier.

Our eyes met briefly and she glanced away. I took the saddle pad from the nearby rack and set it on Remington's back. The colt tensed, but stood still, dropping his head back to see what I was doing. I shadowed the horse with steady, yet firm movements. I wanted Remington to feel my confidence and take notice that I wasn't afraid of him. At the heart of it all, he was a herd animal. The colt wanted to be the boss or to be led by a competent herd mate. Part of the training process was convincing the eleven-hundred-pound animal that he wasn't bigger, stronger, or smarter than me. I had to persuade him that I was the chieftain of the herd and prove that I was worthy of his honor and obedience. With an ornery horse like Remington, the task was easier talked about than actually done.

I couldn't stop the rush of adrenaline coursing through my body that Katie had spoken to me in a somewhat friendly manner. I hated that her words had perked me up so easily, like the invigorating feel of wind whipping my face when one of my trotters was moving effortlessly on the roadway or when I jogged down the stairs on Christmas morning and first inhaled the delicious smells coming from Ma's baking, knowing I wouldn't have to work a lick on that special day. It would be difficult to erase the English woman from my mind but that was what I had to do – forget all the irrational romantic thoughts that had pestered me for years. Katie wasn't mine, and she never would be.

I cleared my throat, trying to sound casual. "Mother and Father are both in good health. Mother is busy making a quilt with the other women for the schoolhouse benefit dinner raffle and Father has grown the organic vegetable farming business. He's even selling produce to several grocery stores in the area. Little Nathaniel is growing like a weed. He'll catch up to my height soon enough."

I flinched, realizing how much information I'd rattled off. It fell quiet again and I peered over Remington's back at Katie. She was chewing on the end of a piece of hay, staring out the open barn doors. I took the saddle from the rack and carefully placed it on the colt's back, grasping the girth and pulling it up to attach the leather tie strap.

"Don't you have a sister?"

Katie's question took me off guard. It was a simple thing to ask, and I suddenly understood how she might have felt when I abruptly asked about her father's death.

Uncomfortable subjects weren't easy to talk about. I didn't want to lie to her but I really didn't want to dig into the muck of what was really going on with Rebecca, either. Remington stepped sideways and I paused with one hand on the girth, steadying him using my other hand on his bowed neck.

"Yes, I do. Rebecca's doing fine as well," I lied.

"She's not much younger than us, is she?"

This was the Katie I remembered, full of curiosity and questions. I might not want to talk about Rebecca but I liked that we were at least talking. "Turned eighteen back in August." I took a breath and looked directly at her. She met my gaze for a change. I leaned against Remington. "Why do you ask?"

Katie shrugged. "I saw her at the feed store a few years ago. I recognized your dad and just assumed she was your sister. She's pretty. You two look a lot alike." Her cheeks reddened and she quickly dropped her gaze.

"I hope you're not saying I'm pretty," I teased, unable to keep the corner of my mouth from lifting.

She snorted and stood up, smacking the loose hay from her jeans. "Naw. I didn't mean that."

I pulled the girth tighter in order to loop the tie strap through the opening. I was distracted and not focused on my charge the way I should have been. Before I had the strap secured, Remington's muscles tensed and a second later he reared up. I reached for the crosstie closest to me but the scoundrel was too quick. He came down with a thump and crow-hopped, jerking his head sideways. The rope attached to his halter on his far side snapped tight and the buckle gave way. The colt almost had his head completely free. I pulled on the end of the rope that still held him, releasing the slip knot and freeing Remington before he could do much more damage.

It all happened like a blur. The golden horse crashed into me, knocking me off balance. I grabbed the stall door to right myself and Remington whirled around like a tornado. I saw Katie shimmy to the right, trying to get out of the way, but the horse was too large. She disappeared behind his haunches just before he bucked, flinging the untied saddle from his back. The saddle hit the wall with a whacking sound, which was immediately joined by the pounding of Remington's hooves as he raced out of the barn. Horse heads that were lazily resting outside of their stalls a moment before, shied back in panic. Nickers and snorts followed the colt as he ran past.

I raced to Katie's sprawled form. Her eyes were closed and I held my breath when I dropped down and touched her cheek softly.

"Katie, are you all right?" I gasped.

Her mouth twitched and then she found her smile again. Blinking, she started to push up into a sitting position. I slipped my hand beneath her arm and around her back. It occurred to me how light she was as I helped her stand.

Katie blew out a shaky breath and wiggled away. I didn't want to let her go, fearing that she wasn't steady enough to stand just yet. I loosened my grip as she pulled away, taking a step with her in case she lost her balance. Her eyes sparked fire and I drew back.

"If that colt wasn't so damn pretty, Daddy would have sold him a long time ago," she said, brushing the dirt from her pant legs.

"Do you need to sit down?" I asked tentatively, trying not to hover too close.

"No, I'm fine." She raised her arm in the sling up and down, wincing a little with the action. "He just bumped me, hard. There's no way Remington will be ready in time for the sale. With his bloodlines and looks, he would have brought a high price. It's such a shame."

I removed my hat and wiped my brow, not taking my eyes off Katie. "Whoa, don't you give up on me or that horse so easy. I told you I'd have all these horses broke by sale day, even Remington, and I keep my promises."

A light flickered in her eyes and her lips parted. She was about to say something and then snapped her mouth shut. She exhaled loudly, shaking her head. "That horse is rogue, Rowan. Every time Daddy or I worked with him it went the same way. For a few minutes he's civil and then all hell breaks loose. He's too smart for his own good and I'm beginning to think he's not worth the trouble." Her eyes narrowed on me. "You could get seriously injured."

My chest constricted with her softer words of warning. I searched Katie's face for something more than just general concern over my wellbeing, but her expression was grim. I had the intense urge to reach out and squeeze her shoulders, give her a gentle shake, and tell her not to worry about me. I wanted to feel her skin beneath my fingers and the thought of doing something so completely inappropriate sent a shiver down my spine. I had once held this woman in my arms and kissed her passionately. Now, I could only dream of touching her again.

I swallowed down the nervous energy bubbling in my gut and reached by Katie to grab the lead rope off the peg.

"Where are you going?" She swiveled toward me.

"To catch that horse. It's going to be a long night."

I turned away and strode out of the barn before Katie could say anything else. My available time to work with her horses was limited and Remington was going to be more difficult to work with than I'd imagined. I was being honest with Katie when I said that I kept my promises. I would get the colts ready in time for the sale, not just for Katie, but for my sister too, who I also owed a promise.

FIVE

Katie

I leaned over the porch railing the next morning, watching the dust billow up from the round pen. Sweat beaded between my breasts and at the nape of my neck, beneath my ponytail.

"That boy must be awfully determined. He's been out there in this heat for over an hour, hasn't he?" Momma stepped up to my side, startling me.

She held out two glasses of lemonade. The ice cubes clinked when I took them. "About that. He started out lunging him with the line, and now he's working with him freestyle. Remington is stubborn, but I believe Rowan might be even more so."

Momma grinned, raising a brow. "He grew up to be a *fine*-looking man."

The wicked look on Momma's face made me snort. I

felt the heat rise on my cheeks, but I didn't really care. She was right about Rowan; he was a *fine*-looking man, and it was good to see her crack a smile for the first time since we'd received news of Daddy's accident and his infidelity.

"Can he really do it?" Momma's face grew serious once again. "Train them horses up by sale day?"

I took a deep breath and looked back at the round pen. The dust had settled and Rowan was standing at Remington's shoulder. The colt's head was dropped and his hind leg cocked in a resting position. The Amish man rubbed the golden fur along the horse's neck and I could see his mouth moving as though he was murmuring something. The man and horse looked about as relaxed as they could be.

"Rowan definitely has a way with horses. If anyone can pull it off, it's him," I admitted quietly.

"I'm surprised he's giving us the time of day after the way your father treated him."

I cocked my head and stared back at Momma. She'd never mentioned the incident before. "Why was Daddy so tough on Rowan? That was the first time we'd ever kissed. Before that, Rowan had all but ignored me."

A sad smile appeared on Momma's lips and her eyes had that foggy, faraway quality that I knew so well. She leaned against the railing and sighed, lifting her chin toward the round pen. "That boy wasn't ignoring you, Katie. He was smitten from the get-go."

My jaw dropped. "How do you know that?"

She shrugged and gave an annoyed shake of her head. "I guess you were too young to read his aloofness but I saw it." Her gaze drifted back to the pen. "I felt sorry for him. He understood that it was impossible to have a relationship with you but the attraction was there, and I know firsthand how difficult it is for an Amish man who is sweet on an English woman.

I set the drinks down on the flat board on the top part of the railing and placed my hands on my hips. Heat fanned my face and my insides twisted. "What are you talking about?" I asked in a low voice.

The fearful look that passed over Momma's face made me hold my breath.

"It's about time I tell you the entire story, Katie, especially since that Amish boy has come back into our lives. Honestly, I never thought we'd see him again up here at the ranch, working with our horses." She shrugged. "Life is a strange journey. Now that your father is gone, there's no more reason to keep secrets." Momma swallowed and lifted her gaze. Her green eyes glistened. "You see, when I was a little younger than you, I met James Coblentz, Rowan's father, at a neighbor's yard sale. Do you remember Mrs. Collins?" I nodded briskly, giving a wave of my hand for her to continue. "Well, my mother had asked me to assist Edna with the yard sale she was having. She was old and her body was riddled with arthritis. She could barely move at the time. I remember that day quite clearly. It was bright and cloudless. The sky was such a pale blue, like a robin's egg."

I was still holding my breath and my head felt light with anticipation. Momma's pause was killing me but I was afraid to say anything to pull her back from those long ago memories. Ever since that day in the barn when Rowan and I had been caught kissing, I'd always thought there was something more than just Daddy being overly protective of me. Something about what he'd said to Rowan, about doing his father a favor, had bugged me for a long time.

Momma sighed deeply and continued. "Edna had an old cart stored in the shed. It was an antique and she'd listed it in the ad she'd posted in the paper. When James showed up to take a look at it, Edna couldn't possibly make the walk to the shed out back so she asked me to take the young Amish man to see it." She smoothed down the front of her pink blouse and took another quick breath. "I was very shy. I hadn't spent much time around Amish folk and certainly not a young man my age." She glanced up from under her lashes and the mischievous look she flashed me made my skin chill. "He was also a fine-looking man – very tall and well built, with brown hair and the darkest eyes. Oh, how my heart pounded on that long walk to the shed. I was a nervous wreck, I think, but then an amazing thing happened. James began talking to me. His steady voice was pleasant. He asked all kinds of questions about my life, and why I was acting so shy; he seemed almost arrogant in his confidence." Momma chewed her lower lip. She was beginning to falter and I reached out, squeezing her arm. The touch seemed to calm her nerves. She wrung her hands. "James ended up buying the sulky and starting up a friendship with me at the same time."

"Friendship?" I said the word with slow emphasis.

Momma made a small huffing noise. "Don't make me say it, Katie. It's hard enough to talk about this as it is. You see, I was already dating your father at the time. All of a sudden I had two men in my life that I was very fond of, and it wasn't an easy time at all."

"But how did you manage to even see Rowan's father, him being Amish and all?"

"He would sneak over to my house after dark and we'd take walks together in the fields. Sometimes, we'd arrange meetings at the little general store at the edge of town. It wasn't easy, and then things got complicated."

"What happened?" I whispered, imagining all kinds of sordid scenarios.

"Your father found out about James. He was very upset and demanded I choose between the two of them. I cared deeply for your father and I didn't want to hurt him, but I had already made up my mind. I wanted to be with James."

"How would that have even been possible?" I breathed.

"That's the crux of it, isn't it? It wasn't possible. At the time I was too naïve to understand, though. The next time I saw James I told him that I was breaking up with your father to be with him."

A tear trickled down Momma's cheek but I couldn't move to wipe it away. Hearing her tell this secret from her past left me frozen. Shock and wonder held me in place.

Momma gulped and sniffed. "That's when James explained that we couldn't be together, that he would never leave his people, and that I would not make a good Amish woman."

"He didn't!" I hissed.

She nodded. "Yes, that's what he told me. He dismissed me like I meant nothing to him. The times we'd shared together had been meaningless." My limbs loosened and I took a step to embrace her but she held up her hands, stopping me. "Your father never mentioned James Coblentz again, until he hired the boy about seven years ago. I was beyond surprised and more than a little uncomfortable having the teenager, who looked so much like his father, coming and going on a daily basis. I never understood why your father would give Rowan a job. It made no sense to me but I didn't question his decision. When he caught the two of you in the barn together and fired the boy, I wasn't surprised in the least. I'm ashamed to say I didn't question it. I was happy to see the boy go. His face had been a constant reminder of the way James had treated me."

I digested what she'd said, my mind reeling. Momma'd had a fling with an Amish man, with Rowan's father. Did Rowan know? If he was ignorant of his father's past, should I even bring it up? I got the answer to my last question immediately.

Momma raised her finger and her threat came out in a low, angry growl. "Do not say a word about this to anyone, especially that boy out there. It's nobody's business. We've all moved on and if news got back to James's wife, Rachel, she'd be devastated. There's no need for any more heartache over a stupid infatuation from the past."

"It sounded like it was more than just an infatuation for you," I said softly.

"I learned the hard way that Amish men are nothing but trouble."

"Couldn't you say that for all men?" After what Daddy had done, it didn't seem fair to single out only Amish males for bad behavior.

"I suppose so, or maybe I've just had bad luck with

men in general." Her face sagged. "I can honestly say that your father's betrayal is nothing compared to the devastation I felt when James turned away from me. My feelings for your father were never quite the same as the love I felt for the young Amish man I used to take walks with. The heart is tricky, my dear. Don't be swept into a forbidden romance the way I was. You'll only get hurt in the end."

I shook my head vigorously. "No, no. You don't have to worry about that with me and Rowan. He's just training the horses so we don't lose the ranch. That's it. I don't even like him much."

Momma looked at me with the arch of her eyebrows that signaled firm wisdom, making me catch my breath. "I hope that's true, for your sake, and that we might be able to hold onto the ranch." She pinned me with a steady gaze. "Mark my words, Katie. If that boy finds out his father and I were in a relationship before his mother came along, he might not finish the job. That's a chance we can't take."

Her warning settled over me like a heavy winter blanket. I didn't like secrets under the best of circumstances, but keeping something like this to myself wouldn't be such a big deal if it weren't for Rowan and his penetrating eyes. He probably thought my daddy was the bad guy, but in truth his own father was even worse.

I nodded reluctantly, agreeing, and glanced back up. I spotted Rowan coming from the barn with the saddle in his arms.

"Oh, great," I mumbled, jogging down the porch steps.

"Wait," Momma called out. She picked up the two glasses of lemonade and followed me down the steps. "He must be dying of thirst by now." When I frowned back at her, she added, "The sins of the father don't belong to the son. As long as you keep the relationship business-only, you'll be fine, Katie. We'll all be fine."

I took the glasses without meeting her gaze. Of course, she was absolutely right. I needed Rowan to train the horses; that's all I needed from him. Any flirty looks he might shoot my way meant nothing. He was probably a player, just like his ol' dad. I'd heard stories of the Amish partying, dating non-Amish, and going wild before they finally settled down in their communities. That was probably what had happened with James Coblentz. He'd taken a fancy to my mom and had a little fun before he found an Amish woman to cook, clean, and warm his bed at night. I wouldn't fall into the same trap as Momma.

As I approached Rowan, holding the glasses in my hands, I admitted to myself that it was a shame the man was once again off limits. He finally noticed me and set the saddle down on the fence railing. I tried not to look at his broad shoulders and slim hips, but that meant looking him in the eye.

When he saw the lemonade, he smiled and tipped his hat. His brows lifted and his eyes widened. He left Remington and shimmied between the fence railings to meet me.

I caught a whiff of his musky sweat mixed with horse hair and leather. When I looked up, shielding my eyes from the sunshine, he stepped closer. His tall frame blocked the sunlight and I suddenly ached for those strong, muscled arms to encircle me.

"You read my mind." He gestured at one of the glasses of lemonade.

I held it out to him but before he took it, he abruptly kneeled in the dirt beside me. I dropped my gaze.

"Hey, girl, do you remember me?" Rowan ran his hands through my dog's fur in the same gentle way he touched Remington. "She must be getting on in years," he commented, still petting Lady.

I nodded once, at a loss for words. Lady didn't like anyone but Momma and me. The electric meter-reading guy couldn't even climb out of his truck for fear of getting bitten. And here she was, after six years of not seeing Rowan, rolling onto her back and letting him rub her belly. She'd turned back into a panting, squirming puppy for him.

Staring at Rowan's crouched form over my dog, I knew I was a goner.

Rowan finished off the lemonade with a swig and handed me the glass. "That was refreshing. Thank you."

"Momma made it," I said quickly.

Rowan smiled a little and grasped Remington's lead line. The horse had been resting in the sun, eyes closed and head dropped. The slight touch on the rope connected to his halter brought him fully alert. His ears pricked forward and he turned to look at Rowan.

I set the glasses onto the ground and crossed my arms over the railing to watch Rowan lead the colt around the pen a couple of times. Occasionally he stopped Remington and turned him in tight circles. The horse moved in a willing way. He almost seemed a little tired.

When Rowan dropped the rope and said, "Whoa," Remington slid to a stop, licking his lips. The mouth action showed that the horse was giving in to Rowan, trusting him as his master.

I cocked my head and studied Rowan's movements. He walked around the horse with a casual demeanor that neither threatened Remington, nor made him feel that Rowan was a pushover. The man's strides were free and easy, his posture loose. He crossed the pen with his head lowered most of the time, seeming to ignore the horse altogether. I wasn't fooled. My trained eyes picked up Rowan's subtle glances and his slightly cocked head and listening ears. He was always aware of where Remington was and what he was doing.

I tried not to notice Rowan's athletic physique and the bulge of muscles where his shirt sleeves were rolled up. Suspenders slipped over wide shoulders, and dust stained the sweaty, cream-colored material. When he spoke to Remington, his voice was quiet yet firm. Even though it had to be over eighty-five degrees, a shiver raced up my neck when Rowan spoke my name.

"Katie, I think we're ready for the saddle."

I almost protested, wishing he'd give Remington a few more days of ground training, for Rowan's own safety, but with twelve other colts to break, there wasn't the luxury of time to go slow with the palomino. I nodded, giving Rowan the go-ahead to try the saddle again.

This time Rowan placed the pad and saddle down on the horse's back at the same time. He probably didn't want Remington to have much time to figure out what was happening. The longer a smart horse like Remington had to think, the more danger the trainer was in.

In a smooth action, Rowan pulled the girth under the belly and secured the tie strap. In an even quicker motion, Rowan slipped his boot into the stirrup and lightly swung his other leg over Remington's back. A warm breeze lifted the horse's white mane, bringing with it the scent of the grass that was curing in the hayloft. I breathed the sweet scent in deeply and then held my breath, waiting for Remington to explode.

Rowan sat deep in the saddle, slightly hunched, with his long legs barely touching Remington's sides. He slid just the toes of his boots into the stirrups while he leaned over and rubbed the golden neck.

"There, boy. That's not so bad, is it?" he asked in a coaxing voice.

When he made the same clucking sound he'd made earlier to get Remington moving off on the rope, I gripped the rail. Lady gave a low whine, as if she understood how temperamental the horse was and that Rowan was in danger.

The barnyard quieted; even the birds seemed to pause their singing to see what happened next.

Remington shifted his weight, spreading his legs further out to the sides, stubbornly not moving. Rowan made the noise again and this time, he brushed his boot heels into the colt's sides. Remington surged forward awkwardly. His balance was off with the man's weight straddling his back for the first time. Rowan lifted his hands, using his expertise to easily control his own balance as Remington trotted bouncily around the pen. Whenever the horse started to lose impulsion, Rowan urged him forward with clucks and his forward seat. I let out a breath and began to enjoy the training session. The horse listened to the man, speeding up and slowing down on cue. When Remington's golden coat was slick and shiny with sweat and his breathing was heavy, Rowan sat back and said, "Whoa, boy," with a firm voice.

Remington remembered the words and their meaning. He seemed relieved when he planted his four feet on the ground and immediately dropped his head to rest.

"I'm impressed," I admitted.

"Strong-willed horses like this one need a job to do more than most. He wants to be a part of a team. He'll make a great horse when we're finished with him."

That he'd said *we're* made me wonder at his choice of words. After all, Rowan was the one training the horse, not me. I let the thought go. My arm was beginning to throb and I had to get ready for work if I was going to make my shift on time. I'd missed several days for Daddy's burial, and although Billy had been more than accommodating with my time off, I didn't want to push the restaurant owner's generosity too far. Besides, Momma and I needed the money.

"How long can you stay today?" I asked.

Rowan looked at his watch and leaned back, resting his hand on Remington's croup. "Our driver should be picking me up in about a half hour, I reckon. I have to work with the building crew this afternoon."

I tried not to let the disappointment show on my face. I knew when I'd hired Rowan that he had other jobs to keep up with and that training the horses wouldn't be his sole priority. I responded with as cheery a voice as I could manage. "All righty. Can you come back tomorrow?"

Rowan lifted the rope and clucked to Remington, waking him from his tired trance. He took a few steps to reach me at the fence and stopped again when Rowan said, "Whoa."

"The schoolhouse benefit dinner is tomorrow night and I'm signed on to help some of the other men put up the tent and clean out the tie stalls for the horses." He must have read the disappointment on my face, because he quickly added, "I can plan to come over after the auction and maybe even later today." He glanced around. "Your barn and pen are well lit and it'll be cooler at night." He pursed his lips, frowning. "That's something I really envy you of: electric lights at night."

I grinned back but I couldn't help asking, "Why don't your people use electricity anyway?"

His spine straightened. "If I had a dollar for every time someone asked me that question—"

I cut him off. "Sorry, you don't have to explain it to me." My skin bristled with agitation that I'd been so stupidly forward. The Amish had their own culture and even though I didn't understand half of why or what they did, their religion deserved respect like anyone else's.

Rowan removed his hat and dragged his fingers through his thick, dark hair. An image of Momma and Rowan's father kissing sprang to mind. I quickly looked down the driveway. Maybe it would have been better if Momma had never told me about her and James Coblentz. The idea of her romance with an Amish man was mind-blowing enough but the images dancing around in my head were downright disturbing. The only reason I could fathom that she'd shared a glimpse into her past with me was to make sure I didn't make the same mistake with Rowan that she had made with his father. Momma had never been good at telling me what to do. Her parenting skills were much more subtle than that. By retelling the story of her disastrous relationship with an Amish man, she'd gotten the message across loud and clear. Even if my friendship with Rowan blossomed into something deeper while he trained the horses, it didn't matter. He was Amish and therefore off limits.

"I didn't mean that I didn't want to explain it to you, just that it's something I figured most people would understand by now." His brow lifted and he managed a weak smile. "You know, there are hundreds and thousands of us, and our communities have spread to most of the States and Canada."

"I hadn't really ever thought about the Amish population before." I shifted my gaze back to Rowan's face.

"We don't use electricity for several reasons but the main one is that it opens our homes up to the outside world through the electric lines."

I scrunched my face, shaking my head. "That doesn't make any sense. What about gas? I've heard your people use natural gas for lights and the stove, and to run your refrigerators."

His smile disappeared and his lips thinned. "Just because it's the way we do things, doesn't make it perfect." His mouth twitched and then broke out into a wide grin.

I snorted out a laugh and began to pivot away when he cleared his throat.

"Have you ever been to the benefit dinner?"

I shook my head. I'd been tempted on a few occasions but I was always working or doing something else, it seemed.

Rowan's voice dropped lower and he leaned forward over Remington's neck. The horse stepped sideways and I guessed he believed his resting session was over. "You should come. There's good food, and we raise the money to pay for our teacher's salary and our little school's maintenance. There's an auction at seven o'clock and everything from wooden furniture and crafts to doves and goats will sell. The quilt my Ma and the other ladies are sewing will be raffled off, too."

"Sounds fun, but I have work tomorrow." I pulled my cellphone from my back pocket, checking the time. "I'm running late for today's shift. I have to go. I'll tell Momma to leave the gate open tonight and tomorrow, so you can come on up and work with the horses after dark, if you have the time."

"You won't be here tonight?" Rowan's voice was guarded, almost rough.

"I normally pull a double shift on Fridays. Sometimes I don't get home until after midnight. It just depends on how busy the restaurant is."

"I see."

Rowan's expression was tight and his eyes downcast. If I was a betting woman, I'd say he was disappointed that he might not see me for a couple of days.

I smothered my satisfied smile with my hand. "You're doing a great job with Remington. He really is the worst of the bunch. After today, I'm hopeful that you might actually succeed and get the training done by sale day."

He tipped his hat. "Oh, there's no doubt I'll have them colts trained up in time."

His confidence caused my muscles to ease and my nerves to quiet. It would still be a small miracle, but the

Amish man was determined, making it a little less of a long shot.

Lady led the way back to the house when Rowan called out, "If you don't mind me asking, where do you work?"

I paused to look back. "At Billy's Diner and Saloon. Have you ever eaten there?"

"Can't say I have."

"I'm sure your standards are fairly high, with all I've heard about how delicious Amish cooking is, but the steak sandwich, with a baked macaroni cheese side, is really good."

"Maybe I'll check it out sometime," he replied.

I turned away and kept walking. I'd never seen any Amish people in Billy's before. Someone had said it had to do with the word saloon in the restaurant's name – and that the Amish didn't frequent places that sold alcohol.

As I climbed the porch steps, my heartrate sped up. I had a feeling Rowan would be true to his word. He'd be the first Amish person to dine in the restaurant and, if my instincts were correct, he wouldn't wait too long to check out Billy's Diner.

SIX

Rowan

W hen I closed the door behind me the smell of baked goodness assailed my senses. I breathed in deeply and looked around. The kitchen was empty and I let go a sigh of relief. I wasn't in the mood for conversation with family. It had been a hot afternoon on the roof of a garage the crew had built for a fellow in town. The beating sun had burned the back of my neck and the side of my temple ached where Martin had dropped a board on my head as I'd climbed up the ladder behind him. I rubbed the throbbing spot and crossed the room to the refrigerator. I grabbed a cold bottle of water from the top shelf and sat down at the table. A dozen pies were lined up and cooling on the counter. The breeze stirring the curtains above the sink was still warm, even though the sun had dropped low in the sky. I still had to feed the horses and calves.

I wasn't surprised that Ma wasn't around. She'd told me that morning that she would be visiting Martha Miller this evening – something about needing a few more stitches on the raffle quilt to make it perfect – and that Father would take her over with the buggy. He wanted to see Tim's new team of Belgian horses anyway. There was a small piece of paper on the table. I reached out and dragged the note over with my fingers.

Your dinner is in the fridge. Nathaniel came along with us but your sister stayed home.

Please keep an eye on her. I don't want her getting into any mischief. Mother

I leaned back in the chair. I'd seen the plate with the pork chop and potatoes when I'd fetched the water but I wasn't hungry and had ignored it. I cocked my head and listened. The house was quiet, except for the dull ticking sound of the old clock on the fireplace mantle in the adjoining room. Where was Rebecca?

Like horses breaking from the gate in a race, my heart began pounding. I stood up and hurried into the hallway, glancing into the parlor first. The sofa and chair were empty. The room was shadowed and only a small strip of the floor was lit by the low, buttery light shining in through the window. I passed the painting of the white farmhouse in the snow, and the scripture verse in the corner popped out at me:

"But godliness with contentment is great gain. For we brought nothing into the world, and we can take nothing out of it."1 Timothy 6:6-7

Even though the house was stuffy, a chill penetrated the skin on my arms. I took two steps at a time as I climbed the staircase to the second floor. Mother and Father had expected me to arrive home sooner. The mischief they worried Rebecca might get into had to do with their idea of her rebellion and had nothing to do with her troubled state of mind. After our conversation about what had become of poor Lucinda, I was more afraid that Rebecca was thinking about death and its promise of freedom from our restrictive world.

I stopped in front of Rebecca's bedroom door and held my breath. The door was shut. Slowly I turned the knob and pushed. The last rays of daylight spilled through the west-facing window. Beneath those splendid rays, I found Rebecca sitting on the floor. Her back was to me and her head was bent. She was very still except for an occasional bob of her head. I hadn't relaxed enough to take a proper breath. Careful not to startle my sister, I stepped lightly. It wasn't until I reached the warmth of the fading sunshine that I saw the white plastic plugs in her ears. They were connected to thin wires that draped around her neck, attaching to a small technology device. It looked like a cellphone, but smaller.

I was close enough to hear the muffled beat of music and realized she was listening to a song. I knelt beside her and leaned over. Rebecca couldn't hear me and her eyes were closed. Her mouth was parted and her lips mouthed silent words. The tight paleness of her face made me shiver, but it was what she was holding in her hands that made me shrink back, rocking onto the heels of my boots.

In one hand she held a drawing pencil and in the other a sketch book. I forced myself to take a closer look at the picture Rebecca had drawn. It was of a girl – or maybe a young woman – with long hair, blowing across her eyes. Her neck was thrown back, raising her face to a dark sky. The girl was naked with a bent leg and her long hair hiding the lower part of her body. A breast was exposed. The fact that she'd drawn such a scandalous picture barely penetrated my mind. It wasn't the girl's nakedness that was shocking; it was the look on her face that held me in a stony grip. The mouth twisted open grotesquely in a scream that I was sure if I closed my eyes I would be able to hear. Then I noticed the girl's fingers digging into her thigh and the blood drops dribbling down her skin. The girl's tightly curled toes completed the tortured image. My gaze quickly lifted to the paintings decorating the pale blue walls.

Rebecca was a self-taught artist. She began doodling as a child. All she'd ever wanted for her birthday presents was painting supplies, and Father had even let her use the back side of the toolshed as a canvas for her ever-changing color experiments. Early on, everyone had praised her for her growing abilities, but over time, Mother and Father became annoyed by the increasing time she spent painting, time that took her away from her many tedious chores.

Now, as I looked at her creations, I suddenly realized just how gifted my sister was. There was a picture of Rebecca's round-barreled black pony standing knee deep in lush, green grass. Butterflies of all colors and sizes dotted the landscape. Wild chicory added blue splashes here and there in the pasture. Another painting captured the friendly warmth of the family farmhouse and red barns surrounded by hills and forest. The picture above Rebecca's bed was of a brilliant red sunset over a cornfield. All of her artwork was expertly painted and beautiful to behold. Even the painting she'd done in the downstairs foyer, with its lonely house on the snowy hill and the melancholy Bible verse attached, was still striking.

But this newest drawing grasped in her hands was something altogether different. The black and charcoal grey strokes were harsh and the image of the pained girl, disturbing. If this was a glimpse into Rebecca's soul, she was doomed.

This drawing was a cry for help if I ever saw one. I reached out and tapped her shoulder. She jumped up and slammed the sketchbook closed. Her gray eyes were wide and surprised.

She pulled the plugs from her ears and groaned, "Why are you sneaking up on me, Rowan?"

The hostile look of betrayal aimed at me made me take a step back. Annoyance prickled my insides. "If you didn't have those things in your ears you would have surely heard me enter the room," I shot back.

Rebecca glanced down at the white ear plugs and then clenched them in her balled fist. "Are you going to tell Da and Ma?" she asked.

I shook my head. "Of course not."

Her shoulders dropped and a small smile tugged at the corner of her mouth before she turned back to her writing desk. She opened the drawer and pulled out a Bible. I inclined my head, watching curiously as she opened the book and set the slender device and the plugs into an opening she'd carved away from the pages.

A short gasp bubbled up from my throat. "Are you kidding me? You chopped up a Bible to make a hiding spot for your phone?"

"It's not a phone – just an iPod." She glanced back

over her shoulder. "You listen to music with it. That's all."

I rubbed my forehead vigorously. "I thought you were going to try to behave yourself, Rebecca. Father and Mother are on to you, and now the bishop is involved. You're treading in dangerous waters."

Rebecca faced me, her arms crossed. She leaned against the desk in a casual way that most people would have found disrespectful. When she was in this kind of mood, it unnerved me the most. Instead of looking back with her usually sad, desperate eyes, she glared at me. Her drawn features were filled with combative tension. I swallowed and braced for her anger.

Her voice was calm and quiet when she spoke. "There's nothing wrong with listening to music while I draw. If I weren't Amish, no one would even notice, let alone think to punish me."

I plopped down on the edge of her bed and stared at the wooden floor. She was absolutely right, but that didn't matter at all. Because we were Amish, our ways were different to the outside world. Rebecca understood that, so there was no point in arguing with her.

"You're smarter than this. If it really is your intention to leave the community, then do it the right way – with a sound plan."

Rebecca's eyes glowed. "You're going to help me?"

I inhaled sharply. "If that's what you really want, yes,

I'll help you. But you have to be patient. It's going to take some time to sort things out."

"What things?" Her eyes were as wide as saucers as she stood up straight and tall.

I sighed. "First and foremost, you're going to need money for a place to stay. Eventually, you'll have to get a car and that will be expensive."

"I'll take on another job," she said firmly.

"Sure you can do that, but you'll still need a place to stay and transportation to travel around."

"Jessica has a cousin who she said I can stay with for a little while until I get my act together."

I couldn't help narrowing my eyes. "You already talked to that crazy driver about running away?"

Rebecca raised her chin. "I hardly call it running away when I'm eighteen years old. I'm an adult and can live on my own if I choose to."

I licked my lips, feeling my face grow hot. I knew I had to be patient with Rebecca but she was making it very difficult.

"That woman has you thinking like an Englisher. Well, you're not – at least not yet." I drew in a raspy breath and blew it out. "Rebecca, if you do this properly and with respect for Father and Mother, it will be better for you in the long run. You don't want to rely on strangers to help and support you. I understand you're fed up with all the rules that our people live by, and maybe you just don't fit in. I get it, but don't be naïve. It's a cruel world out there. In our community, we're always there for each other. Whether it's raising a neighbor's barn, delivering food after a new baby arrives, or when someone is recovering from illness. The Amish are never alone and from what I've seen, that's not always the case for Englishers."

"I don't care about any of that. I'll make a living as a painter. I'll have my own studio and everything."

"You can still sell your artwork as an Amish woman," I argued.

She muffled her bark of laughter with her hand. "Sure. For a little while maybe, but then I'll be pressured to marry and have babies." When I began to protest, she raised her hand and rushed on. "You know it's true, Rowan. If I don't settle down, raise a family, and take care of the house, I won't be accepted. I already have that problem. You don't feel lonely because everyone loves you. You're outgoing and like to talk to them about the same things that interest the other men, like farming and horses." She pushed away from the desk and fell to her knees in front of me. "You like it here and I understand why it works for you. Why, oh why, can't you see that being Amish just doesn't work for me?" she pleaded.

"I do see that! I'm trying to guide you to leave in the right way."

"Is there a right way?" Her hand pressed to her heart. "No matter how I do it, it's going to be a nightmare."

"That's probably true, but you can make it a little easier."

"How?"

"By being as respectful of our parents as you can be. Do the sessions with the bishop and the ministers. It won't kill you, and at least then you can say to Ma that you really did try. She'll see that you made an effort and that might help her better deal with your decision to leave. You never know, you might even change your mind." The stubborn set of her jaw made me quickly add, "I'm training horses for the Porters. I should have enough money saved by December to set you up in your own apartment."

"You would do that for me?" Her lips trembled and I stared out the window. Darkness had fallen and a cool breeze lifted the curtains.

"Father and Mother won't be happy, but yes, if it's your decision to leave the Amish, I'll help you. As long as you promise to see a doctor about your problems." She nodded briskly. "You're a stubborn one, Rebecca, and I know that no amount of cajoling will keep you here if you don't want to stay. I reckon it's better if I assist you so you don't make a complete mess of your life in the process of following your dreams."

Rebecca folded her hands in her lap and smiled

sweetly. "You're a good brother – better than I deserve." She twiddled her thumbs like she was a distracted child again. "I'll do as you say and slow things down a bit. I can survive the bishop's lectures, I suppose." She rolled her eyes. "But I can't wait too long, Rowan. I'll go nuts if I don't get out of here soon."

"You want to be away from us that bad?"

Abruptly, her eyes misted and she dropped her head. "Of course not. It's just so hard for me sometimes. The other day Ma swatted me with the broom because I refused to go to Sarah's baby shower on the only day I had off in over a week. Between working at the butcher shop and doing the household chores, I have no time to paint or even read a few pages of a book most days. I have no say about what happens in my own life at all. It's not that I want to get away from you all, because I'll miss you and Nathaniel desperately. I might even miss Da and Ma after a while. I just can't live like this anymore. I can't."

"Won't it be strange to wear trousers and have your hair down?"

She giggled. "Maybe at first. But you have no idea how uncomfortable these stupid caps are." She adjusted hers with a sharp jerk to head.

"I can't even imagine you driving a car." I rubbed my chin, becoming wary with the conversation.

"It will be a grand adventure to learn so many new things," she said wistfully.

For a moment, pink color flushed her cheeks and her eyes twinkled. Seeing her hopeful, after so many months of mood swings from melancholy depression to frightening anxiety, made all the trouble worth it. And it would definitely be a lot of trouble. In the end, I might find myself being lectured by the bishop. I certainly wouldn't escape unscathed if I succeeded in spiriting my sister away. I would be punished for helping her.

Rebecca stood up. "I'll heat up some dinner for us."

I rose from the bed. "Father asked me to pick up a box of roofing nails today, but I didn't have time. Thomas said he'd drive me into town this evening to get them to save time in the morning, if I wanted." Rebecca stared at me with raised brows and eyes full of confusion. "Why don't we go out for dinner tonight," I suggested carefully.

Rebecca's face lit up. "Truly? I can go to town with you?"

"Sure. I don't think Father or Mother will have a problem with it. After all, I'll pay the driver from my own money and Father needs those nails."

"Where shall we eat?" Rebecca asked excitedly with a bounce.

"Billy's Diner and Saloon."

Rebecca's eyes widened and her mouth exploded into

a huge smile. "Ma and Da will be so angry if we eat there."

"That's why it'll be our little secret. Are you all right with that?"

She drew nearer. "I'm more than okay – and you know I can keep a secret."

"Yes, I do." My heart raced. "I'll call Thomas, and then feed the horses and calves." I glanced at the wall clock. "Be ready to leave in a half hour."

Rebecca bobbed her head and ran out of the room. She had her own chores to finish before we could leave.

My gaze strayed to her sketchbook on the desktop. I had no doubt that it was best for Rebecca to leave, especially after the drawing I'd just spied. Her mind was too busy to ever be satisfied with the ways of an Amish woman. I only hoped that whatever darkness had touched her spirit would be permanently lifted once she got her freedom. Because if it followed her to the outside world, there would be no one there to save her.

Heaviness settled over my mind as I jogged down the steps and went out through the doorway. Was I doing the right thing? Only time would tell. There was one thing that put an extra spring to my step. I would see Katie Porter this very night. It was a foolish thing to do, I knew, but I felt reckless – just like my little sister.

SEVEN

Katie

Tessa looked up from the silverware and napkins she was folding. "I'm so sorry to hear all that, Katie." She shook her head and her mouth puckered as if she'd bitten into something tart. "That's quite a mess your dad left you and your mom in."

I began placing the silverware bundles that were finished into the plastic tub. It was dark beyond the restaurant's windows, but the lights hanging over the booths and tables lit the room with a cheery glow. Couples and families sipped their drinks and munched their dinners while chatting away. Billy's Diner and Saloon was a happy place. The townspeople liked to gather here at the end of the day for some good food and to check in with their neighbors. The tips were pretty good, but that's not why I'd stayed on as a server for over five years. I enjoyed the festive atmosphere and especially working side by side with a group of people who'd become my extended family. I couldn't say as much about my day job at the water company. Bookkeeping was a solitary occupation, and the few people that did occasionally pass through my office were so unpleasant that I didn't even bother with friendships with them. The solitude was nice, though.

I glanced up at Tessa. Her blonde, cropped hair bounced against her cheeks when she got riled up. Her voice would also rise when she became excited or irritated and oftentimes I had to shush her so the customers couldn't hear what we were talking about. On those occasions, she'd raise an eyebrow at me, feigning anger, and then break out with a loud giggle. She was like a sister and one of the few people my age who I honestly called a friend.

Tessa was also my polar opposite. Where she was perky and fun, I was reserved and serious. She was the only person I knew who could actually get me out of my comfort zone. Too many times to count, she'd pestered me to death about going to a club, party, or backyard grill-out, and I'd finally relented and gone. I can't say that I always had a great time, but I usually felt better after those mundane adventures. Tessa was a focused listener and I trusted her advice on most things. On the subject of guys, not so much. She was way too optimistic about the opposite sex. Tessa actually thought most men were good guys – something I highly disagreed with her about. I didn't have the heart to point out that she'd dated five different guys in the past four years – and even been engaged to one of them – but here she was just as single as me. I envied her optimistic nature but thought she was a fool at the same time.

Right now, Tessa's face was troubled, and I wished I hadn't laid all my problems on her at the beginning of our shift.

"Yep. It sucks to find out your father is a bastard right after he dies." I stared at a little girl, sitting on her daddy's lap a few tables away. The child leaned back into the safety of the man's strong arms and burrowed deeper into his chest. I remembered those days all too well. Even though my dad had had a foul temper at times and had never been prone to displaying affection, there were those few blissful moments when he had picked me up and carried me to the car when I was too tired to take another step or when he'd sometimes lift me onto his shoulders and bound up the staircase to tuck me in at night. He'd split story time with Momma, and on the nights when he'd read to me, he'd do all the different voices for the characters. I shook my head and sniffed, blocking the memories from flooding in. He was dead, and I'd learned the truth about him. He was a cheater, who'd frittered our family's hard-earned savings away on a little tramp. Learning that Momma had been involved with an Amish man a long time ago hadn't sat well with me, either. My thoughts popped right out my mouth. "Why couldn't I have had normal parents, like that?" I lifted my chin toward the little family with the girl sitting on her daddy's lap and the mom who was patiently spooning forkfuls of food into the other toddler's mouth.

Tessa followed my gaze and quickly looked back. She leaned across the counter. "I'm sure they have their own problems. Everyone does." She frowned. "Sometimes it's those people who look the happiest and have picture-perfect lives that are actually the most miserable."

I barked out a laugh. "Aren't you just a basket of sunshine today?"

Tessa shrugged. "My experience has been that it's easier to move forward if you focus on the positive. I know this has been a rough week for you, but at least you found someone to train the horses. That's a start."

"What's a start?" Peggy squeezed in behind me, grasping the tub.

Peggy was like a hurricane blowing up on us. Her eyes were huge with curiosity and her mouth rose crookedly in expectation of some juicy news. She was in her thirties, I guessed, and had two adorable children with her partner. Peggy was the type of person you didn't want to tick off, but she was also a valuable ally if a friend ever needed back-up. Her unfailing loyalty was quite impressive.

"Katie hired an Amish guy to train the horses for the sale. If he gets them under saddle in time, she and her mother will be able to pay the bills and save their ranch," Tessa chimed in.

I cringed, clasping my lips tightly closed. Peggy knew some of what was going on but I really wished Tessa hadn't said so much.

Peggy breathed deeply and blew the air back out dramatically. She glanced around and then lowered her voice. "I told you, Jessica and I can lend you a little money. I wish you'd consider our offer."

My stupid eyes teared up and I quickly dabbed them with my fingertip. I struggled to speak without my voice cracking. "I really appreciate that, but the payments are several months behind and the taxes alone are a large sum. If Mom and I are going to make a go of it on our own, we have to get out of this hole by ourselves. Buying a little time won't help us in the long run. We've got to make the ranch earn a profit. If the horses sell for high prices, and I continue to work at the water company and here at the restaurant, we'll be all right."

Peggy rolled her eyes, gesturing to the sling holding my arm. "How are you going to pull that off with that thing on your arm? I don't know why you're even here tonight. You can barely carry a tray." She saw me inhale and raised her hands defensively. "Don't get me wrong, Katie, I'm seriously impressed with your tenacity. But you're injured and your dad just died – sure, he was a dick, no doubt, but there's still a grieving process." She eyed Tessa and glanced back at me. "We're your friends, girl. Let us help you out, for at least a few weeks, so you can sort everything out."

Peggy was right, as usual. She never minced words or danced around subjects the way most people did. I swayed toward her and nodded, as if trying to convince myself. "I need to keep busy. It's just the way I have to do it." I held up my arm. "This comes off next week, so there's that little ray of light."

Kimberly, the hostess, popped up and said something to Tessa, who quickly darted away. Peggy snorted. "You should be doing that job – makes more sense."

I forced a smile. "Well, you know how Kim gets if she has to do the prep work. Best just to let her seat customers so we don't have to listen to her complaining all night long."

"Just like with my kids, spoiling that woman isn't going to improve her disposition any." Peggy paused, staring at the entrance. "Well, I'll be dammed."

I followed her gaze and froze. Rowan Coblentz had just walked through the doorway. Seeing his tall frame standing in front of the hostess station made my cheeks burn. "That's Rowan," I muttered.

"What? You know that Amish guy?" Peggy breathed and stepped closer.

"He's my horse trainer."

Peggy smirked back at me. "Damn, he's cute, Katie. Why didn't you mention you just hired a man who resembles a Greek god in suspenders?"

"Shh." I giggled.

"No, seriously, you should be smiling from ear to ear instead of moping about your troubles."

"He's just training my horses, nothing else, Peggy. Don't get so excited."

"What has it been, two years since you dated anyone?" Her smile was sly.

I grunted and watched Rowan follow Kimberly to a booth. My heart sunk into my stomach when I noticed the young woman following closely behind him. She was Amish and her lavender dress reminded me of Easter flowers. The white cap on her head was stiff and hid her hair very well, except for the few brown locks at her forehead that had escaped. The woman was rail thin and her head was held high as her eyes darted around the room. From her profile, I decided she was pretty.

I sagged a little and sighed.

Peggy whispered, "Ah, don't get all depressed on me. That girl doesn't hold a candle to you."

"He's Amish. It's not like we could ever get together, even if I did like him. And I don't."

Peggy tilted her head and frowned in a way that said she wasn't believing what I was saying.

She began pouring glasses of water and said in a nonchalant way, "I had a cousin who messed around with an Amish girl."

"Seriously? How did that happen?"

"It's a long story, but one worth telling over a couple of beers." She pulled her shoulder-length black hair into a messy bun and put on her apron. "What do you say? Do you want to meet me and Jessica after work?"

I was already exhausted and would surely be even worse in eight hours. I was about to politely decline when Kimberly appeared at the counter. A stud shone on her pert nose and her expression was unfriendly, as usual.

"That Amish man requested you, Katie."

My mouth went suddenly dry. "By name? He asked for me?"

Kimberly shot me a look of annoyance, like I was a dumb. "Uh, yeah. He said, 'Could you please ask Katie Porter to be our waitress? She's a friend.'" She spun away without waiting for my reply.

"Friends, huh?" Peggy smirked, elbowing me.

Her voice was overly sweet and I smacked her shoulder for teasing me. Peggy walked away with laughter bubbling from her lips.

I smoothed down the front of my apron, even though

it didn't need it and took a deep breath. I'd had a wild inkling that Rowan might stop by the restaurant, but mostly dismissed it as wishful thinking. After six years and all the problems I had to deal with, I couldn't shake the teenage crush I still had for the horseman. My knees still got weak whenever he graced me with any attention and my heart felt like it would explode in my chest when our eyes locked. I hated the feeling.

The fact that he'd brought a date along with him made me feel like a complete idiot. He was just the best person to train my horses. He was Amish and I wasn't. It didn't work out for Momma and would never work for me. Story over.

I made my way closer to the booth and Rowan looked up. He saw me and smiled.

The butterflies took flight from the pit of my belly, right up into my throat.

"I didn't think I'd see you so soon," I said curtly.

I couldn't help glancing at the woman sitting across from Rowan. Her head was bent over the menu. I spotted several pins attaching her cap to her hair beneath and I cringed inwardly. It looked uncomfortable.

"Well, hello to you too, Katie," he said in a low drawl. Hearing him say my name sent a little jolt of shivers through me.

I forced a polite smile. The woman looked up and her gray eyes were suddenly laser focused on me. Those sharp eyes passed over my face slowly before her lips formed a crooked smile.

I worked hard to settle the emotions that blew up in my gut. I didn't think I'd ever felt jealousy before, and I didn't like the sickening feeling one bit.

I took a quick breath and smiled as naturally as I could manage. The fact that this Amish man had such an effect on me was embarrassing, especially when his girlfriend was sitting right there, staring at me as if I had two heads.

"Can I start you out with drinks?" I asked evenly. I dragged my gaze away from Rowan, settling it on the young woman.

"I'll have a cola," the woman replied, still smiling.

"An iced tea for me," Rowan added.

I rocked back on my heels to leave and the woman lurched forward. "You don't remember me, do you?"

I searched her oval face. Her pale skin was stretched tightly over high cheekbones, and her eyes were hollow-looking. Dark locks poked out from under her cap, making a striking contrast with the light color of her eyes. The woman resembled a frail china doll. Her gray gaze was wide and innocent at first glance, but there was also shrewdness shining in those depths, and maybe a little crazy too. I searched my memories and came up empty. Although, there was something kind of familiar about her that I just couldn't put my finger on.

My brow furrowed and I looked back at Rowan. "I'm sorry, I can't say that I do."

"This is my sister, Rebecca," Rowan said smoothly. "She came up to your ranch with me a couple of times when I worked there as a teenager and I think you mentioned seeing her at the feed store with my father on one occasion."

A swooshing of relief flooded my veins, giving me renewed energy and snapping me out of the doldrums I'd experienced when Rowan had walked through the door with a woman by his side. Memories of the pudgy little girl in a blue dress exploded in my mind. One time I'd even led her around on my old quarter-horse gelding for a few minutes before I went for a ride. Rebecca had rattled off excitely the entire time about how much she loved to draw horses. I remember thinking how different her personality was from Rowan's. Her brother had barely spoken to me and almost never looked me in the eye back in those days. Now, he seemed to find extreme pleasure in boring holes into my flesh with a broody gaze.

"Wow, I didn't recognize you. You've grown up quite a bit." I said the words slowly, careful not to show my astonishment that the vibrant and healthy-looking girl I'd met years ago was dangerously thin and so softly spoken now.

"I've grown in so many ways," Rebecca murmured, shooting a sly look at Rowan.

His lips thinned and his eyes narrowed at her. She giggled and ignored him. "Rowan says he's going to train your horses."

I nodded uncomfortably. "That's right."

"I would love to see them, Katie. Is it all right if I tag along with Rowan sometimes?"

The grunt that erupted from Rowan's throat drew my attention. His features that were playful a moment before hardened. Before I could say anything, he scolded his sister. "No, Rebecca. Training the horses is serious work and I don't want any distractions. Besides, when you're not working at the butcher shop, Ma needs your help."

Rebecca toyed with her fingers on the table. She snorted out a jarring laugh, raising her brow at him. "Oh, I'm sure you're not too concerned about distractions."

"Rebecca," Rowan growled out in a lower voice.

My cheeks burned. I cleared my throat, trying to defuse the banter between the siblings. "Aren't you a little young to be working at a butcher shop?" I interrupted.

Rebecca eyed me. "I'm eighteen, an adult now. I started there when I was fifteen." She held up her hand and it was then that I noticed the tip of her left index finger, where her fingernail should have been, was missing. "This happened that first year, so I guess you could say I was probably too young to work there back then."

I caught my breath. Heavy anger tightened my gut. "Your parents allowed you to work in a butcher shop when you were just a kid?"

Her grin was wicked. "They're the ones who forced me to go to work there. I would rather have been anywhere else."

"It's not all that bad," Rowan said weakly.

I couldn't stop my eyes from bulging. "Are you kidding? There are laws about child labor – and she lost part of her finger!"

"Those laws don't apply to the Amish," Rebecca said sweetly. She sat up straighter, crossed her arms over her chest, and stared at Rowan. "I can still paint with my damaged finger, so it's not a big deal."

"Stop it, Rebecca. We're supposed to be having a nice dinner. You wanted to come."

Rebecca's expression abruptly deflated from severe annoyance to tired sadness. "Yes, yes, you're right." She tilted her head. "I'm sorry to be so rude, Katie. Rowan was kind to take me out to eat at the restaurant. I'm being a horrible ingrate."

Her change of tone made my head spin. "I'll get you those drinks right way."

I ducked away from the table before either sibling could stop me.

After filling the drinks, I asked Tessa to take them to Rowan's table and also to get the rest of their order. Something about Rebecca's sudden change of personality spooked me. It reminded me of Daddy, and how he could be so rude and temperamental one minute, and then act like nothing had ever happened the next. But Rebecca's despair was real. She was seriously unhappy.

Perhaps that was why Rowan had taken her out to dinner. The lobby was filling up and most of the tables and booths were already taken. It was going to be a long night. I wondered if Rowan still planned to work with any of the horses tonight. The babble of voices and the drone of the country music through the stereo evaporated.

My gaze drifted across the dining room.

Unsurprisingly, Rowan's eyes met mine. He resembled a wolf seeking his prey, and I was suddenly confident that he would be at the ranch when my shift ended and I returned home.

EIGHT

Rowan

"It's late. Where are you going, son?"

Father's voice in the darkness slowed the beating of my heart and I paused my fingers on the saddle riggings. Scout turned his head and nickered at Father when he stepped into the small spray of light from the lantern hanging in the barn aisle.

As I was twenty-two, Father gave me more freedom than he did Rebecca or Nathaniel. I was a grown man and contributed income to the running of the farm and family business. Most evenings, no one paid much notice if I went for a night ride. After all, by the time I arrived home from work, did the evening chores, and ate dinner, it was usually fairly late. But I wasn't surprised that leaving the house at close to midnight had spurred his attention. I had hoped to slip away quietly and unnoticed to avoid just this conversation we were about to have.

Ignoring his penetrating gaze, I stared at the saddle as I tightened the girth. "You're up pretty late yourself, Da. Is something amiss?"

I glanced up to see Father cock his head. He toyed with the end of his beard and his eyes were unusually bright. He grunted. "Turning the questions on me, eh, boy?" Father paused and I didn't speak. He took a step forward and patted Scout's neck. The moon was only a sliver in the sky and the air was still warm for an October night. Something else stirred on the faint breeze that made me stand taller and draw in a sharp breath. If change had a feel, this was it. I sensed things were about to happen to our family, and maybe even the community as well.

When Father finally spoke again, his voice was easy, almost reserved. "I was restless and couldn't sleep." His gaze shifted to the house. "I had a feeling that your sister might be up to her usual tricks, sneaking out after dark, or something like that."

"Rebecca is asleep in bed. You could have seen that with your own eyes without having to come out into the night to investigate," I replied quickly, regretting my harsh words when Father's brows rose in a startled way.

"Yes, I confirmed that she was in her room. But here

you are, Rowan, quietly slipping into the night." Fathered leveled a hard look at me over Scout's back.

"Just the other day you said I'm a man. Isn't it about time you begin treating me as such?"

Father's eyes widened, but he remained calm. "You haven't answered my question. Where are you going, son?"

I was anxious to mount my horse and be on my way. There was a good chance Katie would be home by now. The minutes were ticking away, and I still had to cover the few miles' distance on horseback to the Porter ranch. It was times like this that being Amish was especially inconvenient. For the first time in a while, my lack of freedom to do what I wanted, when I wanted, burned a hole in my gut. Mother and Father had been so caught up with Rebecca lately that they'd all but ignored my comings and goings. It was like a splash of cold water to once again experience the tight leash my sister had been enduring. It was frustrating to be treated like a child when I was a grown man. Deep down, I knew that what was really riling my insides was that I knew Father would disapprove of where I was going – and he was right to do so. My interest in training the Porters's horses wasn't merely business, or even wanting to raise money to help my sister. I had readily agreed to take the job because, more than anything else, I desired to see more of Katie Porter. Father was right to worry about any time I spent with the red-headed English woman. She was dangerous to me in too many ways to count.

There was also the fact that what I was doing would ultimately create a rift between my parents and me. If I helped Rebecca leave the Amish, they might never forgive me. Emotions and indecision battled in my mind as I returned Father's gaze.

I was Amish, and even though I'd been born into this way of life, I'd also chosen to stay in it. When I was younger, I could have left if I'd really wanted to. Being a man, it would have been easy for me. At least, easier than it would be for Rebecca. I had carpentry and welding skills, not to mention my farrier abilities and horse-training experience. If I'd wanted to go English, I would have been able to get work and provide for myself, and eventually, even a family. But I hadn't gone down that path. I'd remained Amish for many reasons, but mostly because the simple way of life was peaceful. I loved to farm the land, like Father, and I respected the old ways – like Church on Sundays and helping a neighbor raise a barn. Transportation by horse suited me just fine. And my faith was much stronger than my sister's. I believed the things taught in the Bible and the close community gave me comfort. The Amish world was my world.

I sighed deeply, knowing in my heart that by helping Rebecca, I'd be going against the rules I'd agreed to live by. I would hurt my parents and bring shame to our family. It would be so much easier if my sister fit in and enjoyed the Plain life as much as I did. But she was what she was. Unless something drastic happened to change her course, she would eventually leave the community, with or without my assistance.

The hard truth set in. I didn't want things to change – for me or my sister. I wouldn't break the promise I'd made to Rebecca, but that didn't mean that I shouldn't do everything in my power to change her mind about staying with us. I knew it wasn't something I could do on my own, though.

With more resolve than I'd felt a few hours ago, I stood up straighter and met Father's steady gaze. "You're being too hard on Rebecca. She's different to us. Her head is always darting around in the clouds, while ours are grounded to the earth." Father tilted his head and was about to speak, but I plowed on. "She's been trying, Da, really she has. She's restless and confused. Maybe if you allowed her to talk to someone outside of our community, it might greatly help her."

"So your midnight ride is because of worry over your sister?" He shook his head. "She's not your concern, and if you allow her to manipulate you into feeling sorry for her, she'll only bring you down when she falls."

I dropped the stirrup leather with a whack that made Scout flinch. Pressing my hand against the horse's neck to steady him, I asked, "Don't you pity Rebecca at all? She's your daughter, and she's struggling."

Father didn't raise his voice. "She's creating her own turmoil, and if she doesn't respond to help from the elders, she'll cause trouble for the entire family." I opened my mouth to argue but he held up his hand to silence me. "The demons in her mind were put there by the outside world. Don't think I don't know what I'm talking about. I've seen firsthand the temptations that are out there, and how they wrap around a person's heart with lies and promises of freedom. Englishers aren't any more unshackled than we are. It's all an illusion that too many of our young people fall for. They don't know until it's too late what they've given up." Father's eyes sparked with emotion but his voice remained steady. "I'm trying to save your sister from herself. I only hope it's not too late. She'd never survive in the English world. It would chip away at pieces of her until nothing was left. Without family, faith, and community, she'd be lost. Just like Lucinda." Father's expression softened and he handed me Scout's bridle from the peg. "Don't let Rebecca trick you into thinking you'd be doing the right thing to help her run away. It would be a disaster for her ... and you – something you'd forever regret."

I swallowed the lump down in my throat. "I have no intention of doing such a thing," I lied.

Father's smile was pinched. "Do you remember that

stray cat that showed up in the barn when you were seven years old?"

A memory of the thin calico sprang to life in my mind, and I was confused.

Father continued. "You carried that cat around in a sack on your shoulder because she was too weak to walk much on her own. You snuck special treats out to her in the morning, afternoon, and night, yet she still didn't regain her strength. You were determined to save that silly cat but it was always out of your hands."

"What are you talking about?" My insides froze and I held my breath.

"Son, she didn't run off like I told you. The cat was sick with an illness that wasn't treatable. I saw it. Your mother saw it. But you wouldn't accept it. One day, while you were at school, I ended the cat's suffering and buried her along the hedgerow. You were still young and I didn't have the heart to tell you the truth of it. You've always had a kind heart, Rowan. I would expect nothing less than for you to take pity on your sister, the same way you did that poor cat. I'm just warning you that some things are out of your control and you must tread carefully or your generous spirit will cause you all kinds of suffering. If I hadn't taken that cat's life, its illness would have surely passed onto the other barn cats. More would have suffered and died. It's a life lesson, son."

My mind spun with the burst of information. It had

been years since I'd thought about that particular cat. Deep down, I guess I'd always thought that she'd gone off somewhere to die, alone and in peace. The fact that Father had sped along that journey wasn't really surprising. It was the comparison he was making to Rebecca's situation that sent a ripple of chills up my arms. I began to wonder if I was doing the right thing by helping my sister leave the Amish. Father was right about one thing. Her problems would follow her into the outside world, and she'd be alone.

Father stepped back as I swung into the saddle. "Enjoy your ride."

I picked up the reins and squeezed Scout's sides. The horse took a few steps and I pulled him around, facing Father.

"I'm training the Porters's two-year-olds up for the December sale. That's where I'm going – to the Diamond E Ranch to get some work done with them tonight. With my work schedule during the week, nights are the only real time I'll have with them."

"I'm surprised Charlie hired you on," Father said in a slow, deliberate way.

"Charlie Porter died in a car accident. His daughter contacted me." Seeing Father's nostrils flare, I quickly added, "It sounds like Katie and her mother need the income to pay for the farm."

"Didn't Charlie take care of things for them?"

I shrugged. "I don't know about the details. Katie hasn't said much. She just seems desperate to get the colts sold."

"I see." Father smoothed down his beard as he stared into the darkness. I waited and after a moment he looked up and his eyes were clear again. "You better get going then. You'll need at least a few hours of sleep before morning."

A weight was lifted off my shoulders. "Thanks, Da. I won't be too long."

Before I had the chance to bump Scout's sides, Father spoke up once more. "Rowan, don't make the mistake of becoming attached to that Porter girl. It's just business, right?"

"Of course. The extra money will come in handy when I start building my house someday."

"I was already married and you were on the way when I was your age. It's about time you find a nice Amish girl and settle down."

I forced a smile. "If I ever find the time, that's the next thing I'm working on." It didn't pass my notice that Father had accentuated *Amish* girl.

"That'll be the best thing in the world for you, son. Having a good woman at your side has a lot of benefits." He winked and slapped Scout on the rump.

I cantered down the driveway without looking back. The moment of relief I'd experienced when Father had

approved of me training the Porters's horses passed
quickly. He'd got his warning in. The worst part of it was
that he was right. I didn't want to become attached to
Katie Porter, and I was afraid I was already in deeper
than I ought to be.

NINE

Katie

I saw the lights shining in the barn when I got out of my truck. Lady ran from the shadows to greet me as I quietly closed the door behind me. Hopefully, Momma had taken a couple of the sleeping pills that the doctor had prescribed, but I still didn't want to risk waking her.

Reaching down to stroke Lady's head, I murmured, "I guess you didn't give Rowan a hard time when he rode up, did you, girl?"

Lady whined her answer. I slipped on my denim jacket and took a wavering breath, forcing myself to walk slowly as I made my way to the barn. I hated the way my heart bounced in my chest.

The red dun filly was tied and saddled in the hallway. Rowan was unsnapping the crossties when he saw me.

His face lit up. I made a mental note that he was very

113

awake for the middle of the night. I stifled a yawn and breathed in the cool night air, trying to revive myself.

"You look tired," he said.

"It was a long shift, and I didn't get much sleep last night." I could have kicked myself for saying the last part.

"Funny, neither did I."

The breath fluttered in my lungs. "This is Laurel," I sputtered out, petting the filly's velvet nose. "She's Dusty's first foal."

Rowan stepped back and studied the filly intently. "I had no idea."

I laughed a little. "She's a lot friendlier than her mother."

"No kidding. This little mare hasn't given me an ounce of trouble. She'll make someone a fine horse." He looked up. "Do you still have that ornery mother of hers?"

"Sure do. She has a five-month-old foal at her side. I'm getting ready to wean it any day now. After you left, it was my number one mission to tame her down. I rode her every day of the week until she finally settled. She became my best trail horse, if you can believe it."

"Sure, I always thought she had potential. She just had to learn to trust people and figure out she wasn't the boss."

The dark sky lit up and we both turned our heads to

the doorway. A low rumble sounded in the distance and at the same time the wind picked up from a soft breeze to a steady drone that flipped the leaves on the trees.

I crossed the aisle and looked outside. A hard gust picked up the dust, sweeping it across the barnyard.

"Looks like we're in for a storm," Rowan said from behind. He stopped beside me, following my gaze to the billowing clouds gathering to the west of the farm.

"It might miss us," I muttered. "We could use the rain, though."

Rowan nodded. "Yes, a little rain would be nice. It's been a dry autumn."

We stood there silently, our sides nearly touching. The wind popped with energy and for an instant my exhaustion was forgotten. So too were the unpaid mortgage and tax bills, Momma's health issues, and my cheating daddy's death. There was just the force of nature beyond the barn, the horses ... and Rowan.

"I'm sorry about the way my sister acted," Rowan said quietly.

I turned to him. "I get the feeling she's a handful," I replied simply.

He graced me with a little smile. "That's putting it mildly." He inhaled and I sensed he wanted to say more so I remained still. "She wants to leave the Amish."

I gasped. "Really?"

He nodded and returned to Laurel, quickly

unsaddling her. I followed him deeper into the barn where Laurel's stall was. With the wind gusting even more, it wasn't a bad idea to get her safely confined.

Once the stall door was latched, Rowan's focus returned to me. "She has problems – depression, sometimes anxiety. It's gotten worse lately. My folks are in denial about it. They think her problems can be fixed by a change of attitude, some Bible study, and social interactions with the other girls. I'm afraid none of that will help her."

He leaned back against the wall, folding his hands across his chest. The sky lit up again, and this time the groaning of thunder was louder. The rainfall started as a few loud taps and quickly turned to a million tiny thuds on the tin roof.

Rowan and I were temporarily trapped in the barn together. The realization sent a thrill through my system.

"She did seem a little unhinged at the restaurant." I mimicked Rowan, crossing my arms and trying to appear as nonplused as he did that we were alone, in a barn, during a storm. "How can she possibly leave your people? I mean, she doesn't even have a proper education, does she?"

The lights in the barn flickered as the wind battered the walls. Rowan wasn't paying a lot of attention to the unruly weather. His eyes were fixated on me, unblinking. "Eighth grade, same as me."

"Wow, I knew you guys didn't stay in school long, but I had no idea you finished before high school. Can she make a living and take care of herself?"

He exhaled. His face was grim. "It's different for the girls. Ever since I was a kid, I've been learning carpentry, farming, farrier work, and even some welding. I could make it just fine wherever I lived, and so could all of my friends, but Rebecca hasn't had any real training in anything, other than cutting meat at the butcher shop and doing the household chores. She's a talented artist, but I don't think she can earn enough money to pay the bills from her art. I'm not sure what she'll do ... and that's my problem."

"Your problem?"

He looked away and back again. A gust swept down the hallway, bringing colder air. Rowan stepped away from the wall and positioned himself between me and the weather.

"She's asked me to help get her out. At first I was thinking that at least she'd get medical help on the outside, but now I'm not sure it's the best thing for her."

I had a million thoughts swirling around in my head about his sister and her leaving the Amish, but I tried not to be judgmental or pushy. I had my own prejudices about the Amish lifestyle and I didn't think I was a good person to offer advice on such a life-changing decision.

Rowan pinned me with a steady gaze. He wasn't

wearing his usual hat and when he ran his fingers through his thick, dark hair with a tug, shivers raced up my arms. "What do you think I should do?"

His question took me aback. Rowan was a determined, confident man. I had just assumed that he was the type who made his own decisions – especially those related to his family and culture.

I recalled Rebecca's pretty face. She had a unique personality that fluctuated from shy to outgoing. I could see a girl like her going wild if there were no guiding hands in her life. "She could still get her GED and go to college. Perhaps a focused goal would be good for her. She could even incorporate her love of art and do graphic design or be an art teacher," I suggested.

"I've thought of all that. The problem is, once she leaves the community, she'll be shunned. My parents and I won't be able to have much contact with her."

The word shunned had the effect of a curse word. I was about to give my opinion on such an archaic response to Rebecca leaving the Amish when a flutter of movement in the shadows above Remington's stall caught my eye.

My heart dropped into my stomach. "Momma must have forgotten to shut up the coop!" I sprinted to the sound and craned my neck to see better into the shadows. The little cream-colored rooster was perched on the railing with its head lolled to the side. I could hear the rattle of his sleeping breaths.

Rowan hovered behind me and I ignored his close presence, reaching for the bird.

"Why don't you just leave him alone for the night? He looks safe enough for the time being," Rowan said.

"Naw. I lost three hens last week. The night we got the news about Daddy, Momma and I completely forgot about closing the coop's door. The hens roosted on rafters in the barn and a raccoon got all of them. I'm not taking any chances with this little guy."

Rowan sidled up against me, his hip brushing my side as he reached up and grabbed the comatose, sleeping bird. He handed me the rooster with a chuckle. "You're as bad as I am about keeping my livestock safe."

I pressed the rooster against my breast and jogged down the aisle.

"Hey, where are you going?" Rowan caught up to me.

"I'm putting him back in the coop. I want to get the door shut for the night," I shouted over my shoulder. The wind was still whipping but the rain had slowed to a spattering of drops. Thunder grumbled loudly.

I rounded the corner at a brisk walk and headed straight for the coop at the far end of the corral. I didn't have to look back to know Rowan was still following me. His boots made splashing noises in the mud and puddles. My nerves had chilled somewhat at the sobering conversation we'd had before I'd seen the loose rooster. Rowan thought his sister's life was complicated, which meant the issue of going English wasn't something he had even considered. Since I certainly wasn't trading in my blue jeans and pickup truck for a polyester dress and buggy, the idea of even a flirtatious romance with the handsome man was insane. We hadn't been thinking clearly when we'd shared a couple of kisses as teenagers. It had been a spur-of-the-moment thing. I shook my head and grunted, angry with myself for thinking so much about Rowan in the past few days. There was no doubt I was attracted to him and I was overly curious about what kissing the man would be like compared to the boy. I was willing to bet it would be even more satisfying than when we were inexperienced kids but I didn't have the time or energy to flirt with a man that I could never have. Momma's story of her past had made me realize that Rowan, like his father, would only be interested in a fling with an Englisher before he settled down with a woman from his community. For my own sanity, I had to forget about Rowan. I had probably just misread his brooding glances as mutual infatuation. In truth, he hadn't said or done anything to show any real interest anyway.

Thunder clapped directly overhead and a flash of lightning lit the sky. The dark clouds opened up and a wall of rain struck. I held the rooster close and stretched out my legs, making a run for the coop. The pelting water stung my cheeks and the air tingled with electricity. I ducked through the open doorway into the small building. Several hens clucked, jumping from their roosting places, frightened. The ceiling was low and Rowan's head almost grazed it. He flung the door shut against the driving rain. The sky brightened with another boom of thunder and for an instant, I saw Rowan's face clearly. His hair was plastered to his face and his shirt was drenched. The thought of what my own appearance must be like rocked me and I burst out laughing. The rooster finally woke from his trance and was startled, flapping clumsily onto the nearest perch.

The tin roof above our heads was assaulted by the frenzied downpour. It was so loud I couldn't hear what Rowan had just said, but I'd seen his mouth move. I took a step closer in the cramped space to hear him better.

The coop shook from the pounding wind and rain, but the storm was just a stray thought in my mind. I stood near enough to Rowan's chest that I had to drop my head back to look up at him. Rowan's intense gaze was fixed on me and a muscle in his jaw shivered. The breath caught in my throat and I was suddenly flooded with heat. There was an urgency in his dark eyes that wasn't there before. The world went hazy for a moment and my legs felt weak. When I focused on him finally, I found his expression full of wanting.

With a surprised grunt, Rowan's hand rose to my face and he carefully pushed the wet tendrils of hair back. The touch sent a shock of vibrations through me. I rocked on my heels and then took a step back. Rowan followed me and I retreated, until my back bumped into the coop's wooden wall. I could feel his breath on my flushed cheeks and his eyes were wide and watchful.

I couldn't breathe. I couldn't move a muscle.

Rowan's voice was rough when he whispered, "I've wondered for a long time what it would be like to kiss you again."

This isn't really happening. I must be dreaming.

When a bolt of lightning lit the small room, it was impossible to deny that Rowan loomed over me. And the look of pure longing on his face was undeniable. Something inside of me snapped, freeing me from inhibition. I sank into him and his arms quickly encircled me. His muscled chest rose and fell against my breasts. Lightning lit up his face, and the intensity of his desire made me lightheaded. I parted my lips and mumbled, "Me too."

My heart felt like it would explode in my chest. When I dropped my gaze, unsure of what the hell I was doing, Rowan brought his fingertips to my chin and lifted it back up, forcing me to meet his pleading gaze.

"May I kiss you, Katie?" he asked in a deep voice that was full of emotion.

The moment swept away any common sense I might have had left. I could only nod and part my lips.

Rowan's mouth touched mine ever so carefully. He exhaled a small groan and his tentative breath made me impatient for more. With a hunger I'd never experienced before, I opened up to him, and our tongues tangled together. He gripped me tighter and I felt his hard bulge pressed into my thigh. Our kiss was slow and deliberate, like we were both savoring what we had been longing for.

Somewhere, way down in my consciousness, I heard a tiny voice. *Are you crazy? He's Amish...*

With Rowan's strong arms squeezing me and his lips moving against mine, I didn't care. I wanted this moment, had needed it for the past six years. Sure, I'd kissed other men since then – and done much more – but Rowan's face had never been far from my thoughts. I'd remembered how perfectly we'd fit together when he'd held me close and then I'd experienced jealousy thinking about him loving another girl. He had come to me on many nights when I'd closed my eyes, even though I'd tried desperately to forget him. I could hardly believe that the man of my dreams was kissing me; a man who was completely forbidden was running his hands up and down my back as he grew bold and nipped at my bottom lip.

"Katie, dear, Katie, you mean everything to me—"

His declaration worked the same as a blast of cold water. I pulled back, breathing hard. Rowan didn't release me and his gaze was flooded with passion.

How could I mean everything to him? We'd just been reunited after years apart. Unless he'd been thinking about me, the same way I'd been obsessing with him, all of these years...

My heart hammered as I stared back at Rowan. I sensed that he was holding back, being overly gentle and carefully controlling his trembling desire. A wolf lurked beneath his skin. I'd seen glimpses of that side of him when he'd watched me from afar. His soft words to the horses and his patience with them was what originally drew me in, but Rowan was also a dominant man. That was why the horses accepted him as their leader. He was powerful and capable – one hundred percent male. And right now, I was experiencing a primal longing for him that scared the hell out of me. The core of my being tingled painfully with anticipation. I was ready to have him take me right then and there in the chicken coop, but Rowan's emotionally charged words sobered me. There would be no one-night stand with this man. I could read it in his eyes that this was very serious to him. The stress of the past week had sucked the life out of me, and I would have been ecstatic for a fun fling with a handsome guy, but Rowan was Amish. It changed everything.

I wanted to leap back into Rowan's arms, but my head got in the way.

I opened my mouth and began to mumble something about slowing things down when a roaring boom of thunder and a loud crash split the stormy night in two. Rowan released me and jumped to the door, flinging it open. Sheets of rain pelted down horizontally and the trees bent in the same direction.

"Do you see anything? Is it the house or barn?" I squealed, trying to push past him.

Rowan grabbed up my arm. "I can't see a thing."

I wriggled against him, attempting to get away.

"Whoa. You're not going anywhere. It's not safe yet," Rowan warned.

I sagged against him, giving up. Another gust struck the coop and the small building rocked. Chickens were dislodged from the rails, and feathers flew everywhere as they readjusted with a flurry of flapping of wings. I pulled my cellphone from my back pocket. The weather warning flashed red and I swiped it, studying the radar map.

Rowan leaned over me, looking at the screen with rapt interest. I wasn't sure how much he'd handled a cellphone or used the internet. In a nonchalant way, I zoomed in and pointed to where the ranch was.

"It's almost past us," he said excitedly.

"Yeah, the worst of it should be over in a minute or two," I agreed.

As if on cue, the rain lessened considerably and the wind died down. The next shot of light was followed by a lower, quieter rumble of thunder.

I reached again for the door handle and paused to search Rowan's face. When he nodded, I rushed outside.

Splashing through the puddles, I ran along the side of the main barn, checking out the roofline as I went. Rowan split away from me and headed around the backside of the one-hundred-and-twenty-foot structure. I held my breath until I made it to the front door. Other than the wheel barrel being blown over and a few empty buckets littering the hallway, everything looked fine.

I turned just as Rowan dashed inside. "The rest of the barn looks all right."

I swallowed and ran past him. The clouds were moving off to the east and I spied a few twinkling lights making an appearance. The sprinkle of rain was only an annoyance as I passed the round pen. Fresh leaves that had been ripped from the tree tops littered the ground under my feet.

The sight that rose up in front of me caused me to screech to halt in the muddy gravel.

"Damn," Rowan said quietly as he pulled up alongside of me.

My mouth dropped and I found it difficult to catch a

breath. Rowan touched my shoulder but I shook his hand away and took two more wobbly steps.

The ninety-year-old oak tree, whose branches shaded the porch in the summertime and protected the north side of the house in the wintertime, was completely toppled. If that wasn't bad enough, it had landed squarely on my red pickup truck.

Rowan's voice came up from behind me. "Do you have insurance?"

"Yeah," I muttered, dazed.

"That's a blessing anyway. At least it didn't strike the house." He stepped in front of me and captured my gaze. "That would have been much worse."

"I know. I know," I lashed out as I took in how my truck had been flattened down to about three feet in height. The tires were the only things that weren't grotesquely distorted under the wreckage of the massive tree. "My poor truck," I sputtered.

Rowan had started to move toward me with his arms lifted, when I heard the shrill gasp from somewhere beyond the branches.

"Mercy, I can't believe that proud tree got struck down," Momma exclaimed. "Oh my word, is that Katie's truck under it?" Momma's voice rose quickly to a higher pitch. "Katie?" she shouted.

"Momma, I'm okay, I'm over here," I managed to answer in my shocked state.

Rowan's arms dropped to his sides and I jogged all the way around the top of the tree to reach Momma. She stood on the bottom step of the porch in her green robe. Strands of her long hair flew wildly around her. I rushed into her tight embrace.

"Oh, I'm so relieved you weren't still in that truck, Katie. You could have died." She shook against me. "I don't know what I would have done if—"

"I'm fine, really I am. I went to shut up the coop after I found one of the roosters in the barn."

Momma abruptly straightened. "Land sakes! I forgot to shut up them chickens. I fell asleep and only woke when I heard the crash."

I smoothed down Momma's hair and shushed her. "It's all right. No worries at all. The horses and chickens are just fine, and I'm sure the cattle made it through the storm. Our dog is right here and the house is still standing." Lady's wet tongue on my hand made me feel a little better.

"Your truck, Katie. What about that?" Momma said indignantly.

I licked my lips and forced out some confidence that I wasn't exactly feeling. "The insurance should cover the cost to replace it. It's not a big deal."

"Not a big deal?" Momma swooned a little and I slipped my arm around her back. "It's just one more thing on your overly full plate." Her hand pressed to her heart. "It might take weeks to replace it."

"I can use your car to drive to work, and I'm sure the Templetons will let us borrow their truck to get bags of feed and bedding for the time being," I rattled off, trying to soothe Momma's worries. She was under way too much stress as it was, and at risk for of an MS attack.

"I'll come by first thing in the morning, Mrs. Porter, to saw the branches out of the way. In the next few days, I'll get the tree trunk moved for you. I'm sure Father will help." Rowan had snuck up on us. He stood a few feet away, wearing an eager expression.

Momma sucked in her surprise. "I had no idea you were here, young man."

Rowan ran his hand through his wet hair in a suddenly self-conscious way. "Sorry, ma'am. I thought you would have heard me trotting my horse up your driveway."

Momma swatted the air. "Those darn pills I've been taking since Charlie died really knock me out." She glanced at me. "I'm throwing the bottle away in the morning."

"I don't know if it's a good idea to get rid of them just yet," I said.

"Nonsense. You need my help and it's about time I get out of the fog."

I snorted. "I'm the one who might need them."

Momma's brows drew together. She looked between me and Rowan, and a tiny smile curled at the corner of her mouth. "I see," she mumbled. Her voice gained solidity when she turned to Rowan. "Thank you for the offer to clean up the tree. We'll take you up on it but I'd rather you didn't ask your dad for help. He's a busy man and I don't want to be a burden to any more of your family."

"It's no trouble at all—"

Momma cut him off with a fierce look that made me cringe. "I don't want that man on this ranch."

Rowan shrank back but his eyes blazed. "Excuse me?"

"Go inside, Momma. I'll be right there," I urged softly.

Momma's lips twitched. "Don't forget what I told you earlier today. Don't make the same mistake I did," she warned in a jerky whisper.

I shooed her up the stairs and inhaled deeply before I joined Rowan at the bottom of the steps.

"Momma hasn't been herself lately. Daddy's death was a shock, and our financial situation at the moment is adding to her stress level. Don't read too much into what she says." I avoided looking directly at him by staring at my truck's shiny, mangled bumper that poked out from under a stubby cluster of limbs.

"She was very determined, almost as if she had a

personal reason for not wanting my father to be here." Rowan spoke slowly, as if he was trying to figure it all out in his own head.

I dropped my head back, rolling my neck until it popped a few times. What a day it had been – starting out with Rowan coming back into my life, like a raging tornado, and making my head spin with the craziness of my attraction to him. Then I find out that Momma had a fling with his father, and following a long night on my feet at the restaurant, Rowan acts as if we've been buddies forever, wanting my advice about his troubled sister. After the best kiss I've ever experienced, I get cold feet and here I am, standing beside my flattened truck, trying to keep a secret from Rowan.

I owed it to Momma to keep her secret, but dammit, Rowan was much more thoughtful than I imagined. He stared at me with narrowed eyes and such intense perception that I knew I couldn't trick him into forgetting about what had just happened with simple denial. I would have to be clever to keep Rowan from finding out about the romance between Momma and his father.

I quickly searched my mind for something reasonable to say.

"Um, Momma had a bad experience with an Amish contractor some years ago. She's a little gun shy now." I hoped my firm nod would get him to let it go.

"Who was it? Someone from the community?" I

shrugged, shaking my head and he went on, "Our people take pride in having happy customers and being fair at all times. I must know who caused your mother to feel this way so I can fix it."

Epic fail.

Annoyance bubbled from my belly, up my throat and out my mouth. "I don't know who it was and I'm not going to bother Momma about it right now," I snapped. "She doesn't want your dad helping with the tree. End of story."

Rowan stared and his tongue slid between his lips. The same tongue that had been exploring my mouth only minutes before. His face dropped and I clearly saw the wall of uncertainty rise up over his brown eyes. I suddenly had the urge to spring forward and jump into his arms, to tell him that everything was all right, and that I wanted to kiss him again ... and again. Instead, I stood like a statue, my arms folded tightly over my chest and my jaw set.

"Understood." Rowan whirled around, skirting the fallen tree and heading for the barn.

The rain had pretty much stopped but drops still assailed me, wicking from the fluttering leaves in the stiff the breeze. I tapped my foot, irritated at Rowan and even more so at myself. Why did I even care that this man, whom I barely knew, was walking away with hurt feelings? I shouldn't give a damn.

Oh, but I did.

My insides quivered and my mouth became uncomfortably dry as I watched Rowan leaving.

"Shoot!" I hissed under my breath.

I sprinted after Rowan, grabbing his arm when I caught up to him. He stopped and slowly turned.

"Are you still going to train the horses?" I breathed.

Rowan's brows furrowed and the corner of his mouth rose in a nasty smirk. "Is that all you want, Katie? For me to train up your colts in six weeks? Is that all that matters to you?"

This is bullshit, I thought. I was just trying to make conversation, to smooth things over. I was almost to the threshold where my temper would spring to life.

"It's important that the horses are fully trained by the sale in December." I worked hard to keep my tone pleasant. "I thought I made that quite clear to you already."

Rowan's features tightened and he nodded to himself. "Sure, I keep my promises." He suddenly leaned in. His lithe body towered over me and I fought to keep from stepping back. "I guess that little make-out session in the chicken coop meant nothing, right?"

My head began to throb with his back and forth of emotions. What did he want from me? Wasn't it just as obvious to him as it was to me that it would never work out between us? Tears threatened to fall from my gritty eyes and the knot of frustration in the pit of my stomach was almost unbearable. More than anything, I wished that Rowan was a normal guy – but he wasn't. He was an Amish man. We couldn't be together. It was impossible.

I closed my eyes, gathered my words carefully for a change, and then opened my eyes again. Rowan was still waiting there. The lines of his heavily muscled arms and chest were visible beneath the wet material and he was close enough that I felt the heat from his skin.

"I wouldn't exactly call it a make-out session but it was fun," I said quickly and without emotion.

Hurt and anger flashed in his eyes. "You must get around with the men quite a bit to so easily dismiss our encounter."

My insides churned to icy queasiness.

"How dare you say something like that!" I growled.

"Don't fret your pretty head about the horses. Like I said, I keep my promises. I'll swing by in the morning to saw up the tree like I told your ma I would. But I won't be back to work on the training for a couple of days. I'll be busy with the benefit dinner at the schoolhouse and these late nights aren't going to work with my schedule. Rest assured, I'll get it done – but the best time for me will be late afternoons, while you're at work."

He took a few steps backward and his stare was cold, unyielding. Losing the closeness of his body was jarring but his words were like being physically slapped.

Tears welled in the corners of my eyes, but I'd be damned if I let him see me cry. I spun on my heels and left him standing in a puddle in the darkness.

That was the second time I'd cried over Rowan Coblentz. He might like to brag that he kept his promises, but so did I. And I made a promise to myself as I jogged up the steps to the front porch that I would never let that man get under my skin again. I was smart enough to take the hint from the universe that Rowan wasn't the man for me.

I paused at the screen door, my fingers curling around the knob. The icy tentacles of despair thawed around my heart, turning into hot anger that burned in my chest.

At the sound of pounding hooves on gravel and splashing through puddles I turned my face. I watched Rowan gallop his horse past the house.

"So you're just like your daddy, huh, Rowan? Going around, all Godly handsome, and acting gentlemanly and flirtatious with an English girl. Then, right when that girl starts to open up a little, becomes intrigued, maybe even infatuated, you squash her heart, just like the tree that took out my truck." I said it out loud, to myself, or maybe I was hoping that my voice would carry on the damp wind, straight to Rowan.

I sucked in a heavy breath. "You're the one who's going to be crying, Rowan. Mark my words, you'll be the one with the broken heart in the end," I vowed.

TEN

Rowan

I set down the last box of donations from the Yoder's store on the dirt floor and straightened up. With hands on my hips, I surveyed the interior of the auction barn. The benches were set up neatly in rows all the way to the back of the building. Father and Elijah were helping the women hang the queen-sized auction quilt from a rafter. Bishop Graber was even surlier than usual, and I tilted my head to listen to his bristly tone. He was complaining that hanging the quilt was a job for the younger lads and asking, rather loudly, where they all were.

I left the barn and surveyed the schoolyard. Dozens of men and woman were already milling about, keeping busy with the tent raising, food preparation, and moving their buggies and horses to make room for the flow of English vehicles that would be arriving soon.

I wiped my brow, lifting my face to the fading sunshine. Thankfully the rain had all but quit the night before and the muddy puddles had a chance to dry out somewhat. The ground was now thickly covered with fallen leaves and the steady breeze was bordering on crisp. I inhaled the change of season, blowing out slowly. It had been an early morning start, and even though the bishop felt justified in his annoyance with the younger men, I'd been working between the schoolhouse and auction barn nonstop since the sun was up.

Going on only a couple hours of restless sleep, I was exhausted – both physically and mentally. I raised my hand to cover the huge yawn that I couldn't stop from opening my mouth.

"It's all very boring, isn't it?"

The female voice instantly woke me. I turned to find Miriam Graber standing behind me. We'd grown up together and were the same age so her playful tone didn't sound strange to me. She was a wispy little thing, her head barely reaching my shoulder. Her blonde hair was perfectly tucked beneath her white cap, and her brown eyes matched her brown smock.

I smiled back. "It's been a long day and I didn't get much sleep last night," I said casually.

Miriam's brows rose and her pert nose lifted. "Oh,

really?" She grinned broadly. "Were you out in the dark, up to no good?"

Miriam wasn't one to shake the barrel, being able to keep a secret well, especially if it was something that might get one of her peers into trouble. Still, I wasn't going to confide in her about training horses at midnight and kissing my new employer in a chicken coop during the storm. I didn't want to even think about it, let alone talk about it, but it was difficult. Nearly every step I took that entire day, thoughts of Katie's warm skin beneath my fingers pestered me. Whenever I closed my eyes, her lips were brushing mine, and a hot longing would stir in my groin. The only thing that saved me was to remind myself how flippantly she'd commented that kissing me had been *fun*.

All the nights of dreaming about a girl I could never have, and then finally holding her in my arms had meant something to me. Hope had stirred in my heart for a moment, until she'd pretty much admitted that the entire encounter hadn't meant anything more to her than having a little entertainment. I wasn't interested in Katie Porter, or any other woman, for a good time. I wanted a deeper relationship that would someday turn into a holy commitment. Even though Katie was English – and I knew she wasn't right for me – I still had a spark of hope that maybe we could be together. She'd shot it down with one sentence, and the heavy resentment had overwhelmed me at sunrise, dimming the autumn splendor into gloomy muted tones. That anger helped to keep thoughts about Katie at bay, so I embraced the hard feeling happily.

"Naw. I took Rebecca out for dinner then I spent some time at the neighbor's training a horse," I said simply.

Miriam nodded but her smile remained and so did her inquisitive eyes. "That was quite a storm. Did everything hold up at your farm? Part of our greenhouse blew down."

An image of the huge oak tree pressing Katie's truck into the mud, flashed in my mind. "No damage at our place. That's too bad about your greenhouse. That must be why your father is in such a cranky mood."

She giggled. "That among other things."

Now it was my turn to raise a brow. She ignored my look and gestured to the bottom of the hill where the buggies were parked. "Would you care to help me bring a box of pies to the kitchen?" She blushed and glanced sideways. "It's an awkward size and I fear I'll dump all my hard work on the ground before I even reach the schoolhouse."

"Of course I will. Lead the way," I told her.

Miriam mumbled a thank you and began to make her way down the hill. She walked at a slow pace, almost leisurely, talking the entire way. She mentioned how nice it was of me to spend time with my sister and that she had noticed that Rebecca seemed rather glum lately. Then she rattled off everything she had done the previous week, and all that needed to be done the next one.

"What are your plans for the week, Rowan?" Miriam asked cheerfully.

I raised my hand for her to stop. Little Jeremy Mast, who couldn't be more than five years old, struggled to pull a shaggy miniature pony up the hill toward the barn. The stubborn beast planted its hooves into the grass and refused to move. I smothered my chuckle with my hand as I knelt down beside the boy.

"May I?" I pointed to the rope in his small, dirty hands.

Jeremy nodded, handing me the lead. His plump cheeks were beet-red from exertion and angst.

"He's a mean pony, he is." Jeremy spoke to me in our language, a form of German that most people called Pennsylvania Dutch. Kids his age were just learning English and relied mostly on their birth language when speaking within our community.

I answered him in kind. "Yes, perhaps, but even a mean pony can be tamed when handled the right way." I took my free hand and placed it at the boy's back. "Here you go. Stand up straighter and lift your chin. You must have an air of authority about you without looking too much like a predator." Jeremy stood tall and proud. His eyes were saucer-sized as he listened to my every word. "That's right. Very good. Now pick up the rope here." I moved his hands to the proper place, and keeping my hand right beside his, I twirled the end of the rope in the air. "Hold on tight. He's going to find his feet again and you want to be ready." Jeremy nodded. "Take the end of the rope and with a flick of your wrist, swat right behind him – no need to make contact at this point. It might only take a little coaxing, or a lot, but always begin with the small things," I instructed.

Jeremy had a sure hand, even for his limited size. He snapped the rope behind the pony and the movement of the rope out of the corner of the animal's eye was enough to wake the beast back up. He jerked forward, passing the boy. It was the pony who ended up leading the boy straight up the hill at a smooth trot.

"Thanks, Rowan!" Jeremy exclaimed, without the ability to turn back.

I laughed, shaking my head. I recalled those long-ago days of being dragged around, and sometimes even trampled, by difficult ponies. Every child had to begin somewhere.

"You're very good with kids," Miriam said softly.

I had forgotten all about her. "Ah, it's nothing. I only like kids when there's a horse or pony involved."

Miriam giggled as she continued on her way. "Won't you have a house full of your own children someday?"

Her question stunned me. I rubbed my fingers together and looked straight ahead. Just as we reached her father's buggy, which was parked in the middle of the long row, I realized our talk might be entering an inappropriate territory. Such thoughts hadn't even entered my mind when I'd been in Katie's company. The tension-filled banter we'd shared was very different to the polite conversation with Miriam. It was just mundane pleasantries between us, but with Katie it had felt like the beginning of something more. How wrong that perception had turned out to be.

I stepped between the buggies and really looked at Miriam for the first time. We had sat beside each other in school for eight years, so what I saw didn't surprise me in the least. I'd always favored Miriam, even considering her for courtship at times. The main drawback had always been that she was a bishop's daughter. Things could get complicated being Elijah Graber's son-in-law and I had always kept away from the politics in the community. Miriam was a pretty woman with a quick mind and a friendly manner. She got along well with all the other girls and could be found working diligently next to her mother and sisters whenever our family visited hers. She seemed as content with baking pies and hanging laundry as she was with bouncing a toddler on her knee or reading picture books to little girls. Unlike Rebecca, Miriam liked being Amish – at least, that was the impression she'd always given me. She wanted the same things I wanted: a family, a farm, and community. And she was Amish.

The best way to rid Katie Porter from my mind once and for all was to invest my energies into a woman like Miriam – and never look back.

"Yes, I will have a full house in time." I swallowed down the nervousness that made my heartrate soar and took a chance. "Is that the kind of life you want, Miriam?"

She glanced at her feet and then back up at me again. There was only a hint of a smile on her curved mouth. "I dream about having an entire bushel load of babies and making the perfect home for my future husband."

My mouth went dry. A rush of panic reached my head but I forced my voice to sound regular. "Would you mind if I drove you home in my buggy this evening, after the auction?"

Too quickly she answered, "If Da agrees, I'd love you to take me home tonight."

I was a little disappointed that she so readily agreed, and the thought of speaking to the bishop, in his current foul mood, was not something I looked forward to in the least.

I lifted the box from floorboard, ignoring the scents of sugar, cinnamon, baked apples, and cherries. The knot in my stomach made it impossible to enjoy the sweet aroma.

"Elijah, may I have a word with you?" I asked.

The bishop dragged his attention away from the sales list he was leaning over and looked up at me. Cars were beginning to line up in the driveway, creating a small traffic jam at the intersection. Horses whinnied and the voices of many conversations drifted into the office from the open window. The scent of roasting chicken was also in the air and I hated that I probably wouldn't enjoy my meal one bit. I was wondering what insanity had taken me over when I'd asked to drive Miriam home. It was an impulsive thing to do and I wished I'd given it more thought beforehand. Our people took courtship seriously, and relationships that soured between young people could affect the balance in the community. Elijah and Father were close friends. If it didn't work out with Miriam, there could be consequences for the entire family. Then again, there wasn't any reason to think it wouldn't work out, and getting Katie off my mind was my main concern at the moment. The very worst thing for me would have been to become so enamored with the English woman, that I left the Amish to be with her. It's something that had never really entered my mind before, but Katie was just the type of girl to make me lose my mind enough to fall into that kind of mistake. Instead of the rolling disappointment I felt toward her, I should be thankful that I learned of her true intentions, or lack of them, so quickly.

My last thought made me resigned. "May I drive Miriam home this evening? It won't be late," I added quickly.

Elijah sat back in his chair and considered me for a long, uncomfortable moment. The buzz of the ever-growing crowd beyond the walls didn't hurry the bishop at all.

Finally, he spoke. "Rowan, I know my congregation very well and I observe everyone, all the time – especially the young people. I have seven daughters, as you know. Six of them are now married women, and Miriam, being my youngest, is my only child left. She's very special to me. I guess the baby of the family always is."

He paused, giving me the opportunity to speak. "I understand, sir. I will treat Miriam with the utmost respect at all times."

Elijah scowled, waving his hand. "I would expect that, of course. I've seen with my own eyes that you're a quality, hard-working young man, with a gentle soul – just the sort of man I'd welcome into the family." He ran his fingers through his bushy beard. "What ails me is my own wisdom on the subject of our people." He leaned forward, crossing his arms on the desk. "I have found from many years of observance that families that have one troubled child – a child who leaves the fold – usually have at least one more that follows them out the door."

"Your worry is because of my sister?" Adrenaline coursed through my veins and I paced the length of the small room and back again. "Her problems are not my own."

"Have you ever had thoughts of leaving our way of life, Rowan?" The bishop's voice was cool as steel.

"Of course not," I lied. Just the night before when Katie was pressed up against me, the thought of running away with her had definitely crossed my mind. But I wasn't like Rebecca. I was satisfied right where I was and I certainly wasn't seriously contemplating leaving my people for an Englisher. "I am content to farm the land and work the horses, same as my father," I assured him.

"I hope so. I will not have my daughter's heart fooled by a man who doesn't know what he wants." Elijah's lips thinned and he eyed me shrewdly. "I want Miriam home by ten o'clock, not a minute later," he said.

"Yes, sir. I won't be late. Thank you."

Elijah pushed away from the desk and stood up. "Let's get this over with, so we can all go home."

I ducked around the auction barn, exhaling loudly. My goal was to get to my buggy where I might be able to sit quietly for a few moments, gathering my breath, but I was intercepted by Rebecca. Her shoulder bumped mine and she glanced over with a look that stilled my heart.

"What?" I asked worriedly.

Her lips spread wide and she flashed white teeth. "I just heard a very tasty bit of gossip, dear brother."

I slowed my steps, rolling my eyes. I waited until a group of giggling schoolgirls passed by, their colorful dresses looking like a rainbow in the crowd of dark coats, pants, and hats, before I leaned in. "Dare tell me," I teased, feeling instantly better. Rebecca's mood was as light as the puffy clouds dotting the sky for a change. I wouldn't do anything to burst her bubble of cheer.

"It came from an extremely reliable source that my older brother is driving Miriam Graber home this evening." Her wicked look made my heart sink. Why was she enjoying the revelation so thoroughly?

"It's not a big deal," I said.

She swatted my arm. "It is so, brother, and you know it." She whispered, "She's the bishop's daughter. What game are you playing?"

I avoided her piercing gaze. To have my flaky sister admonishing me was something new. "Where did you hear about it, anyway?"

"From Miriam. I overheard her telling the other girls the *exciting* news." She folded her arms in front her pale blue dress, inclining her head. "Really, Rowan. Couldn't you at least pick a girlfriend whose mind isn't as shallow as a puddle?"

"She's not my girlfriend. I'm just driving her home," I insisted in a low voice. I began walking again until the crowd thinned and we had reached the long shed where the horses were tied. Finding Scout, I sidled up next to him and patted his neck. Of course, Rebecca intruded, following me straight into the dim light of the overhang.

Rebecca ran her fingers along Scout's side, burying them in his thick fur. She was comfortable with silence for only a moment. "I like Katie better," she said in a humming voice.

"Are you nuts?" I hissed. "Good Lord, you've lost your mind."

"You like her," she said firmly.

"Why would you say such a thing?"

She shrugged, but her face was wide and alert. "I could tell at dinner last night. When she stood by our table, taking our orders, you stared at her like a lovesick fool." She ignored my snort, raising her voice. "And then, when she didn't come back, you kept looking around for her, even though you tried hard not to let me see what you were doing."

I opened my mouth to rebuke her words, but snapped it shut again. Rebecca had always been perceptive.

"I think she likes you too," she offered quietly.

"Why do you say that?" I hated that I cared so much, and even more that I wanted to talk to my sister about Katie.

"I couldn't help but feel the connection between the two of you. It was like a pulsating ribbon stretching from you to her and back again." Rebecca's eyes became foggy as she looked past me, remembering. "She's so pretty, and I love her red hair and blue eyes. I like her. She has spunk."

Oh, Katie was spunky, all right. I rested against Scout, dropping my head. I wished my sister hadn't reminded me of Katie's vibrant beauty. She was a firefly in the dark night – completely different from Miriam's subdued prettiness. Katie was hot to the touch in a way I couldn't imagine Miriam ever being, and the Englisher's boldness and independent spirit would be a prize for any man. Any man that wasn't Amish, that is. I pictured the sway of her hips when she walked and the way she pursed her pouty lips when she was annoyed. Katie was the type of woman that other men would covet, a woman who might cause even the most tolerant man to become jealous. A woman who would never settle down with a simple farmer.

"It doesn't matter anyway. She's not Amish, so nothing can ever come of it," I said.

"I'm sorry. I can see the situation bothers you

immensely." Rebecca's eyes misted and I knew her sympathy was genuine.

"I'm still going to train her horses and I'll use that money to help you get out," I promised.

Rebecca looked over her shoulder, searching for anyone spying on us. When she seemed satisfied that no one was close by, she said, "You must not do that." When I shook my head in wonder, she raised her hands. "It will only put you in ill favor with the bishop, and that would ruin your chance with Miriam."

"I thought you didn't like Miriam?"

"I don't, but I also will not be the reason that you're kicked out of the community. That must be your decision when the time comes."

"When the time comes? I have no intention of leaving the Amish. I believe I can still help you, though, Rebecca. First, I have to save up the money."

Her small smile was sad. "I hope so. I can't stand being here." She pressed her hands to her temples. "My head hurts all the time that I'm here." She glanced up, her cheeks pale. "I will stay strong for as long as I can, but you must promise me something."

Her tortured eyes made me answer quickly. "Anything."

"Be open to change, brother. That's all I ask." She paused her hand over where her heart was. "I have a feeling – a strong one – that your destiny isn't your own."

Her statement startled me and I was about to pester her for a meaning, but she dashed away before I could.

Rebecca was a strange girl. She was deeply troubled but her mind was special. Sometimes she seemed like one of the fairies in the books she read – almost as if she knew things and saw things that other people didn't. There were times I thought she only had one foot in our world – and I meant the world that included the English and the Amish.

I gazed out at the ever-growing stream of cars and buggies parking side by side and watched the mixture of Amish and English make their way to the schoolhouse and auction barn. The women were chatting away and men slapped each other on the back. A pair of girls, one English and the other Amish, raced by. The Englisher was in denim jeans and a bright, puffy, purple jacket. Her long hair streamed out behind her. Her Amish friend couldn't have been any more different. Her hair was neatly pulled up beneath a cap and the green dress she wore was mostly covered by the simple black coat she wore. Even for the blatant differences, the girls held hands and whistled together.

In this atmosphere, my people were open to interactions with outsiders. After all, it would be their money-making donations into the box for the roasted chicken and mashed potatoes. They would also be bidding right along with the Amish on the barn full of sale items, from handmade furniture to goats and fancy pigeons. They were our neighbors and business partners. We needed these people, and our elders knew it. That's why on nights like this, our people lightened up a bit and welcomed interactions that normally would be frowned upon.

The scene before me made me frown. I had never had cause to think much on it, but now I did. Two very different worlds came together for this one festive night. Tomorrow, things would go back to normal. Sure, business between our people and theirs would continue but the young people wouldn't be allowed to mingle and the women's chatter would lessen to the occasional telephone calls to hire drivers for grocery shopping.

That's why I had made the right choice to court Miriam. Unlike Rebecca, I didn't want to lose my family or my community. This was my place; this was where I was meant to be.

"Rowan, why are you hiding in here?" Martin popped into the shed. "It doesn't have anything to do with a certain bishop's daughter, does it?"

I grabbed the horse brush off the ledge and tossed it right at Martin's cocky smile. He was quick, catching it in the air before it could damage his face. He laughed, wagging a finger at me.

I joined him with a resolved set to my jaw. I wouldn't listen to Rebecca, even though I had a strong inkling what she meant.

She would be sorely disappointed if she thought I was going to someday join her in the outside world. I would make my own destiny.

ELEVEN

Katie

P eggy's eyes became slits. "You mean he kissed you and then accused you of being loose with the guys?"

That wasn't exactly how it had gone, but I didn't want to get into my own anxieties about committed relationships and how Rowan's intensity scared the crap out of me. I *did* need the distraction of angry friends commiserating with me, though.

"Basically," I replied, wiping the serving counter with wide, sweeping movements.

Peggy shook her head, frowning. "Men. You can't let him get away with it," she growled.

Peggy's wrath finally made me smile. She would be a great friend to have if you'd murdered someone, and needed help burying the body. She was loyal to a fault. "I don't plan to," I assured her.

Tessa's jaw dropped. "Katie Porter. What are you thinking?"

"I know Rowan likes me. He just wants things his way—" I began, but Peggy interrupted.

"Now, Katie, I admit the man is as good-looking as a man can get." She bumped Tessa's side with her elbow and smirked. "If you're into that kind of thing. Maybe it's a good turn you found out how controlling he is before it went any further. He is Amish, after all. What more were you expecting, except a couple of rolls in the hay?"

I drew in a shaky breath. I wasn't sure if I should laugh at her choice of words or cry. There would never be any rolls in the hay now, and for some reason it really bugged me. My emotions were a mess, but the taint of anger was still strong, probably obliterating any common sense I might still have.

"You're right. I'm sure it was all for the best," I admitted, feeling sullen and depressed that I couldn't have a chance with the only guy I'd ever really liked.

"Good girl." Tessa patted my back, then she untied and removed her apron.

"I'm still going to make him pay," I said firmly.

Tessa and Peggy stared at me. Tessa looked worried but Peggy was definitely proud.

Tessa looked around. The restaurant was in between

meal times and relatively quiet. When she spoke, she made sure to whisper. "Seriously, what do you have in mind?"

"I'm going to lure Rowan back in and then break his heart. That's what I'm going to do."

"That doesn't sound like a very good idea," Tessa offered.

"Why not? Katie can't let him get away with that kind of disrespect," Peggy chimed in.

"There are so many things that can go wrong," Tessa argued. "He might get her feelings hurt even more. Or even worse, she might be the one falling for him." She shook her head vigorously. "That's not you, Katie. You're not that kind of woman."

"Hey, guys, I'm right here." I tapped my fingers on the counter and they turned to me. Suddenly, feeling completely exhausted, I sighed loudly. Tessa was right. I wasn't a vengeful person, and as frustrated as I was with the situation I found myself in – falling for a guy I could never have – I wouldn't take it out on Rowan. I'd acted like a bitch the night before. It wasn't Rowan's fault, even if his nasty words had hurt me. "Don't worry, Tessa. I'm not going to do anything mean."

Tessa whispered under her breath, "I hope not."

"But I want to get him out of my head. And the only way I think I can accomplish that is if I have a civil conversation with him and explain that we can still be friends, but that's all." I blinked, imagining saying the words under Rowan's steady gaze.

"I think you're being too nice as usual, but if it makes you feel better, why not. Isn't he still training your horses? Why not talk to him then?" Peggy asked. Her voice was subdued, but the look of disappointment on her face that I wasn't going to give the handsome Amish man a piece of my mind was unmistakable.

"Yeah, but he said he'd come by when I wasn't around," I replied.

Peggy snorted and Tessa interjected. "What about the schoolhouse dinner thing you were talking about? Won't he be there?"

"That's tonight, and I don't get off work until nine o'clock. It will be over by then." I slumped on the counter, glancing out the long row of windows. The sun was already low in the western sky. On any other day, I would have admired the reds and golds of the brilliant sunset filling the sky. Not today.

I barely caught the sideways look Tessa shot Peggy, which I immediately understood.

"Oh, now you want to facilitate Katie's next interaction with the rogue Amish dude?" Peggy grunted when Tessa shrugged, grinning.

"Peggy, I wouldn't let you take my shift for something stupid like this. Doesn't Owen have a game? I thought you were going to meet Jessica at the soccer fields?"

Peggy's loud snort came out like a bear's growl. "I was, but you never ask me to fill in for you, and you're always taking my shifts. Jessica will understand. She really appreciates how we can depend on you when the kids are sick or they have a game or something, especially when Jessica is working and I need to be there. I owe you one – or two – favors."

"You don't have to do that. It's not that important," I countered, but Peggy threw her hands up.

"I insist. You know there's no use arguing with me. You won't win." She shooed me toward the door. "Now get out of here before a busload shows up and the boss decides to keep us both for the evening."

"Thanks, Peggy. You're the best." She quickly turned away but I saw how red her cheeks were first.

Taking off my apron, I joined Tessa and we walked out the front door together.

I bumped into her side. "So. How do you feel about eating some Amish food?"

Tessa's smile was brilliant. "I wouldn't miss it for the world!"

Tessa insisted on driving so I wouldn't have to borrow Momma's car, and I was sure glad she did when we pulled into the crowded parking lot.

"Watch it!" I burst out.

A little boy ran right in front of her SUV and Tessa, who was already moving at a crawl, had to hit the brakes to avoid bumping into the child. Then a horse started backing up, instead of going forward, directly in front of us. Tessa couldn't go into reverse because of the horse and buggy directly behind us. She closed her eyes, and I held my breath.

"Tell me when it's over," she begged in a quivering voice.

When the buggy's back wheels brushed the car's front bumper, I flung the door open, jumping out. With long strides, I passed the buggy to reach the panicked horse. With my trained eye, I knew the gelding was young, maybe only a three-year-old.

"Dumb place to train a horse," I muttered, grabbing the rein closest to me.

A girl was in the driver's seat. She was barely a teenager, if I had to guess. Her cheeks were pink and her mouth puckered as she snapped the reins and shouted words at the horse that I couldn't understand. Somehow the horse's blinder had dropped down right over his right eye. It wasn't just tunneling his vision, it was completely blinding him, and rubbing his eye to boot.

"Stop it!" I shouted, jerking the rein hard enough that the Amish girl finally noticed me at her horse's head.

She scrunched up her face, but relaxed her hands on the reins.

"Whoa, boy. I got this. Easy, easy," I coaxed as I reached up and grasped the buckle. The bridle was on way too loose, almost as if it was meant for a bigger horse. With quick action, I flipped the blinder back into place and tightened it up a couple of notches. Once the gelding's view was clear, he dropped his head and took a step forward.

I looked back through the small window in the front of the black canvas-covered buggy. The girl leaned forward and caught my gaze. I pointed to an open spot between two other buggies. "Is that where you want to go?" I called out to her.

She nodded briskly. I stayed with the horse's head and walked him into the spot. Tessa craned her neck out the window and shouted, "I'll park over there."

I nodded, waving her on.

The sun had disappeared and was replaced with the low grayish light of dusk. I zippered up my jacket against the suddenly cooler air and waited while the girl climbed out of her buggy. Seeing how short she was, I changed my judgment of her age. She couldn't have been more than eleven or twelve and it struck me as idiotic that a child was allowed to drive a thousand-pound beast on the roadway along with speeding cars and trucks. She wasn't even old enough to get a driver's license, and as far as I knew, the Amish didn't do buggy driving tests.

"Your horse's blinders weren't adjusted properly. The eye piece blocked his right eye and even dug into it. That's why he was freaking out," I explained to the large-eyed girl.

She craned her neck to study the piece of tack that I was pointing to. Curly brown hair poked out from beneath her cap and when she met my gaze, I noticed her eyes were the same muddy color.

She shook her head. "It's Buster's bridle. That's why it didn't fit."

"This isn't Buster?" I asked.

"No, he's Sox. We bought him a week ago." She dropped her gaze and sounded contrite. "It's my fault. I was in a hurry to leave. I must have grabbed the wrong one."

"You drove this horse here all by yourself?"

She placed her hand on Sox's shoulder. "Naw. My sister, Melanie, came too."

"Where is she?" I asked slowly. I was extremely bothered by the entire scene. Didn't anyone keep tabs on these Amish kids? They seemed to be running wild and left to their own devices much of the time.

She gestured to the top of the hill, at the schoolhouse.

"I dropped her off there. She had to carry in the loaves of bread."

The bottom of her navy-blue dress billowed in the wind and she dug her black tennis shoe into the cut grass. Her shoulders sagged and she looked quite pitiful. I suddenly felt sorry for the timid-looking girl. She was doing the best she could. She certainly didn't seem comfortable fooling with the jumpy horse.

"I'm Katie. What's your name?" I held out my hand and her face instantly brightened.

Her back snapped straight and she shook my hand. "Sarah Yoder."

My phone buzzed in my back pocket and I pulled it out. Tessa's text told me that Jimmy had called her. She was going to call him back before she met up with me, if it was okay. I couldn't even remember which guy Jimmy was – probably a new love interest, I figured. I responded with a thumbs up emoji and put my phone away.

"Hey, do you want some help unhitching your horse and tying him up in the shed we passed back there?"

"Oh, yes. I would appreciate that very much," she replied happily.

As I worked alongside her, unfastening the shafts, I noticed how unsure her hands were. Going slower, I showed her how to do things the best I could. Daddy had had an old cart that I used to hook up to my pony and drive her around the ranch. This harness rigging was close enough to the same thing, and I was able to figure it out as I went along. Realizing that the girl wasn't as knowledgeable as I was, I tried to teach her a few things for her trip back home.

"Where are your folks?" I asked when we were leading the horse, side by side, to the shed.

"They're working in the auction barn. Da is helping the bishop with the numbers and Ma is selling the quilt's raffle tickets." As if in anticipation of my next question, she quickly added, "They left early, so Melanie and I had to drive the new horse separately."

"This isn't something you do very often, is it?"

She shook her head and leaned over, cupping her mouth toward me with her free hand. "I don't even like horses much. They always step on my feet."

I laughed and patted her on the back. "Maybe next time you ought to speak up for yourself and tell your father that you don't feel comfortable driving the horse. He might not know your feelings," I suggested.

"If there is a next time, I'm definitely going to tell him. I about fainted back there when I thought Sox was going to crash into the car." She looked up. "Thank you for helping me."

"You're welcome. I have horses, so it just came naturally to get involved."

"I'm glad none of the boys saw what happened.

Josiah would never let me hear the end of it if he saw that I couldn't control my horse."

"Is Josiah your friend?"

Sarah stared straight ahead but I caught her cheeks turning a brighter pink and she reduced her volume to a whisper. "I'm not really sure. Sometimes he's kind of mean to me."

I held in my smile. Typical. Even little Amish girls had to deal with annoying boys. "He probably just likes you."

"You really think so?" She looked up eagerly.

"That's usually why boys are rude. If they don't like you at all, they typically ignore you all together."

Sarah made a humming noise. "I'm not sure how I feel about that."

I couldn't stop myself from laughing. "Don't worry, Sarah. You won't have to worry about Josiah's intentions for a long time. Just have fun being a single, independent, little woman while you can."

For a second, I worried that my advice wouldn't be well taken by an Amish preteen, but when Sarah glanced up, her grin was huge.

"Just like you?"

"Yeah, just like me." Sarah's lopsided smile made me almost forget why I'd originally come to the Amish benefit dinner in the first place. But then I spotted Rowan's wavy dark hair and wide shoulders ahead. He was leaving the shed with another Amish guy. I ducked behind Sox so he wouldn't see me if he turned this way. Feeling pretty foolish, I peeked around Sox's rump as Sarah tied him to the hitching rail. Rowan strolled up the hill, talking to his companion. My stomach did a somersault when my eyes locked on him. He moved with wiry athleticism, making me once again compare him to a wolf in suspenders.

Sarah appeared at my side. "He's all set."

"Very good," I commended her.

"Are you eating alone?" she asked, tilting her head.

I checked my phone and didn't see any new messages. "My friend is talking to someone. She should be joining me any moment, but who knows?"

"You can eat with me," Sarah offered.

"Are you sure that's all right?" I glanced around, noticing all the people for the first time.

"Sure. No one will care. Especially since you helped me and all." We began trekking up the hill and she didn't stop talking. "I've never seen you before. Is this your first time coming?"

"Yep. I live just up the road a few miles, but I never made it to one of these dinners before," I mused.

"How come you came today?"

She was a precocious child. Her English was flawless but still, there was a slight lilt to her voice, as if she was speaking a second language. It made me wonder about the Pennsylvania Dutch the Amish also spoke. Which language did they speak first?

Feeling brave and curious at the same time, I decided to tell the truth. "Rowan Coblentz told me about it. He recommended I come." I gauged the girl for any reaction. "Do you know him?"

"Sure, I do. He's Nathaniel's older brother. He's really tall and rides horses all the time."

"Yes, that's him all right. He's training some horses for me."

"Why don't you train the horses? You're awfully good with 'em."

I held up my arm. I had removed the sling that morning and was testing it out a little more, hour by hour. My doctor would throw a fit if he knew, but what difference would a few days make? It didn't throb too much.

"I was thrown off one of my horses a few weeks ago. My arm is still healing and I have to be careful. I won't be able to do any serious riding until it's one hundred percent. Training colts is grueling business."

"The way you handled Sox, I had no idea you were hurt," she commented with awe in her voice.

I shrugged a little. "I probably shouldn't have done that. I actually kind of forgot all about my arm when I ran up to help with your horse."

We lined up behind a family that was waiting for the

crowd to thin out before they entered the schoolhouse building. The woman wore a floral-print dress, and her cap was smaller and made of lace. The two little girls on either side of her wore dresses just as brightly colored. The man carried a baby boy in his arms and he had on regular store-bought denim jeans. I smiled back at the baby who eyed me, and wondered why this family was dressed differently.

Bending down, I whispered to Sarah. "Are they Amish?"

She shook her head and whispered back. "Mennonite."

A few more minutes went by and we finally crossed the threshold into the building. There were a lot of non-Amish inside, but mostly the giant room was filled with Amish people. A basketball hoop hung above our heads and I realized that the space where we were standing must be a gymnasium of sorts. At around ten-foot intervals, gas lamps protruded from the walls. The light emanating from them was slightly dull, but there were enough of them to light up the interior with enough brightness. I caught the whiff here and there of the burning gas, which I'd experienced before. The Amish market on the corner of Bayberry Road had the same types of fixtures.

Sarah continued to be my little guide, pointing out different children and their parents, telling me their names. I wouldn't remember half of them in ten minutes, but a few people did stick out – like the burly man with the bushy blackish-gray beard and eyebrows. His sharp, stoic features reminded me of a hawk seeking prey, or maybe a fox was a better comparison. I also spotted Rebecca from across the room. She sat at a table with a dozen other teenage girls and young women, but slightly apart. I watched for a moment, noticing that she never turned to talk to anyone, intent on eating her meal with her head mostly bowed. Another girl looked up and our eyes met. She was blonde and her face was oval and smooth. She continued to stare at me, even when I looked away several times. Finally I whispered in Sarah's ear, describing the girl to Sarah and asking who she was.

"Oh, that's Miriam Graber, one of the bishop's daughters."

"The bishop?"

Sarah nodded at the fox-like man I'd noticed earlier. "Miriam isn't a girl though. She's twenty-one, I think."

"Really...?" Trying not to look obvious, I raised my eyes again. Sure enough, Miriam was still watching me. Her gaze sent a cool chill over my skin. She looked a lot younger than me at a glance, but now that I brazenly stared back, I noticed that her cheeks didn't have any youthful plumpness and the curve of her neck indicated a young woman instead of a teenager. Our staring match became a competition for me. I never in a million years thought an Amish woman would be so rude. I also wondered where the hell my friend was. How long could Tessa talk to a guy? But I already knew the answer: a long time.

"Miriam thinks she's the prettiest girl in the community."

"She does, huh?"

"That's why she's looking at you – because you're so pretty. She's probably jealous."

The kid was outspoken, that was for sure. "Thanks for saying that, Sarah, but I'm no different to any of the other women in this place. It must be something else."

When I narrowed my eyes, Miriam finally broke her gaze away. She whispered into the ear of the girl to her left and then that girl looked up at me, nodded, and then they went back to their huddled conversation. The encounter made my insides twist but that feeling was nothing compared to the hot jolt that made the hair at the back of my neck rise. With the feeling came a thumping of my heart and I knew before I even turned my head what was making my body go nuts.

Rowan Coblentz sat on a bench at the long table in the next row over. The guy I saw earlier was still at his side, but now there were a dozen other young man sitting along the same table with him. When our eyes locked, I forced a polite smile. He didn't return the favor. Rowan's face was as still as a statue. I wished desperately to know what was going through his surly mind at that moment. My face grew hot when he lifted a questioning brow and I straightened back up. We had just reached the serving girls. I nodded for the first girl to put a roasted chicken leg on the plate. Mashed potatoes, green beans, coleslaw and bread followed, until my plate was nearly overflowing with food. Each fresh-faced girl quickly deposited food on the plate, hustling me to the next.

A can of cola was handed to me and I stuffed it under my arm. When I saw the hundreds of pieces of pies waiting, I wondered how I would manage to pick one up. Sarah saw my dilemma and helped position one of the peanut-butter cream slices on a second plate and into my free hand.

While Sarah picked out a slice from a cherry pie, I glanced over my shoulder. Rowan was still looking at me and I quickly turned away. Staring competitions with hot guys weren't the same as ones with stuck-up women.

Something did just occur to me all at once and I bent down to Sarah. "Aren't the guys and girls allowed to sit together?"

Sarah led the way toward the long table where all the females were sitting, giving me an answer before she even spoke. "I don't know if it's a rule exactly but the girls do sit together and so do the boys. She gestured toward the inside rows that were filled with non-Amish and Amish families alike. "Families mix together, but the girls my age, all the way up to the ones that aren't yet married, stay together."

She picked a spot that would barely have fit one of us, but when she talked to the closest girls, they squeezed down further to make room for us. I lifted my leg over the bench and was happy to deposit my plates on the table. The throbbing in my arm had grown into a dull pain. I winced a little when I sat down.

"You can rest your arm now," Sarah said.

I smiled back at her. She was a nice kid. I did my best to ignore Rowan, who was sitting several rows away. It wasn't too difficult since my back was to him but still, I fought the urge to twist in my seat to see what he was doing.

Miriam was across the table, a few seats down. Her eyes strayed once again to me. I couldn't ignore her penetrating gaze.

"Hello," I said to Miriam. "Do I know you?"

Miriam's eyes widened for a second and then she was composed again. "Are you Katie Porter, the owner of the Diamond E Ranch?"

All nearby faces turned my way. I liked to keep a low profile and was more likely to be found sitting in a corner, quietly observing everyone else in group situations. I definitely didn't like being the center of attention of a bunch of strangers. I pursed my lips and focused on slowing my rapidly beating heart. "My mom is, and I help her. Why?"

The brown-haired girl sitting beside Miriam nudged her and said, "I told you."

Before I could get to the bottom of Miriam's strange obsession with me, she abruptly stood up with her empty dinner plate and left the table. Several girls followed suit, disappearing into the crowd with Miriam.

"I wonder why she did that," Sarah said, staring after the group.

"You and me both," I responded, taking a bite of the chicken. It was perfectly spiced and melted in my mouth. My bad mood was momentarily stifled by the good food. I took another bite and raised my hand when I spotted Tessa making her way to our table.

"Finally," I chided. She took the open space on the bench across the table from me and sat down.

"Sorry about that. I was making weekend plans. Looks like I have a date," Tessa chirped.

I hated being a downer, but I had to feign interest in Tessa's cheerful proclamation. "Who's Jimmy?" I asked between bites.

"He came into the diner last week. You remember – tall, blond, and with the sweetest smile." I shrugged, searching my memories, but coming up empty. "Well, we got to talking, and he loves the theatre as much as I do. We're going to see a show."

"This weekend?" Seemed to be moving kind of fast to me.

"We're going for coffee and a movie tomorrow night. We'll make plans for the theatre then." She took a sip of her cola. "I really like him."

I worked hard to form a believable smile. At least this Jimmy dude went to the movies. That was something Rowan wasn't even allowed to do. The thought flitted in my head, then disappeared. It didn't matter anyway.

"I'm rooting for you. Just don't get your hopes up too high. Try to take it slow," I advised.

"Coming from the girl who makes out with Amish guys after one day of employment." She quickly recognized my not-so-happy expression and pivoted the conversation. "So where is the handsome horse-trainer? Have you spotted him yet?"

My gaze shifted to Sarah, who was chatting with the little girl on her other side. Thankfully, I didn't think she'd heard Tessa. Then I searched for Rowan. He wasn't sitting where he had been. A sweep of the crowded room didn't reveal him.

"He was right over there. Now he's gone." I felt like a balloon that had been poked and deflated.

Tessa held up her fork. "Even if you don't get to talk to him, and upset yourself further, the food's delicious."

I lowered my voice. "Do you really think seeking

Rowan out for a brief conversation is the wrong thing to do?"

Tessa looked at me with thoughtful kindness. She exhaled. "You have so much going on in your life at the moment. Saving your ranch and keeping your mom healthy should be your priorities, not bothering with a guy you kissed once."

"A few times now," I corrected.

"You know what I mean." Tessa was becoming impatient. Her face was flushed and I could feel her foot tapping the floor from a foot away. "What good would it do anyway?"

I couldn't tell her about Momma's romance and subsequent poor treatment by Rowan's own father. I'd promised not to say a word about it. But I felt the quiet need to set Rowan straight about our relationship so I could finally move on and forget about him. "Probably give me a few minutes of deep satisfaction," I mumbled. "You're right. I need to get my priorities straight."

"What you need is another guy to get your mind off of Mr. Suspenders." Tessa raised her chin, jerking her head toward the front the door.

Dillon Wilder stood in line with his best buds, Barton and Luis. I was surprised to see him at the Amish event. It never occurred to me that he'd spend part of his Friday night eating wholesome food and hanging out with neighbors. His parents did live right beside the community and they were farmers, so maybe that was why he was here. When we'd dated during our senior year, he hadn't shown much interest in doing anything other than drinking beer and making out. That was why we weren't together very long.

I ate some of the pie and rolled my eyes. "Been there, done that."

"I've heard Dillon has straightened himself out a lot since high school. He got his degree and is apprenticing with his uncle at the funeral home."

"Yeah, as a mortician. It's kind of a creepy occupation, if you ask me," I said with a shiver.

"There's good money in it, and a never-ending source of work." Tessa chuckled at her own attempt at a joke. She thought she was so clever but I just shook my head.

A blond flash in the corner of my eye made me catch my breath. "Dammit, he's coming over here," I coughed, nearly choking on the gulp of pie I had to force down quickly.

"Oh, be nice," Tessa ordered.

Dillon took long, quick strides and I only had a few seconds to collect myself before he leaned over my shoulder. "Katie, it's been a while. How've you been?"

The bristly fuzz covering his jaw made me realize just how much Dillon had grown up since we'd parted ways. His hair was thick on top and buzzed at the sides, and he was relaxed in blue jeans and a gray hoodie. I had to admit, he looked pretty good.

Sarah quickly rose. "I have to check in with Ma. I think I'm supposed to sweep the kitchen." She turned toward Dillon, but didn't raise her gaze. "You can have my seat. I'll see you later, Katie." And then she was gone. The arrival of an English guy, on top of Tessa's outgoing personality, must have been too much for the poor kid.

Dillon raised a brow and I motioned for him to sit down. He said hello to Tessa and they made pleasantries for a moment about what she was up to. She asked him if he knew Jimmy and of course he did. Dillon knew almost everyone our age in the county. Their dull conversation about what a nice guy Jimmy was made my mind and eyes wander.

This time when I searched the room, I immediately found what I was looking for. Rowan leaned against the opposite wall. He was surrounded by other guys, old and young, but he wasn't talking to any of them. Instead, he was staring directly at me.

His dark gaze made my insides melt in a warm shudder.

"Did you hear, Katie?" Reluctantly, I brought my attention back to Dillon. His eager face made me feel bad that I hadn't been listening at all. He didn't seem to mind, though, and he rushed out, "My uncle is making me a partner in the business."

Tessa's eyes rose expectantly from across the table. She obviously thought Dillon's career advancement was something to get excited about.

I nodded, offering a pinched smile. "That's great, Dillon. Congratulations. I thought it was your dream to own your own bar."

Tessa's head dropped forward into her hands and I shrugged, wondering what her problem was. I was trying to be nice and make small talk, like she was always bugging me to do.

"Yes, well, that was my ambition for a short time but I changed my mind when I attended my cousin's funeral."

"He committed suicide, didn't he?" The words tumbled out of my mouth before I could stop them.

Dillon didn't even flinch, which I instantly gave him credit for. "Yes, he did. We weren't close – he was ten years older and all – but it was a miracle how my uncle prepared him for the viewing. He had shot himself in the head, you know. Yet he looked as close to himself as he could have, following such a violent death. My uncle did a brilliant job and I guess you could say, it inspired me to go into the family business."

Being a mortician would be creepy but also fascinating. A dozen questions trickled in, but I held them at bay, fearing Dillon might never leave. I risked a look back at Rowan. He frowned at me and then at

Dillon. There was a dazzling flash in my mind and I suddenly understood. Rowan was jealous.

I didn't feel one bit guilty. After all, he was the one who had accused me in so many words of being promiscuous.

Dillon leaned in closer, as if on cue. Since we had been an item for about six months, and there had been a lot of make-out sessions in that time period, his near proximity was a little bit of a jolt. I stayed planted on the bench, resisting the urge to scoot away.

"I'm really sorry about your dad. Luis mentioned it to me the other day. I was going to stop by, offer you and your mom any assistance you might need, but I had certifications I had to complete this week." He paused, maybe expecting me to say something, but I didn't know what. When I remained silent, he continued, "Do you need anything? I'm here to help."

A stupid tear threatened to form in my eye. I sucked in the jarring emotions and swallowed. "That's really nice of you. I appreciate it, but Momma and I are doing just fine."

"Are you sure about that, Katie?" Tessa quipped.

I shot her a look that made her draw back.

"Yes, I'm sure," I told Tessa, then brought my attention back to Dillon. "We really need to go. I have an early morning tomorrow."

Dillon rose right with me. He hesitated, and with a

sudden burst of surety asked, "Do you want to go out sometime? Maybe we could see a movie and have dinner"—he glanced around—"in a quieter place."

Tessa's lips thinned with warning. When I was opening my mouth to politely refuse, she piped up. "You two can join Jimmy and me tomorrow night. If I remember correctly, you're on day shift, aren't you?"

I could have kicked Tessa. She was bound and determined to play matchmaker. It wasn't such a bad thing. Dillon was attractive and he had a good job. Now that he'd outgrown his party days, we would have a lot more to talk about, and making Rowan squirm a little certainly was a plus. But my mind was a scrambled mess and Dillon was a nice guy. Did I dare go down the road of hurting his feelings because I was frustrated about Rowan?

"It would be fun to join Tessa and Jimmy, don't you think?" Dillon asked.

I heard the slight waver of his voice. Dillon knew me all too well. After I'd broken up with him, he'd called me every day for three months straight, trying to get me to change my mind. I was stubborn and he knew it. In the end, I didn't budge and we moved on. He'd probably faint if I actually accepted the date invite, after all of his previous begging from a few years ago.

It was a combination of Dillon's tentative expression and Tessa holding her breath that prompted me to finally say yes. We made our plans and I quickly exited the building with Tessa. The cold shock of air on my face when we walked outside into the moonlight made me take a deep breath. I filled my lungs with air, hoping the cool oxygen would wake me up. The gas lamps inside made me feel flushed and sleepy. I wanted to be alert enough to get home safely and crawl into bed. Sleep was the only place I could escape the craziness that my life had become.

We reached the beginning of the long line of parked buggies in silence. Tessa was probably afraid to say anything to set me off. I viewed her behavior as a complete ambush, and rolled it around in my mind, searching for any other reasons that going out on a date with Dillon Wilder was a good thing, when someone touched my shoulder.

I spun around.

"Can we talk?" Rowan said in a demanding yet low voice.

Tessa turned and stared at me hard with her mouth pinched shut. When I gave her a curt nod, her eyes shot skyward but she muttered, "I'll be waiting in the car for you."

"I can take you home, Katie. Your friend doesn't have to wait," Rowan said firmly.

"Hey, I can sit in my car all night—" Tessa began, but I cut her off.

"It's okay. I'll go with Rowan." My heart pounded madly in my chest. The desire to spend some time with the Amish man was making me do something stupid. His sudden appearance had shocked me and now I just wanted to hear what he had to say.

Tessa shifted her weight to go and hesitated. "You're still going tomorrow night, right?" I nodded briskly and she added, "Text me later."

The instant she began walking away, Rowan grasped my hand and pulled me into the shadows between the buggies.

TWELVE

Rowan

I didn't want to let go of Katie's hand, but I did. The quick touch was enough to shoot adrenaline into my heart. Watching Katie from afar, without being able to approach her, had been torturous. Especially when the blond man joined her at the table. They seemed to be well acquainted, which had agitated me even more.

"Where's your sling?" I flicked a finger at her arm. The dull moonlight made her red hair look brown and her usually rosy cheeks pale, but there was no mistaking the flash in her eyes. I braced for her wrath.

Surprising me, she glanced down and back up again, studying me with confusion and a scrunched mouth. "That's why you yanked me over here? To ask about this?" She thrust her arm up. "I'm scheduled to take it off on Monday anyway and it feels great, if you have to know."

When she dropped her arm to her side, she winced, and I knew she was lying. "It's better to have the doctor make sure it's healed properly before you take it off. You could make it worse and slow the healing process jumping the gun like that."

She rolled her eyes and crossed her arms. A few strands of her long hair blew across her face. I fought the desire to reach out and push her soft locks back. I remembered the smell of her hair – vanilla and wildflowers. If I inhaled deeply, I was sure I'd catch her scent on the wind. It was getting awfully chilly and I wanted to reach out, pull her close, and wrap my arms around her to warm her. But I didn't move a muscle.

The silence was strangling. I was afraid to say more, so I waited for her to do something. She was usually as temperamental and jumpy as a fresh filly. I was impressed at the brewing patience she was exhibiting.

She continued to stare at me with wide eyes and her full lips pursed. How I wanted to kiss those pouty lips.

All the reservations I'd felt earlier for Katie Porter had flown out the window when I saw her in the schoolhouse. I couldn't stop looking at her. She filled my head with a throbbing need to be with her. What my sister had said about my destiny flashed before my eyes and I worried that she could be right. Katie might hold the key to my future.

Nearby laughter brought my head up and I glanced over my shoulder. A small group of Amish women, each carrying a baby or holding the hand of a toddler, walked by. They were chatting away about how much the quilt had sold for. I took a step forward, obscuring Katie with my body.

"Are you afraid someone will see you talking to me?" she snapped.

I smiled, glad her spunkiness had returned and she'd spoken to me. "Of course," I replied honestly.

"Why? Are you ashamed or something?"

I shook my head. "Certainly not. If anyone from my community saw us together, they'd speculate that we were having a forbidden romance. It wouldn't take long for my parents to hear, and that would cause me a heap of trouble."

I watched her expression fade from agitation to calm understanding. There was also a hint of something else – something, dare I say, mischievous about the look on her face – that made me shudder.

She leaned over and whispered, "Is there any place we can talk where you won't get into trouble?"

I wasn't sure about the swing of her mood but I let any doubt slip away when I reached past her to open the door to my buggy. "No one will know if we're in here. The auction will go on for a couple more hours, keeping most of my people away until it's over."

She pursed her lips and her voice was playful. "Are you just trying to get me into your vehicle so you can take advantage of me?"

"Absolutely not. I would just like to talk for a minute. I'll be a perfect gentleman. You have my word," I assured her, standing up straighter.

"You and your promises," she huffed, before sliding through the opening, into the cab of the buggy.

I quickly joined her and latched the door behind us. Since the buggy wasn't hitched, it was a little wobbly and I was careful to balance my weight to keep it from rocking too much. That kind of scene would definitely bring prying eyes.

Katie leaned back in the seat, rubbing her hand over the velvet cushion. There was very little room inside. When my leg rested against hers, she didn't jerk away.

"Your seats are fancier than I expected," she said.

I laughed. "They're hardly fancy. That's just the way they usually are. I did have mine made with the royal blue covering, though. I thought it was a sharp color."

She pulled her phone out and turned it into a flashlight for moment. The small light shone around the interior and then she turned it off. "It looks nice. How much does one of these things cost?"

"Depending on the size, anywhere from six to ten thousand dollars. Add another five or six thousand for a solid driving horse to pull it and you might spend as much as sixteen thousand dollars."

She whistled. "That's more than I thought it would be."

My shoulder brushed hers in the darkness and blood surged through my veins. I held my breath steady, determined to keep my promise. "It's about the same as you'd spend for a truck," I said.

"Depending on the make and year, I suppose," she agreed in a subdued voice.

The cab became quiet. Beyond the small, fogged-up window, I could faintly hear the auctioneer's rambling calls. Children's laughter came from the direction of the playground and the roar of the occasional engine starting filled the air, but the sound I listened most intently to was Katie's rhythmic breathing.

At that moment I wished more than anything that Katie was Amish ... or that I wasn't.

"I'm sorry," I said.

She faced me and her leg slipped beneath mine in a very intimate way. I don't think she even noticed, though. The whites of her eyes shone with interest.

"For what?"

"I shouldn't have insinuated that you spent time with other men. It was mean and wrong." I thudded my head back on the headrest. "I only behaved that way because it upset me that you didn't seem to take our kiss very seriously."

In a softer voice, she said, "It was only a kiss. Why make such a big deal out of it?"

"It was more than just a kiss to me, Katie. I wouldn't have ever opened up to you in that way if I didn't have strong feelings for you."

She rested her hand on my thigh in a comforting gesture, not realizing that her slightest touch made my skin burn with desire.

"It's only been a few days since we started talking again. Don't you think you're rushing it a little? We hardly even know each other."

The fire in my belly subsided with her cold words. I didn't want to get angry with her again. Licking my lips, I tried to imagine what it would be like to be in her boots. She was an English girl, not an Amish one. English girls might have several beaus before they settled down. Our girls usually married the first boy they courted. Rarely, a couple broke up. Katie and I were looking very differently at the idea of what a relationship was like at this early stage, very differently.

"I guess I feel like I've known you for seven years. I'm sorry you don't feel the same way."

She snorted. "For six of those years, we didn't see or talk to each other. That makes a big difference, but I see what you're saying." She hesitated and then rushed the words out. "It kind of feels like we've been friends all along. We just picked right up where we left off – kissing and everything."

I chuckled, breathing easier. It was so easy to talk to Katie. I was tempted to share my every secret with her, but I was careful not to startle her again. She wanted to take it slow and that made a lot of sense. Even though it was extremely difficult to do so.

I grew bold. "You didn't mind me kissing you?"

"Hah. I thought I was the one kissing you." She patted my leg. "Of course not. If the storm hadn't blown up, downing a tree on my truck, we probably wouldn't have stopped with just a kiss."

My face burned. She was correct. It would have been difficult to pull back from the sheer joy of holding her in my arms. That night, after I'd returned home, even though we'd argued, I still dreamed about touching Katie's naked skin ... and doing other things.

"I should have controlled myself," I forced out.

"Why? Because it was a mistake?"

"No," I breathed, grasping her small hand. "I scared you off, and now your feelings have changed."

"Who said my feelings have changed? I still want to kiss you. A lot." She leaned a tad closer and I drew in her fresh scent.

Frustrated, I dragged my hand through my hair with

a tug. "Please, don't tease that way."

"I'm not joking."

She shifted suddenly and climbed into my lap in a smooth motion. Her bottom pressed into my groin, causing an electric jolt to spiral outward, making me gasp.

"We're twenty-two years old, Rowan. Don't you think we're old enough to make out?"

I didn't answer her with words. My mouth closed on hers and she sighed hungrily, encircling my neck with her arms. There was an urgency to our kiss that was different to before. Oh, good God, she tasted so sweet. I couldn't resist slipping my hand up beneath her jacket. I made sure to not to lift her sweater, but she broke from the kiss and quickly shed the jacket. She took my hand and brought it under her sweater until my hand was cupping her breast. Even though she wore a bra, I still hesitated and she held my hand there.

"It's all right," her silky voice muttered into my ear. With my free hand, I traced her cheek and then her jaw. Her breath warmed my face and I kissed her swollen bottom lip. There were so many factors working against us but I didn't care. Nothing else mattered at that moment, except the girl in my arms.

She repositioned herself on me without breaking from

our kiss. As she straddled me with her knees bent, and without much thought or practice, I grasped her behind, pressing her against my bulge.

"Katie, you're ... driving me crazy," I sputtered between kisses. "I'm trying to be good and you're making it ... very difficult."

Her giggle came out husky and low, and then her mouth found my earlobe. I tilted my head to give her access. Slowly, she trailed kisses and small licks along my jawline and down to my neck. The grunt that erupted from my throat was a primitive sound that I was sure I'd never made before.

There wasn't enough room to lay her down on the short bench seat, but I shifted my weight, still holding onto her, trying to get even closer. The buggy shook and dipped an inch or two and we both stopped moving.

Katie rubbed her face against mine and laughed quietly. Even though every part of me was on fire, I laughed with her.

"Rowan, are you in there?"

The small voice from beyond the buggy made me bolt upright. Katie froze in my embrace and I didn't let go.

"Rowan? Father needs your help at the sales table..."

It was Miriam. I had forgotten all about her. I found it hard to catch a breath and my heart thumped nearly out of my chest. "I was just trying to catch a moment or two of shut eye. I'm feeling a little off," I forced the words out. That was putting it mildly.

"Do you need assistance? You can take me home now, if you want. I'm sure Father won't mind, with you being sick and all." She grasped the door handle and I reached over Katie, having to scrunch her tighter into my lap to catch it before it opened.

"No," I nearly shouted. Lowering my voice again, I added, "I'm fine, really. Just give me a few minutes and I'll come up to the barn. Don't wait for me. I'll be right there."

I held my breath, waiting for Miriam to answer.

"All right, then. I'll see if Mother has any medicine in her bag. I think we should leave early, anyway. It will give us time to talk." She paused. "I'll look for you in the barn."

The last part sounded almost like a question. "In a few minutes. Just give me some time."

There was only silence outside of the buggy for some long seconds and I pressed the latch, opening the door a notch. I could just see Miriam's backside as she walked back up the hill. With a huge release of breath, I leaned back. My heart slowed to normal. Then I noticed how suddenly rigid Katie was. She looked away and I cupped her chin, trying to force her to look at me. She pushed off my lap, wriggling away, until she was sitting beside me.

I tried to digest what had just happened and how it had affected Katie. I was too worried to even speak.

Katie didn't have that problem. "You're taking Miriam home tonight?" she asked in a low hissing voice.

"Don't get mad, please. It was arranged earlier. I thought you didn't want to talk to me anymore—"

She cut me off. Her eyes were wide with hurt. "More like you figured I'd never know. Then the next time you saw me, we could make out like we just did." She punched my upper arm. I didn't move a muscle. "Thought you could get a little on the side, huh?"

"What are you talking about?" Annoyance crept into my voice. "Miriam is just a friend. She asked if I would take her home and I agreed. You're making too much out of this."

Katie tried to leave, but I blocked the door with my arm. She slumped back onto the seat and let out a frustrated sigh. When she spoke, her voice sounded tired.

"You had better open that door, Rowan Coblentz, or I'm going to scream my lungs out. Can you imagine all the Amish that will bring running over here, including your *friend*, Miriam?"

A small part of me was terrified she'd actually do it, but I couldn't let her leave the buggy upset with me.

"Be reasonable and sit back down. Please." I used my most coaxing voice.

Katie hovered in front of me, her limbs ready for flight.

"Please," I asked again, in an even softer tone.

The moon had risen higher in the sky and its soft glow brightened the inside of the cab. She avoided looking at me. I watched the rise and fall of her chest with her agitated breaths.

She lowered her head to her knees, covering her face with her hands. "Why should I listen to you?" Sitting back up, she glared at me. "Now I understand why that bitch was giving me the death stare at dinner."

The fog lifted from my head. "What? Why would she do that? She doesn't know anything about us."

"Does she know you're working for me?" Katie inclined her head, the sour look still hardening her features.

"I might have mentioned it. Still, there's no reason for her to jump to conclusions."

"It was her friend who recognized me. Maybe Miriam doesn't like competition." Her words trembled and I tried to touch her but she snatched her hand back as though she'd been bitten. "I'm not stupid. You've already made it very clear that the Amish treat dating seriously. You wouldn't be taking her home tonight if you didn't have some interest in her." She grunted, spreading her hands wide. "Is this – you and me – some kind of a game to you?"

I shook my head, snatching her arms from the air and pulling her closer. She struggled but I held firmly until she stopped moving. "Katie, this is no game for me. I have feelings for you. You must believe that."

"What good do feelings do if you're Amish and I'm not? We can never be together and you know it. You just wanted to have a little fun before you settle down with Miriam."

"That's not true—"

"Do you deny it?" she interrupted. "That it's impossible for us to be a couple?"

When I should have spoken my heart, I hesitated. She was right.

"See," she breathed. "We've been ignoring the obvious elephant in the room but we both know the truth of it. Just admit it out loud," she demanded.

I drew in a heavy breath, clearing my head. I didn't want to lose Katie. "There are ways it could work..."

Her eyes narrowed to slits. "I'm never going Amish, if that's what you have in mind. The rules you have to live by are ridiculous. You're twenty-two and you have to sneak around, and girls have hardly any rights at all in your society."

"That's not true. Women are highly valued and are usually partners with their husbands in everything they do," I argued.

"Yeah, that's why your poor sister lost her finger

working in a butcher shop at fifteen years old. She can't just go to a doctor or psychologist or whoever and get the meds she needs." She crossed her arms. "Why are you trying to help her escape if your culture is so good for her, huh?"

"Rebecca is an unusual case and I won't discuss my family's troubles with you like this, in a fit of anger. My community is different to yours, of course, but that doesn't make yours better."

"Let me out, Rowan," Katie said in a breathy voice. "Please."

"What about us?" I dared to ask, not moving to open the door.

"Obviously, there is no *us*. I believe you when you say that you made plans with Miriam last minute, and I don't blame you for doing it. Before a half hour ago, I had no idea we'd be slobbering all over each other inside a buggy. There's a chemistry between us that we can't deny, but there's also the fact that we're from different worlds. And neither one of us is going to the other side. So it's for the best that we just end this now and get on with our lives. I still need you to train my horses and I'll behave myself until you get the job done."

I was going to lose her. In a swift motion, I leaned forward, bracing the back of her head with my hand and pulling her forward. My mouth met hers and she opened to me. Our tongues touched and a low moan escaped her lips. I kissed her long and slowly, imprinting every second to memory.

I lifted my face ever so slightly. "Can you really walk away from this?"

She trembled beneath my touch and I experienced a surge of hope in my gut.

"Yes. I have to," she whispered.

I loosened my hold on her and slumped back. She snatched the door handle, climbed over my legs and stepped from the buggy.

"Wait!" I stopped her. "I can still take you home. Let me explain things to Miriam."

Katie frowned. "So you're going to skip out on taking her home like you agreed to?"

"Yes. She can ride home with her parents. You don't have a ride."

"Actually, I do, Rowan." She lifted her chin to the small group of men making their way down the hill. I recognized the tall blond who she had been speaking to earlier.

"No, I said I would take you home and I will," I insisted.

"You also made that same commitment to another woman and since she's one of your people, she takes priority. You owe me nothing."

She spun on her heels and walked quickly to intersect the group. I watched her talk for a moment and then continue on with them. Craning my neck, I saw two of the men split off and then Katie climbed into a truck with the blond man. My head throbbed and I turned away, unable to stand the sight any longer.

I was such a fool. If only I hadn't fallen prey to Miriam's flirtations, I would still be touching my dear Katie. Only now, matters were even more complicated. I'd asked the bishop for his blessing to court his daughter and he'd accepted, with a fair warning. If I really did back out of that commitment, it would ruin me within the community. I wasn't even sure Katie would have me now. Her prejudice against my way of life was unreasonable. There was so much she didn't know. I could understand her reservations, though, as I felt the same way about becoming English. I'd heard too many stories about my people leaving the Amish to be with an outsider and it almost never worked out well.

I wiped my face with my kerchief and climbed out of the cramped space. Katie's scent still lingered in the cab so I left the door open, hoping Miriam wouldn't smell it.

Up until that moment, my family and community had been the most important things in the world to me. But something had just changed. With the force and suddenness of a bullet, Katie had claimed a spot in my heart. I wasn't ready to walk away from my life, but after tonight, I was certain about one thing. Even if it was impossible to be with Katie, I would never get her out of my mind.

The best plan, and probably the only thing I could do at the moment, was to tread carefully moving forward.

I had to trust in God and that it would all work out for the best but there were trials to come.

The first being how to handle Miriam and her father.

THIRTEEN

Katie

"So what happened with Tessa?" Dillon asked with a sideways glance.

It had taken a lot of work to pull myself together, walk up to my old high-school buddies, and ask for a ride home. I think I did a pretty good job of acting like nothing was wrong and Dillon had immediately and happily offered to drive me home.

I scrambled to come up with an acceptable lie. "She had a family emergency." Seeing his raised brows of concern, I quickly added, "Nothing too serious, just something she had to leave to take care of." I licked my lips, hoping I sounded convincing. My heart still raced uncomfortably from before. "I thought I'd just ride home with my neighbor, so I told Tessa to go on without me.

Unfortunately, I didn't get a chance to talk to my neighbor before he left. So, here I am."

"Worked out perfectly, if you ask me. I'm glad I got the opportunity to rescue you from the Amish event." He smiled broadly and I worked up a weak smile.

Miriam's voice and face still swirled around in my head. I had no doubt that she had put serious moves on Rowan. After all, he was a handsome man from a quality family in the community – a prime pick for any Amish girl. I couldn't stop the slow burning simmer that I was experiencing from head to foot, but I tried to think rationally about everything. I cared about Rowan, probably more deeply than I had any business to after such a short time, but our relationship was hopeless. The entire plan of trying to make nice with Rowan, convince him and myself that we were simply friends, had backfired on me completely. I'd gotten so caught up in the heat of the moment that I hadn't been able to stop myself from getting lost in Rowan. The way he kissed me was different to how I'd ever been kissed before. His touch was all consuming, as if he was trying to absorb me into himself. It was overwhelming and, if I had to guess, a passion I'd never experience again in my life. But it was wrong – all wrong. I had no business leading him on. I realized his feelings had been hurt and that was why he'd lashed out at me with angry words. Hell, I did the same thing when I was riled too. He was an honorable guy, and he deserved to have a chaos-free life with an Amish woman in his own world. I just wished the girl didn't have to be Miriam.

Dillon turned into the driveway, slowing down to navigate around the fallen branches that still hadn't been moved out of the way. He whistled when he saw the downed tree. Rowan had sawed up a large portion of it that morning, but the main part of the tree's trunk still lay sprawled over my pickup truck.

"Have you talked to the insurance company yet?" He parked in the only space where the tree didn't touch and shut off the engine.

"I will on Monday. I took a lot of pictures, though. It should be covered in full – just a pain in the ass to do the paperwork." I wanted to check on the horses and fill up their water buckets. When I looked over at Dillon, I saw anticipation shining on his face. More than anything I just wanted to be alone, but he had been nice enough to drive me home on short notice. I also had to start getting on with my life if I ever had a chance of driving Rowan out of my mind. "Do you want to see the horses?" I asked quickly before I could change my mind.

"I'd love to." He was out of the car before I was.

We walked side by side down the gravel lane to the barn. Dusty was hanging her head over the railing. Her foal was laying down in the grass, close by. When the mare spotted our approach, she nickered, and I changed course. She was usually grazing down in the lower part of the field by the creek this time of night so I was surprised to see her waiting for me.

"After we broke up, I missed seeing the horses." Dillon stepped up to Dusty and began rubbing her forehead. "You were a great instructor. I think I had a real knack for riding by the time you got through with me."

I looked away so he wouldn't see me roll my eyes. A small laugh escaped my lips. In those days, it had been my sole mission to make Dillon a horseman. Looking back, I think I was trying to get him to measure up to Rowan in that department, but it was impossible. Some things you're just born with and horsemanship was one of them. Especially if the first time you sat on a horse was when you were eighteen years old. I'd been raised riding horses, starting before I could even walk properly and so had Rowan. It made a difference to start early. Rowan also had an extra pinch of something else that made him an extraordinary horseman, a quality that even I didn't possess.

I glanced over at Dillon. He clucked to the foal, trying to coax her to get up and come to the fence. He had definitely made a real effort with the horses. I had to give him credit for trying.

"Have you been on a horse since then?"

He shook his head. "After we broke up, horses reminded me of you so I kept away. Later on, I got so busy with college classes, I wouldn't have had time to ride even if I'd wanted to." He draped his arms over the fence. "I have the time now."

I laughed out loud. "Whoa. Don't you think you're being a little presumptuous?"

"I know you, Katie. If I don't act quickly, I'll never have the opportunity again."

"I'm not a fish in a stream. I'm not going anywhere." I wondered why I was being so nice to Dillon. Then it occurred to me: I just wanted the distraction. Shame washed over me. Dillon had feelings, just like I did. I had to take it easy on him. "I'm not ready to jump into a relationship – just warning you."

I left the fence and Dillon caught up.

"Certainly. I wouldn't expect you to. You've just lost your father. I'm sure you and your mom need time to heal." He lightly touched my arm to get me to face him. "I'm a patient man. If it's friendship you want then that's what I'll give you."

I swallowed the lump in my throat. Dillon was the first and only guy I'd slept with. It wasn't passion that had made me pick him. It had been convenience and the desire to just get it over with. By the time I was eighteen, none of my friends were virgins anymore and I didn't want to be one either. Dillon had been kind and outgoing. He'd also had a wiry, athletic body from years of playing soccer. He had been a virgin too, so there had been that as well. We had both been ready to explore our sexuality and learn what it was all about. I jerked my head away, knowing I was blushing when I thought about all our clumsy attempts inside the hayloft of the barn. I had insisted on protection and he'd taken care of it on his own, which I had also admired.

Sadly, after all of that, I had no more feelings for Dillon than the day he first asked me out. Sure, we were friends and all, but the Amish boy had never left my mind. Even back then, Rowan was annoying me with some invisible connection I couldn't break. Dillon's partying ways weren't really the issue. It was that I felt hollow nothingness from his touch. When I'd realized how wrong it was to be using Dillon as my personal guinea pig, I broke up with him. Afterwards, I'd regretted that I had lost my virginity to a man I wasn't in love with. After experiencing the passion Rowan fanned inside of me, I was doubly irritated with myself.

If I was a betting woman, I'd put money down that Rowan was still a virgin. Being Amish, it kind of came with the territory. Up until the time that he was in a deeply committed relationship or married, he wouldn't cross that line. Until now. He might have made love to me in that buggy if Miriam hadn't shown up. If not right then, it would have been soon, either in the barn after a training session, or I would have enticed him into the house when Momma was away. There was no way we could have kept our hands off each other.

My heart dropped into my stomach thinking about what Rowan would think if he knew I'd had sex with someone else. I was sure it would upset him greatly. Unlike regular guys, who didn't expect their twenty-something-year-old girlfriends to have saved themselves for them, an Amish man surely would expect it. Just another reason we were destined to go our separate ways, I reasoned. It still hurt like hell but at least I was able to check off items in the cons column of dating an Amish man, in a sensible way.

I raised my eyes. Dillon waited patiently, just like he'd said he would. I'm not sure what came over me, but the sudden curiosity to see if his kisses had gotten any better made me take a step forward, right into his bubble. Could Dillon make my legs go weak, the same as Rowan had?

I saw the look of surprise on his face as I rose on tip toes and leaned in, planting my mouth on Dillon's. He recovered quickly and brought his hands around my back. It was a familiar feeling. He still smelled faintly of the same brand of men's fragrant soap I'd gotten used to in high school. His mouth tasted equally the same, and his tongue slid around against mine with ease. It was comfortable, even a little nice, but my heart was quiet, almost bored, and the juices in my core didn't stir.

He sighed in pleasure, rubbing his hands up and down my back. I didn't want to jerk back rudely. After all, I'd initiated the kiss. So I faked it for another minute, letting it die off naturally. When I stepped back, Dillon looked more confused than ever.

"What was that for? You just said you wanted to take it slow." He followed my movement, standing close. "Don't get me wrong, I'm very happy you took the initiative but I have to understand what you want from me."

I felt like complete crap. Once again, I'd used Dillon and it wasn't fair. I swallowed a gulp and decided to come clean with my old boyfriend. "I'm sorry, Dillon. You're going to hate my guts when I tell you the truth." I pushed my fingers through my hair, digging into my scalp. Moonlight sprayed the barnyard. The sound of horses munching on hay in their stalls and the smell of the crisp air tickled my senses. I had gone a couple of years without kissing anybody and tonight I'd had my lips on two different men. It wasn't my style at all and I felt icky all over. Dillon deserved the truth, even if he stormed away, never talking to me again.

"There's another guy in my life." I pressed my lips together and reconsidered. "Well, not anyone serious, I guess, just someone who I've been hanging out with the last few days." Dillon's eyes widened but he didn't say anything, so I plowed on. "I like this guy, but I don't think it's going to work out. That's why I kissed you; I wanted to feel if there still was a spark between us."

After the words spilled out of my mouth, I felt much better, lighter and freer at the same time.

Dillon nodded a little and stuffed his hands into his jacket pockets. "How was it then? Any sparks for you? Because I sure had my share."

His mild tone and encouraging words took me off balance. I was anticipating him to stomp away in a puff of anger. Instead, he was still standing there, telling me that he had experienced something that I hadn't when we'd kissed. The feeling of relief I'd felt an instant before disappeared. I slumped, inhaling deeply.

I couldn't bring myself to completely ruin his night. If I had left him alone and just walked the three miles to the ranch, he'd be home right now, probably on an online dating site, arranging a meeting over coffee with a deserving girl.

No matter what I did, I just couldn't stop making a mess of things.

"It felt good," I lied.

"Are we still going to the movies tomorrow?"

He looked like he was holding his breath. It wasn't right to mislead Dillon, but going out for an evening with friends was very appealing and a way to keep my mind off Rowan.

"Sure, I'd like to get out. I can't make any promises about where we'll end up, though."

Dillon's mouth spread into a smile. "I'm fine with that, Katie. As long as you give me a chance. That's all I ask."

To get away from any more talk of romance, I quickly changed the subject. "I could use some help filling up water buckets. You interested?"

"You bet," he said.

As we walked into the darkness of the barn and I fumbled for the light switch, I was grateful to have Dillon there. Regardless of whether we ever kissed again, he was a friend. I needed all of those I could get at the moment. Especially since visions of Rowan and Miriam began pestering me.

It was just about the time they'd be leaving the auction, and my stomach clenched. I couldn't help but wonder if Rowan would test the waters with Miriam, the way I had with Dillon.

FOURTEEN

Rowan

I snapped the reins over Scout's back and he stretched his gait into an extended trot. There were a few buggies in line ahead of us but they were a fair distance away. We had split from the driveway onto the roadway about ten minutes before the auction would end, getting a head start on the traffic jam building behind us.

I slid the side window open, glad for the cold air on my face. The minutes had ticked slowly by after Katie had left. I had done my best to act like nothing was wrong, and thought I'd fooled everyone sufficiently, but I still hadn't let my guard down for one minute. Father and Mother had been pleased to hear I'd be taking Miriam home and I did nothing to diminish their good moods. My main goal was to get the day over with as quickly as possible. In the light of morning, I would talk to Father and convince him that a match with Miriam wouldn't work out. Tomorrow couldn't get here quickly enough in my book.

Miriam sat very still beside me, her side bumping mine ever so slightly with the shifting movement of the speeding buggy.

"Father said it was a successful dinner and auction – maybe even better than the spring event," Miriam broke the silence.

"Uh-hmm," I muttered.

It had come to me as I called out the numbers in the crowded barn that if Miriam didn't like me, she wouldn't pursue me any longer. Driving her home once didn't necessarily mean that we were a couple. If we mutually decided we weren't a good fit, no one would care, even our parents. Timothy and Miranda had courted for a month or so the year before and they called it quits, without any hard feelings between the families and the elders had accepted their decision. Of course, that had been mutual. Problems arose when one party wanted in and the other wanted out.

"Did you know I'll be helping Emily Yoder teach classes after the holiday break?" Her voice was still cheerful.

It was news to me. "I hadn't heard. Will you get paid a wage?"

"I will and Emily hopes I can take her place next year."

"Is she quitting?"

She dropped her voice as if she were telling me a secret. "She wants to have another baby, and is planning ahead."

I counted the teacher's kids up in my head. "Doesn't she already have eleven?"

"Twelve, actually." She giggled.

"I would think that's quite enough for her," I commented, mostly to myself.

"I agree. I'd like to have five or six – no more than that." She fell silent, and only the sound of the striking of hooves on pavement filled the cab.

We passed the Troyer farm and I slowed Scout to a walk. He was breathing heavily, and even though I wanted to drop Miriam off as soon as possible, I wouldn't push the horse too hard.

Steam from Scout's back rose into the chilly night air. The reflectors on the buggies in front of us became small dots in the distance. It was a lonely stretch of road.

"Your employer is very attractive," Miriam commented out of the blue.

I felt like groaning out loud but I didn't. It wasn't surprising that she'd mention Katie. Actually, I'd been mentally preparing for her to bring the subject up.

"She's not my employer, just someone who hired me

to train her horses. The job will be over in December," I replied matter-of-factly.

"Are you two friends?" When I didn't immediately answer, she went on. "I mean, how'd you get the job?"

I flopped the reins over Scout and clucked once. He picked up speed, back into a trot again and I sat forward on the seat, looking straight ahead.

"I worked at Diamond E Ranch when I was a teenager for about a year. It was the best job I ever had. Being paid to ride and care for horses was a dream come true." The image of Katie's fuming father rose in my mind. "Unfortunately, after a while my services weren't needed anymore, so I began working on the building crew. Katie contacted me a few days ago about training up the colts. Her father died and it seems he left her and her mother in a bind." I shrugged. "So, I want to help them and it's a great way to make some extra money doing something I love."

I'd probably said way too much but if I was going to be convincing, I needed to be willing to elaborate. Having a moody mother and a troubled sister, I already knew that women liked to talk.

"Oh, I see." Miriam's voice lightened again. "Thank you for telling me. I didn't want to pry or anything but if we're going to be courting, I should know what's going on in your life, don't you think?"

I bristled at her words and inhaled slowly to gather

my wits. "About that, Miriam. We've been friends since we were little kids, and you know how I am. I take time making my mind up on most things. I don't want to jump into anything serious right now but I would like to get to spend some time with you. Does that make sense?"

Miriam folded her hands on her lap. "I feel the same way, Rowan. It's a scary thought to settle down with a person. That's why I'm twenty-one and still available." She gave a good-natured snort. "I guess you could say I'm picky too."

"I don't think I'm picky—" I began.

"Of course you are." She waved her hand at the front of the buggy. "Take your horse for instance. He's a fine buggy horse but he's got some age on him, and you probably should have traded him in a long time ago. I know John Yoder offered to sell you one of his younger harness horses and you said none of them suited you."

My lips pinched together as I digested what she said. It turned out that Miriam was a lot more observant than I'd ever thought.

"That's true. I wasn't interested in replacing Scout with one of John's horses but not necessarily because I'm arrogant about the horse that pulls my buggy. Scout's the best working horse I've ever owned. He's just as willing under saddle as he is in harness. He's a smart one, too." I smiled fondly. "I have to admit that after fifteen years together, he's one of my closest friends. It's difficult to replace that kind of horse."

Miriam swiveled in her seat, facing me. "That's the sweetest thing. I'm proud of you. Everyone else just sells their old horses when they start to slow down. The fact that you aren't in any hurry to upgrade, is a sign that you have a gentle soul and a good spirit, Rowan."

If Miriam knew what I'd been doing with Katie in this very same buggy, not an hour ago, I didn't think she'd be so proud. I let the thought go, wishing to put the English girl out of my mind for the rest of the night.

"Scout will be with me for the rest of his life. I'll never sell him, but a time will come when this kind of work is going to be too much for him. Then he'll be retired to pasture with our old ponies."

"It's a good life for a horse," she said.

I pulled on the reins, slowing Scout to make the turn into her driveway. A moment later I pulled up to her house, stopped, and faced her.

"Here you go." I hoped I didn't sound rude, but I was impatient to get away from Miriam. Especially because of Katie. It wasn't right for me to be with her at all when it was Katie who had captured my heart.

"It will be a while before things are closed down at the schoolhouse. We have some time before Mother and Father are to return home." She fidgeted with her fingers in her lap in a nervous way. "You could stay and we could talk some more."

I felt sorry for her. She hadn't done anything wrong. If my mind wasn't full of Katie, I would have liked to court Miriam. If I wasn't meant to be with Katie, Miriam would have been a good match for me in a lot of ways.

"We have to take it slow. We don't want to make a mistake and honestly, I'm not sure if I'm ready to settle down."

"When will I see you again?" she ventured in a steady voice.

"I'm not sure. Probably for Sunday church service," I said.

"I'm fine letting you take your time, Rowan, but if we don't actually spend time together, we won't know if we're right for each other."

"It's a very busy time for me right now, what with the building jobs and training Katie's horses," I rushed out, just wanting to be on my way.

I saw Miriam stiffen when I said Katie's name and I instantly regretted the mistake.

"I think you're just avoiding me," she said, the pitch of her voice rising.

I couldn't deal with this right now. I'd simply dropped her off at home. We'd never even held hands and I was supposed to feel guilty that I wasn't spending enough time with her? I knew if we were English, this wouldn't be happening.

Just to get away, I said, "Maybe after the service I'll be able to spare some time."

"That sounds perfect. I'll look forward to it." She rested her hand over mine, startling me. "See you Sunday."

She swept out of the buggy. I waited, making sure she made it into the house, and then I snapped the reins, trotting down the driveway.

My mind was made up the second Miriam touched my hand. I had felt nothing at all. There weren't any sparks or heat from that contact. Sure, I believed attraction could grow slowly over time, and sometimes the best wives were the quieter ones who made a cozy home and took good care of the children.

After the passion I'd experienced with Katie though, nothing short of that kind of connection would ever do. Katie was the only woman for me. I just had to find a way to make it happen.

FIFTEEN

Katie

The sky was dark and the air chilly when we walked out of the movie theater. A gust of wind picked up a flurry of leaves from the curb, scattering them across the parking lot. It was still light outside when we entered the building so the change was a little disorientating.

Dillon placed his hand on the small of my back as we walked and I tried to ignore the pressure of his touch. He'd been the perfect gentleman all evening, making light, animated conversation during dinner, buying the popcorn and colas for the movie. It was extremely easy being around him. I just wished he set my blood on fire the way Rowan did.

Thinking about Rowan made me wonder what he was doing on this cloudy evening. Was he snatching a few kisses with Miriam behind a shed? I shook the distasteful image from my mind. I'd called Momma from work several times to see if he had shown up to train the horses, but he hadn't made an appearance. I hated that I cared so much what he was up to.

"Do you guys want to stop by The Roadside Pub for a drink?" Tessa piped up.

She and Jimmy were walking a few strides ahead of us, holding hands. I'd spotted them kissing in the theatre, like a couple of teenagers. The problem with Tessa was that she got too excited about a having a new man. She moved way too fast and usually regretted it later on. I could hardly judge because I hadn't exactly taken it slowly with Rowan, but with other guys, I had a rule: no hand holding or kissing on the first date. Maybe that was why I rarely got a second date. Whatever it was about Rowan, I hadn't been able to resist him right off the bat. I just wondered how Tessa had the stamina to bring that kind of passion into every single relationship she got into.

"That sounds perfect," Dillon replied. He nudged me. "What do you think?"

Embarrassingly, I'd fallen asleep during the movie and Dillon had had to wake me up when the credits began rolling. I was still tired but that little nap and the brisk wind had reinvigorated me. What else did I have to do? Pining away over Rowan when I got home was something I wanted to stall.

"Sure," I said, forcing enthusiasm. "We'll meet you over there, Tessa."

Dillon wanted to discuss the movie. It was a thriller about a woman whose family had disappeared and she was under suspicion by the cops. She was a sympathetic character that the audience was rooting for the entire movie, but in the end and, with a big twist, it was discovered she had murdered her entire family so that she could run away with a man she hardly knew but had become completely obsessed with.

Since I had slept through the most important part of the movie, I was relieved when we walked into the pub and joined Tessa and Jimmy at a booth, thus ending our conversation. The idea of becoming so enamored by a man, to the point where you're willing to kill your own kids, was extremely disturbing, and it stayed with me right up until the instant the waitress placed the bottle of beer in front of me.

"How did you like the movie?" Tessa leaned over the table. She couldn't have gotten any closer to Jimmy without sitting in his lap.

Dillon sat a respectable several inches away from me on our side of the booth, which I was grateful for. "It certainly wasn't a feel-good experience," I said.

Tessa laughed at my choice of words and began debating the characters and storyline with Jimmy and Dillon. My gaze wandered around the room. The place was crowded tonight and I recognized several people sitting at the bar.

I took a swig of my beer and was about to join the conversation when someone caught my eye. My heart rate spiked as I sat up a little straighter and craned my neck to get a better view.

There was a young woman sitting on a stool, drinking what appeared to be a mixed drink. She was dressed in a short skirt that showed off most of her slender legs, straight up to her thigh. Her sequined blouse sparkled brightly and looked a little dated, like something that would be worn in the seventies. Long, dark brown hair spiraled down her back, and she kept sweeping it away from her face with flips of her head. All those things were just side notes in my mind. It was the woman's pale, frail-looking face that made it difficult to swallow.

I must be mistaken, I told myself, pushing out of the booth and mumbling to the others that I was going to the restroom.

I walked slowly to the bar, not taking my eyes off the young woman, even when I said hello to someone squeezing by.

The woman threw her head back and laughed. It was then that I noticed the man sitting with her. I guessed he was in his late twenties and decent-looking, in a rough, almost scary way. Dark stubble shaded his jaw and ink traveled from his hands, under his t-shirt, and up around his neck. It wasn't just the initial visual appraisal that made me slow down. It was the four shot glasses in front of him and the pistol at his hip. Most drinking establishments didn't allow open carry, but The Roadside Pub was a lot on the shady side. Fights broke out regularly and occasionally a good guy with a gun might be needed to offset the bad ones. I wasn't sure which category this guy fell into.

I had almost reached them when the guy bent forward and whispered something to the woman. She nodded and he left his stool. I watched him move in the direction of the restrooms. Taking the opportunity, I sped up and sat on the available stool.

The woman didn't look up. She was scrolling on her cellphone.

"Hello, Rebecca," I said.

Her eyes popped open wide and her mouth dropped open.

I waited for the initial shock to wear off and watched in fascination as her entire demeanor quickly settled. The corner of her mouth rose and she took a sip of her drink which, from the tall glass, lemon slice and brown liquid, I took to be a Long Island Iced Tea.

"Hi, there," she said, tilting her head. "I thought you'd be with my brother."

I didn't like the way she'd turned the tables. Before asking her what the hell she was doing in a bar, dressed like a slinky trollop, I had to respond to her snarky comment about me and Rowan.

"Why would you think that?"

Her smirk deepened. "He's sweet on you, you know. I think it goes all the way back to when he worked at your ranch years ago." She took a gulp to finish off her drink and motioned to the bartender for another one.

The swift, experienced action told me she'd done it a few times.

"My brother has always been the good boy, the perfect son, and a steadfast Amish man." She circled her finger in the air and then pointed at me. "I think those days are soon coming to an end, and all because of you."

Now it was my turn to drop my jaw. Rebecca was a real piece of work. All the sympathy I'd felt for her went straight out the window.

"I haven't done anything," I argued.

"Oh, maybe not yet, but I know my brother well. He's completely smitten with you. Since you don't seem like the type of English girl who is clamoring to lose your freedom and trade in your jeans for a dress, I'd bet it will be my brother who will have to leave his world to be with you."

"That's absurd." I narrowed my eyes and leaned over. "You're nuts. There's hardly anything going on between me and Rowan. He isn't going to have to leave anything because we aren't together anyway."

"*Hardly.*" She stretched out the word seductively. "That means you've done almost everything, except *the deed*. Hah. It won't be long."

My stomach twisted into knots. This wasn't about me.

I lowered my voice to a harsh whisper. "I wonder what Rowan or your parents would say if they found out you're spending time in rough bars, drinking alcohol and hanging out with unsavory people?"

Just then, the man returned and I shot him a warning look that pushed him back a step.

"Everything all right, sweetie?" the man asked Rebecca.

She smiled broadly, twirling the end of her long hair between her fingertips. "Nothing I can't handle. I'll be out in a minute. Just let me finish off this last drink," she drawled.

When the man was gone, she turned back to me. "You wouldn't dare say a thing about finding me here."

"Why is that?" I was amazed at her audacity.

"Because you aren't that type of person, Katie." She swallowed her drink down in three gulps, set the glass roughly on the counter, and bounced off the stool. Bringing her lips close to my ear, she said, "You're just too damn nice to do something like that."

She sashayed by me, wobbled a little at the door, and

then disappeared into the night. A quick blast of colder air invaded the smoky warmth of the bar and I shivered.

Good grief. I had really underestimated Rebecca Coblentz.

"I had a really nice time. Did you enjoy yourself?" Dillon asked.

I was so distracted, that I barely remembered the rest of my time in the bar and the drive home. I hadn't even finished my beer so it wasn't intoxication, either. I just couldn't stop mulling over what Rebecca had said. Was I really too nice or was that a form of manipulation to get me not to narc on her? It seemed to me that if she was trying to use reverse psychology, she wasn't doing a great job – or maybe she was completely brilliant. I wasn't so sure anymore that her problems could be fixed by medication and weekly talks with a shrink. She would have even the most wizened therapist wrapped around her finger. She was just that good.

"It was fun. Thanks for getting me out of the house on my night off. I needed it." That was the honest truth despite the troubling encounter with Rebecca.

"When can I see you again?"

As great as the date had been, I wasn't ready for any

more right away. "We'll talk next week and figure something out," I offered, hoping he'd let it go.

When the barn came into view, I saw Rowan's horse tied to the hitching rail. My heart jumped into my lungs. The quivering excitement that shot through my body irritated me deeply. I really was a stupid fool.

"You can let me off here. I'm going to check in on the horses."

"Do you want some help?"

"No, no. It will only take a minute and then I'm going straight to bed."

There was an awkward moment of hesitation by Dillon before I exited the vehicle. I think he was hoping for a quick kiss.

"Be careful going home," I said, opening the door and jumping out of the car before he said anything else.

I stood and watched Dillon drive away. When his car disappeared around the bend, I took a deep breath to quiet my nerves and headed to the barn.

I loved the feeling of walking into the barn at night. The lights were shining but the horses still looked sleepy in their stalls. Remington was tied in the hallway. His golden coat was glistening with sweat but he was breathing normally. Rowan was busy wiping him down with a towel.

"Did he have a good workout?" I stepped up to the colt's face and slid my hand down his nose.

"Sure did." Rowan didn't look up from his work. "I'm taking him for a ride up the path. You can ride Scout if you want to come."

"At night?" The surge of anticipation in my chest was almost painful.

"Ah, it will be all right. We have the moonlight to lead the way. If I remember correctly, that path is clear and safe."

Feeling a little bit challenged by his words, I readily agreed. A few minutes later, I swung my leg over the saddle on Rowan's tall gelding and bumped his sides to come abreast with Rowan and Remington.

I studied Remington's movements. He walked forward with confident strides, tossing his head from side to side – not in agitation, but more in curiosity as he looked around into the dense foliage on either side of the trail. Rowan had been right. Remington just needed a job to do.

"That horse has come a long way in just a few rides," I said.

Rowan reached down and rubbed Remington's neck. "He's a good boy. We just needed to come to an understanding. He should fetch a pretty penny."

The trail narrowed and Remington, for all his usual bravado, stepped closer to Scout. I couldn't help my knee rubbing against Rowan's. I glanced over to see him sitting relaxed in the saddle. A blade of hay protruded from his mouth and I fought the urge to snatch it from between his teeth.

My thick jacket kept the cold breeze from penetrating, and with gloves and a knit beanie, I was quite comfortable. A spray of leaves pelted us from above when our horses walked into a stand of poplar trees. It was quiet except for the squeaking of the leather saddles and the horses' breath.

"Where were you tonight?" Rowan finally asked.

I'd been waiting for him to broach the subject so I was ready. "I went out to dinner and the movies with friends."

"Did you have fun?" His voice remained neutral, almost disinterested. But I wasn't fooled.

"Yeah, it was a good time." It gave me satisfaction to utter the simple words. Whatever was going on with him and Miriam, at least he knew I wasn't sitting at home pining away for him.

"I've always wanted to go to the movie theater," he said.

I swiveled in the seat to look at Rowan. He met my gaze. "Would you really get in trouble if you went?" He nodded solemnly. "What about when you have your own farm and you're married? Can't you just hire someone to drive you into town? No one would even know."

"I would know." He exhaled and I watched his breath puff out in front of him. "Our culture only works because we're faithful to it. If everyone began doing their own thing, we wouldn't be honest and we wouldn't be Amish anymore."

"But it's just a movie."

"Where does it end? If I sneak off to a movie, next thing I'll be listening to music and eventually my heart will yearn for things like cars and electricity."

"Don't you like music?"

"Of course. Our work crew has a driver who always plays country music on his radio between driving to different sites. Father is all right with it because Mr. Murphey is a reliable man and Father doesn't want to lose him."

"I can't imagine all the rules and restrictions you live by. Is it really worth it?" I twirled a piece of Scout's mane between my fingers.

He was slow to answer. "Sometimes I'm sure it is, other times I question everything." He tossed the piece of hay to the ground and exhaled loudly. "I'm sure you think our ways are backwards." He snorted. "I don't even own a vehicle or a cellphone, which are a couple of things that seem to be very important to outsiders." His voice gained volume and emotion. "But there are so many things you don't understand, Katie."

"Like what?" I slanted a look at him.

There was just enough moonlight to see the corner of his mouth rise. "For instance, think about your own situation. Your father passed away, leaving you and your mother in dire straits. That wouldn't happen in my community. My people always join together to help other families in need. Amish folks never suffer alone. We help each other in ways I don't see happening on the outside. It's the truest sense of community you'll find anywhere. Following the rules is a small price to pay for that kind of peace of mind."

He fell silent and I thought about what he'd said. The unconditional support within an Amish community did sound kind of appealing, from the way he described it. It would have been nice to have that kind of support when Daddy died. But what Rowan didn't understand was that Peggy and Tessa had both volunteered to help us and I was sure that Momma had received offers too. We were just too proud to accept. I guess since Rowan's upbringing was different, accepting assistance from a neighbor in a time of need wasn't a big deal to him.

He continued to quietly stare off into the distance, rocking back and forth in the saddle, giving me the feeling he had something else on his mind. I didn't want to pry though. What I'd seen and the conversation I'd had with his sister earlier that evening was heavy on mine.

Rebecca was wrong about me being too nice to tell Rowan. He was on her side and the reason he'd taken the job training my horses was to help her leave the Amish.

Was it really the best thing for her to run away if she was going to get drunk at bars and go home with questionable men?

Being nice meant that I should do what I could to keep her from ruining her life, or worse, end up buried in a shallow grave out behind some redneck's abandoned house.

"Does your sister ever go out at night?" I asked carefully.

Rowan glanced over. "Not very often. Why would you ask?"

Any reservations I had disappeared when I recalled Rebecca's cocky smile and how she'd downed two Long Island Iced Teas in a matter of minutes.

"What about tonight? Do you know where she is?"

"I'm so busy most of the time that I don't usually keep tabs on her. As far as I know, she's babysitting for the English neighbor this evening." I snorted and Rowan turned fully in his saddle. "Do you know something about Rebecca?"

Our horses broke out from the darkness of the trees into the wide, open field. It was the same spot that I'd come off Dusty during the storm six years ago. I could point out the exact place I hit the ground. Remington sped up into a nervous prance and even Scout perked his ears when we stepped onto the grass.

"Do you promise not to freak out?" Knowing how

seriously Rowan took his promises, I would make sure he agreed before I said anything.

"I will try not to, but I guess it depends on what you have to say," Rowan said.

He was protective of his sister; I got it. She was only eighteen and needed to be reined in before it was too late.

I looked him in the eye. "Rebecca is getting in over her head."

"What do you know?"

"Tonight, after the movies, we stopped by The Roadside Pub for a little while."

"Isn't that a bar?" His mouth was drawn into a tight line and his voice shook.

"Yeah. I'm twenty-two years old, Rowan. It's perfectly legal for me to be there."

"That's why I smelled cigarette smoke on you. Did you drink alcohol?"

His nosey questions about what I had been doing made me mad. "Not really, but your sister sure did."

"What are you saying ... that my sister was at a bar?"

"Not only at a bar, but drinking heavily and she left the joint with a guy that I would be afraid to get into a car with."

"That's impossible," he murmured. "She's at the Tippersons's house, babysitting. Maybe you mistook someone else for her."

I rolled my head back. "Afraid not. I sat down with her and we even talked about you before she left with that guy."

He rubbed his jaw. His posture was as tight as a drawn bow.

"How could this happen?" he asked in a dull voice.

"She had a cellphone so she must be hiding it somewhere. She was also wearing a mini skirt and a gaudy top that she might have picked up at a thrift shop." I softened my tone. "Maybe she met the guy at the butcher shop or something. There's something else—"

"What more could there be?" He sounded completely defeated.

"It wasn't her first time there, Rowan. She's done this before, probably a lot. Your sister has had a secret life for a while."

"I'm not shocked, exactly, more ... disappointed. She's been so troubled for so long that we've all grown accustomed to her strange behavior. Thinking back on it, there were times when I thought I smelled cigarettes in the house or noticed that Rebecca was overly exhausted on Sunday mornings. It all makes sense now." He reined Remington to a stop and I pulled up next to him. "What am I going to do with her? I thought funding her escape from the community was the right thing to do but I'm not so sure. If she's behaving so irresponsibly, she might get hurt."

"I worried about that too. Is telling your folks out of the question?"

"How can I *not* tell them? She's their only daughter. They have a right to know what she's doing. She's only eighteen."

"Yes, she's young, but she's also a legal adult. Your parents will only punish her and I don't think discipline will work with her. She was almost taunting me to turn her in. I think she wants to run away. She won't wait for you to raise the money and make the special arrangements for her to leave properly. She wants out now."

"I can't just ignore what you've told me. She needs help, Katie."

He looked sick to his stomach. "I know. I'm here for both of you."

He glanced at his watch and back up. "This is asking a lot, and I hate to put you in this position, but will you take me to this bar so I can get my sister?"

"She already left there. Who knows where she might have gone."

"I'll ride Scout home and check if she's in her bed yet. My parents are sound sleepers; they won't wake. If she isn't there, I'll call you. I want to go to that bar and ask around; maybe we can find out who the man is that she was with."

My head was spinning but I was all in. Rowan and I

might not be destined for romance but he was a friend. If I could help him, I sure would, although worry tickled my senses. Anything could go wrong with the crazy plan.

Remington felt Rowan's nervous energy and his prancing turned into a crow-hop and a little buck. His rider stayed glued to the seat, impressing me. Rowan looked at me with expectation, holding his reins slightly up, ready for action.

I couldn't say no to Rowan Coblentz. "You can count on me."

SIXTEEN

Rowan

I glanced over at Katie. She'd been relatively quiet since she'd picked me up on the side of the road in her mother's car. It was embarrassing that she couldn't drive straight up the driveway, but the sound of the engine might have woken my parents. At times like this, I was resentful of my heritage. My little sister was drinking in bars and running around town and I couldn't go out in the night on my own to find her. I wasn't allowed to drive or own a car. My parents still kept tabs on where I was and the girl I really wanted to be with was out of reach.

I stared back out the window. It was just shy of midnight and the streets in town were vacant. A feeling of hopelessness washed over me and I rubbed my temple and exhaled.

"You okay?" Katie asked.

"I'm still digesting what Rebecca has gotten herself into. Her difficult nature has always worried me, but I never dreamed she'd do something as reckless as going out drinking with a strange man. I'm still not sure what we can do to stop her self-destructive behavior."

"She obviously needs professional help but there's something else going on with her. It's like she's lost, and is trying to fill a void, or possibly she just wants attention." She slowed the vehicle before pulling into a small parking lot. The bar was a one-story brick structure that looked like it had seen better days. Straight off, I noticed the grass growing out of the gutters and the broken pavement stretching up to the entryway. For all that, the parking lot was full and people milled around outside, as if the interior was too crowded to hold everyone.

Katie parked the car and shut off the engine. She turned to me with a small frown. "Let me do the talking. You're too emotional and no one will say a word if they think you're going to get them into trouble." She cocked her head, staring at my shirt. "I didn't even think about that," she said under her breath. Her eyes suddenly brightened and determination etched her face. "Take your suspenders off and unbutton the top of your shirt. Untuck your shirt, too."

"Why? What's wrong with the way I'm dressed. I'm looking for my sister, not trying to impress anyone."

She snorted, rolling her head. "Yeah, how many people are going to talk to us if they see you're Amish? Huh?" When I dropped my gaze, she continued. "An Amish man, not trying to conceal his identity, coming into a place like this in the middle of the night, will freak everyone out. Trust me on this. It's best if you just blend in as much as possible and let me do the talking. Guys won't notice you much if they're focused on me."

Everything she said made sense. I just wanted to find my sister and bring her home, but the thought of Katie flirting with men to locate Rebecca made my stomach churn. "I don't want you to do this," I said firmly. "Let me ask around. I talk to Englishers all the time on the job. I can handle it," I insisted.

"That may be true, but we only have one shot at this. If you blow it, we're out of options. Do you really want to take that chance?" When I stubbornly stared back at her without moving, she shook her head. "It's not like I'm going home with anyone else. I'm simply talking and that's it. You'll be standing right there with me."

The strong smell of stale cigarette smoke drifted in through the crack in the window. "I don't like this place. It's dangerous, I can tell."

Katie graced me an indulgent smile. "At this hour, it's

a little riskier, for sure, but I wouldn't say it's dangerous. People are just in there having a good time on a Saturday night. Don't overthink it. We'll be in and out in no time." She paused and then added, with a less enthusiastic voice, "Fingers crossed."

"All right, but if anything seems amiss, we're leaving immediately. I'm not taking a chance with your safety, even to find my sister."

I unclasped my suspenders and unbuttoned my shirt a little. What I had just said was unreasonable, and I knew it. Katie had been in this place with her English friends earlier that very same night. That fact left a heaviness in my gut that I was still coming to terms with. Katie was her own woman. We weren't committed to each other and she could come and go as she pleased. If Rebecca went English, she would also have that kind of freedom. The only difference was, I believed Katie was responsible enough to take care of herself. My sister wasn't.

Before we stepped inside, Katie looked me up and down and smiled. If I was correct, she was satisfied with the appraisal she gave me and she liked what she saw. My stomach muscles that had been coiled since we'd left the car loosened and my face flushed. She carried the same air of authority that she possessed when she was in the barn or riding a horse. Instead of her red hair being pulled back in the usual ponytail, it draped across her shoulders and I caught a whiff of vanilla when the breeze stirred her stands. She wore blue jeans and a satiny, purple blouse. The knee-high black suede boots matched her jacket. Other than the loop earrings that adorned her earlobes, she wasn't wearing any jewelry. Her attire wasn't inappropriate in any way, yet she was still incredibly seductive. I hated the idea of other men ogling her, but I was proud that she was by my side.

When our eyes met, a funny look passed over Katie's face. She reached out and I offered her my hand. "We've got this." She squeezed and let go.

I missed the warm pressure of her touch but didn't dwell on the loss of it. The burly, bald-headed man blocking the entrance caught my attention. Katie leaned in and spoke to the man, who only glanced my way once. He stepped aside, motioning us to enter.

I was surprised at how well lit the inside was. A smoky haze and loud music filled the air. I recognized the song as one that I'd heard on the work truck's radio. I followed Katie through the throng of standing people, past several pool tables and a crowded dance floor. I'd always wanted to play pool, and I glanced back over my shoulder to see a short, bearded man draw the long poker back and strike the balls. When I straightened back up, a curly-haired woman was right in my way. I tried to swerve around her, but she squeezed by me, holding a beer bottle in each hand. Her large breasts rubbed my chest and she flashed a wide grin. I jumped sideways and hurried to catch up with Katie who had just reached the bar. Much in the same way the blonde woman pushed past me, Katie leaned in between two men sitting at the counter. I didn't like to see her so close to them but I remained silently standing behind her. I'd agreed to keep my mouth shut and let Katie take the lead, and I aimed to keep it, as difficult as it might be.

She tapped the counter to get the bartender's attention. The woman who leaned forward to listen to Katie was gray-haired and wrinkled. Her age didn't fool me, though. The leathery skin, hard-edged features, and sharp eyes hinted at a tough old woman.

I couldn't hear what Katie was saying or the woman's response. The music was so loud that the drum beat vibrated my insides. I glanced back toward the dancers. One couple weren't really dancing. They were rubbing against each other in very sexual movements. I quickly averted my eyes, feeling my cheeks burn, but the image was seared into my mind. The idea that my sister or Katie would willingly come into this horrible place made my heart thump wildly.

When I turned back, Katie was speaking to the two men she'd squeezed between at the counter. One of them appeared to be close to our age. The other was middle-aged and balding. I saw the wedding ring on the older man's finger and wondered why he wasn't home with his family. The younger man held a beer in his hand, but unlike most of the other patrons, he was clear-eyed. I watched as he cocked his head toward Katie and then whispered something back into her ear. I stood frozen, trying to remain cool at the close contact. In my world, a man and a woman who weren't a married couple would never get so close in public. This wasn't my world, though, and I swallowed down the hot juices, looking away.

I felt a light touch on my arm and I jerked it back.

"Hey, buddy, you want to buy me a drink?" the woman asked. She was short and slender with cropped black hair.

My lips thinned in disgust. "No, of course not."

"Oh, come … on, you handsome … thing. I'll make it worth your while." Her words slurred together, and she placed her hands to my chest as she pressed closer.

I grasped her shoulders gently and moved her several inches away. "It appears you've already had enough to drink, ma'am. Please be on your way."

"Ma'am?" The woman mouthed the word. "Where did you come from?"

Out of the corner of my eye, I saw the middle-aged man reach forward and place his hand on Katie's hip. He was trying to get her attention back from the younger man, but that didn't matter to me. I took a couple of strides, grabbed his hand, and flung it away from her.

The man jumped off his stool and faced me. He was taller than he had looked sitting down, matching my height.

"What the fuck did you do that for?" the man demanded.

"This is my girlfriend. Don't ever touch her again," I ordered.

"Is that so?" The man took a step forward. His chest bumped mine, like he was a puffed-out rooster.

I held my ground, balling my fists. Katie's hands sliced between us, pushing both of us back.

"Whoa, boys, no need to fight over me," she said.

The other man poked me in the chest with his finger. "Is he really your boyfriend?"

The music still vibrated loudly in my ears and the nearest patrons were staring our way. I noticed several back away. Some of the men actually stepped closer. They were the rowdy-looking ones and their eyes popped with excitement.

Katie looked up at me. "Yep, I claim him." She grabbed my hand and tugged me sideways.

"Are you a true ginger?" the man snarled. He grasped his groin. "There's only one way to know for sure."

Katie rolled her eyes and my fist shot forward, striking the man squarely in the face. He wobbled and stumbled into me. I shoved him away and he tripped over the stool.

"What the hell!" he shouted, wiping the blood that dribbled from his nose.

Katie's hands clutched my entire arm. "Come on, let's go," she hissed.

One of the men from the group of onlookers stopped our progress to the door by grabbing my shoulder and yanking me from Katie's grip. I ducked and his hand missed its mark, but his forward momentum and large size brought us tumbling down on an innocent fellow sitting at a table. A woman screamed, bolting out of the way as the three of us and the chair struck the floor. The man who'd been in the chair jumped to his feet, dragging my attacker with him. He began pummeling the other man with rapid punches that left me staring in shock.

In another blink of an eye, the man I'd originally struck kicked me in the side with his boot. I rolled, unbelieving that someone would actually strike a man while he was down. The large, bald man that had guarded the entrance suddenly appeared. He was in the process of separating the other two men when Katie flew out of nowhere. She jumped on the back of the man kicking me and, like a crazed crab, wrapped her legs around him and smacked him in the head with her good hand.

I lurched to my feet and tried to reach her but the crowd

folded in between us. Grunts and shrieks joined the music's momentum as fists flew and men crashed together. I'd never seen anything like it. A hand came out of nowhere, striking me in the eye. I didn't even know which direction it came from. I pushed my way toward Katie, my eyes never leaving her flailing form, still clinging to the man's back.

A gunshot exploded and the music stopped playing. Everyone quit what they were doing, and all eyes shifted to the doorway. The old woman stood there, legs apart, holding a twelve-gauge shotgun on her hip.

"That's enough, you bunch of buffoons!" she shouted.

Disheveled women helped groaning men off the floor. I moved quickly to reach Katie who leaned against the wall with round eyes. Her hair was a tangled mess on her shoulders and there was a red blotch on her cheek.

Katie fell into me and I hugged her tightly, sucking in the sweet smell of sweaty vanilla. The embrace only lasted a few seconds. She wiggled out of my arms and, still holding my hand, she tugged me forward.

She slowed when we reached the old woman with the gun. "I'm so sorry," she said in a quietly pleading tone.

The woman's glassy blue gaze landed on me. She tipped the barrel of the gun at my heart. "Katie, I don't want to see this one in my establishment again."

"No, he won't be back," Katie assured the woman who still hadn't lowered her gun.

The woman eyed me, shaking her head and making a huffing sound. "Child, you better run back to the Amish community and keep your damn ass there if you know what's good for you."

Sirens wailed in the distance and Katie shot me an anxious frown.

I chuckled. "Ma'am. Don't worry. Trust me, I won't be back."

The woman nodded and then raised the gun. Katie didn't waste a second. She pulled me through the doorway without looking back.

Once we were in the car, driving away, she bellowed, "What the hell were you thinking?"

I opened my mouth to explain that I had been protecting her virtue when she made a whooping sound, causing my heart to leap into my throat. Then she began laughing loudly.

She waved her injured arm in the air, wincing, but didn't stop her fit of laughter. For a second, I thought she'd lost her mind, but then the image of her streaking through the air and jumping on my attacker made a gurgle rise in my throat. I thought I had been the one protecting her but in reality, she had come to my rescue in a way no woman ever should do. She could have been seriously injured.

I stared at Katie. The window was down and cold

wind pummeled her red cheeks, whipping her hair around her in a crazed halo.

What a woman.

I couldn't contain my mirth any longer. I laughed right along with the beautiful woman at my side, knowing at that moment that I'd never let her go.

SEVENTEEN

Katie

The adrenaline rush made my hands jittery on the steering wheel. I was finally able to stop laughing and I glanced sideways at Rowan. He was smiling back at me from a swollen face. A half circle of black and purple bruising spread out from his left eye. I reached for him and carefully touched the discolored spot.

"Does it hurt?"

"A little, but I'll survive." He snatched my finger from the air and brought it to his lips. His kiss of my fingertip sent a shock wave of pleasure coursing through me.

I cleared my throat and returned my hand to the wheel. "What will your parents think when they see you have a black eye?"

Rowan settled back in the seat and rocked his neck, popping it. "I'll tell them one of the colts knocked me down. It's happened often enough. Believe it or not, I'm no stranger to bruises." He flashed his white teeth in a wide grin.

I hated to bring him down from his bar-room-fight high, but it was unavoidable. "That guy at the bar, the one you didn't punch, told me who Rebecca was with and where he lives. We'll be there in a few minutes."

Rowan drew in a sharp breath and nodded. "You did well, Katie. I'm sorry I started that mess"—he thumbed his finger over his shoulder—"back there. I couldn't stop myself from reacting when that man put his hand on you."

I snorted. "And you weren't even drunk. I can only imagine what a wildcat you would have been with a few beers in your system." Seeing Rowan's somber face, I wished I'd kept my mouth shut. "No need to say sorry. That's the most fun I've had in ages."

"I must admit, I wasn't expecting my actions to create a riot," he said.

"Well, when a fight breaks out in the middle of a bunch of drunk people, everyone wants in on it." An image of Rosemary Black hitting Tommy Morehouse over the head with a chair flashed in my mind and I almost started laughing all over again.

"Has that ever happened to you before?" Rowan asked in a slow, deliberate fashion.

"Nope. I witnessed a bar-room brawl last year, but I

didn't get my hands dirty." I chuckled and then quickly sobered. "I lost my mind when I saw that guy kicking you on the floor. That wasn't a fair fight."

Rowan thudded his head back. Whatever thrill he'd been experiencing moments before was gone. With his droopy appearance, he resembled a sad dog. I was as shocked as anybody that he'd actually punched that guy, but right beneath the skin I was secretly delighted. A man had never protected my honor before and even though I didn't need protecting, it was a very romantic thing to do. It showed just how old-school Rowan was, and that was one of the things that made him so damn attractive.

"I'm ashamed," he said quietly and then added, "not about punching the man. He deserved it. It shames me that I had to go into a place like that in order to find my sister. I'm sick to think about what Rebecca has gotten herself into."

"The Roadside Pub isn't all that bad. We just went in there right about the time when people surpass their alcohol consumption limits." For Rowan's own state of mind, I continued, "You shouldn't think too poorly of Rebecca. A lot of kids go through a wild spell when they hit eighteen. It's not that unusual for teenagers to spread their wings by sneaking into bars and drinking."

He sighed warily. "Even our children go through it.

It's just a shock when it's your little sister acting out like this."

I pressed the brakes, entering the trailer park. I didn't have a trailer number. I was looking for a jacked-up black pickup truck with a confederate flag streaming from its bed. Should be fairly easy to spot. I cringed inside at the absolute stupidity of the Amish girl to pick a guy like that to act out her rebellion with.

Just like I thought, the red flag with its starred cross stood out plainly. I pulled up behind the truck and shut off my engine.

"This is where he lives?" Rowan sat up, peering out the window.

"Yep."

The trailer's paint was faded to a pale, yellowish blue. Boards on the porch railing were popped out and a trash can was knocked over on the path, spilling garbage into the yard. Two pairs of eyes glowed back at us from scavenging raccoons.

"Dear God," Rowan breathed.

I completely agreed with him.

"Let's get this over with," I said, clutching the door handle.

Rowan grabbed my arm, pulling me back. "Stay in the car. I'll go to the door."

"I'm coming with you," I said firmly.

"No, it's not safe. I'm not going to put you in any danger. She's *my* sister; *I'll* go after her."

"Sorry, but you can't tell me what to do." Rowan's brows shot up, and I wagged a finger at him. "We're going to do this together, as a team." I pulled out my cellphone and held it up. "I have the sheriff's office right here in my contacts. If anything goes sideways, you'll need me to make the call."

"You could do that from the safety of the car," he pointed out.

I shrugged. "I'm not staying."

With a heavy sigh, Rowan nodded. "This time, you're keeping behind me."

I couldn't really argue with the logic of that.

The raccoons scurried away into the shadows when we approached. To either side of the trailer were vacant, overgrown lots. The bushes pressed up against each end of the trailer, scraping eerily on the plastic siding. Rowan reached his hand back without looking, and I gladly clasped it.

Just as Rowan placed his foot on the bottom step of the wooden stairs leading to the front door, there was a jingling sound and my heart froze. A huge, snapping dog streaked out from under the porch in a blur of movement. It raced up behind us, so the only way to go was forward. Rowan picked me up in a whoosh, shoving me behind him at the far edge of the landing. The porch light came on and when the door flung open, the barrel of a rifle poked out from the opening. The dog's barking echoed in my head and a gob of saliva splashed on my boot, but the beast had reached the end of its tether, just a few inches shy of where we were huddled.

"Who's there?" an angry voice shouted.

I took a gamble and prayed that the scary-looking guy I'd seen leaving with Rebecca would have an ounce of hospitality in his bones. "Please, please get your dog away." I called out from behind Rowan. "Please," I begged.

The man poked his head out. His gaze traveled first over Rowan, before he saw me peeking around from his back. He scowled at me. "Charlie, come here boy." When the dog ignored the man, he stepped onto the porch and grabbed the chain, jerking it hard. The dog fell backwards with a yelp. "Now, get off the damn porch," he yelled. The dog slunk down the steps and back into the dark hole beneath the porch that he'd rocketed out of.

"What do you all want?" the man growled.

With sudden clarity, it occurred to me that this was the second time that night that Rowan had experienced a gun pointed at him. No wonder he thought bad things about the outside world.

"Is my sister here?" Rowan took a step forward, ignoring the rifle.

I held my breath. Charlotte, the owner of The

Roadside Pub, would never shoot an unarmed man, but this guy might do it without even blinking. I prayed that Rowan didn't get too cocky. My fingertips brushed the cool screen of my cellphone. I was so close to whipping it out and calling the police.

"That depends on who your sister is," the man's raspy voice teased.

Rowan was opening his mouth when a wispy voice called out from inside the trailer. "Who's that, Ben?"

"Rebecca, it's Rowan. Come on out here." Rowan inched closer to the door, stretching his neck to see inside.

"Whoa, stop right there. The girl isn't going anywhere she doesn't want to," Ben said, his heavily stubbled mouth twitching.

I left the protection of Rowan's back but he thrust his arm out to block me. "Are you saying if Rebecca wants to leave, you'll let her?" I asked in a shaky voice.

The man considered me. "It's up to her, but I doubt she wants to go back to those backward people." He raised his chin at Rowan.

"How can you say something like that when you live in filth?" Rowan demanded. "My sister's coming home with me."

I gasped and ducked under his arm. Placing my hands on his chest, I held him back. "Let me go talk to her, Rowan. She might listen to me."

Rowan shook his head fiercely. "No. You aren't going in there."

The man chuckled behind me and I looked back. He seemed highly amused with the little argument between Rowan and me.

"The girl can go in." He thrust his rifle at Rowan. "Not you."

I turned back to Rowan. "It's the only way we're going to get her home tonight." Indecision clouded Rowan's face and I quickly added, "Ben will be out here on the porch with you, and I'll be in there with Rebecca. It's all right."

After glaring at Ben, he reluctantly nodded.

I swept past Ben before either of them could change their minds. My heart hammered as I rounded the corner and found Rebecca sprawled on a sofa. She was wearing nothing but lacy panties and I controlled my shock by moving into action. I scooped up her mini skirt and the sparkly blouse off the floor, tripping over a small backpack. I picked up the pack and unzipped it, finding a hunter-green Amish dress wadded up inside. Beneath the dress was a white cap. Pushing the coffee table back, I ignored the empty beer bottles that tumbled onto the stained carpet to reach her faster.

I flapped the dress out and placed it over her pale breasts, bending down to her ear. "Rebecca, get dressed. We have to leave. Rowan is outside that door and I don't know how long he'll stay there. You don't want him seeing you like this, do you?"

Rebecca stirred, finally opening her eyes. Her pupils were dilated and the muscles in her face were loose. "Go away." She tried to roll over but I grabbed her arms, holding her in place. "Fuck off. I'm sleeping," she growled.

I glanced at the front door and my temper unfurled. Dammit. I could be home, asleep in bed with my dog, but nooo. I had just been in a bar fight, had been almost eaten by a crazed dog, and now feared that the psycho redneck, Ben, might kill us all. I was not in the mood for Rebecca's drunken theatrics.

Grabbing the dress off her lap, I pulled it down over head. But her hands were clasped tightly together. Straddling her, I pried her hands apart. She tried to bite my arm, but I was too quick for her fumbling attempt to make contact. Something fell from her grip, and rolled off the sofa, but I was too intent on shoving her arms through the sleeves to look down. Once I had pulled the dress down to her knees, I slid off the sofa and plucked the black tennis shoes off the floor. As quickly as I could manage, I put her shoes on and tied the laces, just like she was a toddler.

"Is everything all right in there?" Rowan called out from behind the door.

"We're just fine," I quickly replied, hoping it was true.

Rebecca heaved and I ducked to her side. Grasping her long hair and pulling it up, I got it out of the way in the nick of time before she threw up. This wasn't something new for me. In college, I'd held Tessa's hair back several times while she'd vomited – only, all of those occasions were outside in the grass. I reached for a discarded t-shirt – presumably Ben's – on the arm of the nearest chair and wiped her face with it.

"Stop it." Rebecca swatted at me.

Sitting beside Rebecca, I grasped her face in my hands, forcing her to be still. "Listen to me. I know you don't feel well, but you have to trust me. In a minute you'll be asleep in the car and everything is going to be all right. Just quit fighting me. I'm trying to help you."

Something bumped into my hand and my gaze dropped to the carpet. It was a pill bottle. I picked it up and read the label. Tramadol. I shook it and could hear the pills rattling around inside. I held it in front of Rebecca's face and asked in an urgent, low voice, "Did you take any of these?"

Rebecca groaned in reply and I stuffed the container into my pocket, pulling her up beside me. "Hold on to me," I ordered. Thankfully, Rebecca finally did as I asked.

Her legs were like Jell-O, but she managed to take the steps needed to reach the open door. Colder, fresher air touched my face, erasing the smell of vomit and cigarettes from inside the stuffy trailer. When Ben saw us appear in the doorway, he smirked. The look sent a chill down my spine.

"You're good, carrot top, I'll give you that, but we had an agreement. Rebecca has to want to leave," he said in an all too confident tone.

Rowan tried to step forward, but the point of Ben's rifle held him back. My mouth went suddenly dry when I turned to Rebecca, who was leaning against me. I lifted her chin and blew in her face to get her to open her eyes. Her eyes were bloodshot and the pupils were still large. "Can you hear me?" I asked. She nodded. "Rowan and I are going to take you home. We're not going to tell your parents about this"—I searched for the right word —"night. It's our secret. Please let us take you home."

Rebecca wavered a little in my arms and I tightened my hold on her. She raised her gaze to look at Ben and beneath fluttering lashes, managed a sickly smile. "It's been fun, but I'm going home now."

"Are you sure? Earlier, you said you never wanted to go back."

She nodded stiffly. "I changed my mind."

Ben licked his lips and a quick glance at Rowan told me he was holding his breath. I returned my attention to Ben and the man's gaze narrowed on me. "I guess you won … this time. Better be quick about it. Once I step inside, I can't say what my dog might do."

Ben moved aside and Rowan sprang forward, taking Rebecca's other side. Together we guided her down the steps and to the car as fast as we could.

True to Ben's word, once he closed his front door, the dog streaked out from under the porch, but we were just closing the car doors when the dog's front paws hit the passenger-side window. I backed up until he fell away, the chain jerking him backwards.

I made a squealing U-turn and kept my eyes straight ahead until we were out of the trailer park and speeding down the road toward the Amish community. Finally, I took a deep breath and glanced in the rearview mirror. Rebecca was already asleep in the backseat.

Rowan rubbed his face and I dug the pill container out of my pocket, handing it to him. "Read the label, and count the pills inside," I told him.

He didn't hesitate, pouring the pills into his hand and counting. "Did she overdose?"

"I'm not sure. How many are there?"

"There's eight, and it says take one morning and night for pain, for five days. It's got Ben's name on it."

I blew out a breath of relief. "Then I'm guessing she only took a couple, which will knock her out for sure, but shouldn't seriously harm her unless it's laced with something else. I doubt it is, since it's his own prescription. He probably hustled a doctor into prescribing something strong by saying he had back pain or something."

"How do you know so much about this drug?"

"My mom has MS. She uses opioids to control the pain sometimes."

Rowan looked into the backseat. "Why would Rebecca take drugs on top of the alcohol?"

"Because she's seriously messed up. She's in emotional pain, and the drinking and drugs take that pain away."

Rowan's voice became soft. "How did she look when you found her in there? I can't imagine she was already dressed in her regular clothes…"

I quickly debated how much I should tell Rowan. Even though he was a sexy grown man, there was still a naivety about him. I worried that an image of his half-naked sister, passed out on a stranger's couch, would haunt him forever.

"Look, it wasn't pretty, Rowan. You don't want to know all the details."

"Do you think she had sex with him?" he said with a rasp in his voice.

"I would think so. Let's not focus on that. At least we got her out of there and we're all still breathing."

"She could be pregnant." His eyes glistened with moisture.

I rolled my own eyes. That was the furthest thing

from my mind. "Oh, come on. Let's not get paranoid and make up even more trouble than we already have." I shook the thought away with a trembling jerk. "She's a hell of a lot savvier than you think. She would have taken precautions. The last thing Rebecca wants is a baby."

"But she's drunk," Rowan said stiffly.

True. She could be pregnant, but I'd worry more about an STD if I were her. A slight throbbing pierced my temple and I rubbed it. I never dreamed that through Rowan, my Amish neighbor, I'd be dragged into the town's underbelly. I had my own problems to work out – like saving our farm and taking care of my mother. Was being close to Rowan worth all this chaos?

Just then, as if he could read my thoughts, Rowan reached over and placed his hand on my thigh.

"Thank you, Katie."

His voice was husky velvet in my ears and the heavy warmth of his hand made the pounding of my heart quiet.

As frightening as it was, I already knew the answer.

Yes, he was.

EIGHTEEN

Rowan

I pushed Rebecca's bedroom door open slightly and peeked in. From the slow rise and fall of her chest, I determined that she was still sleeping. I blew out a breath of relief and shut the door. She hadn't said a word when Katie dropped us off and when I'd gently shaken her awake in the backseat, she'd kept her eyes downcast. I was still disoriented from the night before. The scenes at the bar and the run-down trailer had replayed over and over in my mind before I'd finally drifted into a fretful sleep only a few hours before the sun had risen.

It was hard to picture my sister in the rowdy bar or doing God knows what with that dishonorable man back at his place. I wasn't completely sheltered. I'd snuck out a few times in my late teens with some of the other boys. We'd hung out with English kids our age and drank beer. There was one particular Englisher who we'd visit in the middle of the night sometimes, but our secret outings to his house included playing video games on his Xbox and watching old John Wayne westerns on the television set. That was about the extent of my rebellion. Soon enough, I'd decided that the chance of getting into serious trouble just wasn't worth video games and movies. I never really liked the taste of alcohol either, and I was repulsed by the way it sometimes affected the others in my group who were drinking. Things were said and actions were committed that were regrettable the next day. It turned me off to that kind of lifestyle. When Abe Schrock had died in the car crash with his English girlfriend, and Lucinda had hanged herself after spending only a few months in the outside world, I was done with it. Leaving the Amish didn't appeal to me anymore.

For years I felt content and happy with the path I'd chosen. Then Katie Porter blew back into my life, and thoughts of actually quitting the Amish had reared up in my mind. Now, the terrible events of the previous night had me more confused than ever. Was it a sign from heaven that an English life wasn't for me?

Pushing the question far back into my mind, I jogged down the stairs, yawning the entire way. It was going to be a long day. I had to keep my wits about me if I was going to make it through the church service. Smells of frying potatoes and strong coffee brewing filled the kitchen when I walked in.

Mother looked up from the stovetop, greeting me. "Morning, son. What happened to your eye?"

"It's nothing. A horse bashed me with his head yesterday."

Just as I suspected, her face didn't show any surprise or suspicion.

She grunted. "Are you feeling well?"

My breathing slowed and Mother came into sharper focus. Why would she ask such a question?

"Fit as a fiddle. Why?" I managed to say.

"Just checked in on your sister. She's running a fever. I'm going to let her stay home from church today. Don't want to wear her out too much or she'll miss work this week."

I scratched my chin, pouring a cup of coffee. It was still murky gray beyond the kitchen window and Nathaniel's head lay flat on the table. He was snoring. I thumped his head when I passed by to take my seat. He groaned, slowly sitting up and rubbing his eyes.

"I'm sick too, Ma. Can't I stay home?" he asked in a whining voice.

Mother swatted him with the end of the dishrag that a second earlier had been folded over her shoulder. "There isn't anything wrong with you. Don't tempt our Lord's anger with ya by lying like that."

He groaned louder but began eating from the dish Mother placed in front of him.

She handed my plate over and I dug in, suddenly feeling hungry.

"Where's Da?" I asked, glancing up from the scrambled eggs.

"He's already in the barn, getting the horse ready." She stopped in front of the window, glancing outside. "He didn't sleep well last night – tossed and turned, giving me fits. No telling what the man has on his mind."

I ate quickly and deposited my plate into the sink.

"The way you wolfed that food down, wouldn't be surprised if you don't feel sick too soon enough," Mother commented.

I was glad she didn't look up from her sweeping. If she had, she would have seen my worried frown.

"I'll go help Da." I snatched my coat from the wall peg.

When I opened the door, cold air struck my face. I buttoned up and stuck my hands into my pockets as I made my way back to the barn. It felt like winter was right around the corner. When I returned from the church service, I'd have to use the Bobcat to deliver round hay bales for the cows.

I found Father running a cloth over Sully's black coat. He glanced up and nodded. "Did you get your breakfast?" he asked.

"Sure did." I took the collar from the stand and carried it over to Father, handing it to him. He placed it around Sully's neck.

"That's quite a shiner," he noticed.

"I had a little trouble with one of the colts."

"You had a late night with them horses, eh?" Father waited until I looked over and met his gaze.

His voice was casual but his eyes were intense.

"It's a big job to complete in six weeks. Since they have lights in the barn and the pen up there, I can work well into the night. The horses seem a little less energetic at that hour, too. Works out well," I said as I retrieved the rest of the harness.

"Is Anne's daughter, the redhead, hanging around when you're doing your training?"

The question was very pointed and I saw exactly where Father's mind was going. What struck me as odd was that he referred to Katie's mother by her first name.

"Do you know Mrs. Porter?" I asked.

Father's demeanor changed. His shoulders drew back and he ran his fingers through his scruffy beard with a tug. I stopped what I was doing and stared at him.

"Actually, I do know her, son." He blew out a breath. "It's not a time of my life that I'm too proud of. It is what it is."

My heartrate accelerated and my mouth became dry. I

was almost afraid to ask. "Is there a story I don't know about?"

Father took a seat on the nearest bale of hay. He slumped back in a tired way. "I don't want to talk about it but perhaps this is the right time – with everything going on with your sister, and the uncertainty of her future. There's also the fact that you're a man now. I haven't seen that girl for a lot of years, but if my memory serves me, she resembled her mother, making her a temptation for you indeed."

My face must have shown my surprise at his choice of words. He quickly said, "You must promise me that you'll never mention this conversation to your mother. It's water under the bridge and means nothing now, but it would hurt her feelings and there's no need to do that to her."

"Of course. You can confide in me." I folded my arms over Sully's back and waited.

"A long time ago, before I began courting your mother, I met a young English woman. I remember that day well. It was hot and sunny and I was still a wild buck at the time. I had stopped by a yard sale to look at a used cart. I bought the cart and made a friend." He paused, staring past me, as if caught up in the memory. He grunted and went on. "The Englisher was Anne Porter, of course back then she wasn't married and went by the name O'Leary. She was like a butterfly that had just broken from its cocoon – all bright and lively. I'd never met a girl like her and I admit I was quickly smitten with her."

I hardly breathed, listening with such incredible focus. The barn disappeared as I imagined my straight-laced father with Katie's mother.

"We spent time together. A lot of time."

"How is that possible? Didn't Papaw or Mamaw find out?"

"Things weren't much different in those days to how they are now. I snuck out after dark, when your grandparents were asleep in their beds. I wasn't proud of my actions but I had to see that girl. When I wasn't with her, she was constantly on my mind. I thought I was going crazy. Just when I was about to up and leave the Amish community behind, to be with the lovely Anne, your mother came into my life. Her family had just moved here from Ohio and because our mothers took a liking to each other, we found ourselves thrown together."

"You were involved with Mrs. Porter while courting Mother?"

He shook his head. "No, son. I didn't ask permission to court your mother until I had ended things with Anne."

"What made you choose Mother over Mrs. Porter?" I could hardly believe we were having this conversation. I felt sick to my stomach, but I couldn't take my eyes off Father, either.

He sighed heavily. "I cared deeply for Anne, but there was something about your mother that immediately overwhelmed me. It wasn't just her beauty. Anne rivaled your mother in looks. No, it was the peace I felt in your mother's presence. She was the calm in a storm, the welcome canopy of branches and leaves on a blistering hot day." He tilted his head, meeting my gaze. "Where Anne brought carefree and thrilling experiences into my life, your mother represented balance and harmony. In the end, I realized Anne was like a hot flame that couldn't be controlled or even reasoned with sometimes. Because our spirits were so different, I knew I couldn't keep that fire going. I loved your mother and realized she was the right woman for me, so I broke it off with Anne."

A memory trickled in, something Katie's father had said the day he'd fired me. *I owed your father a favor…*

Father stood up and I walked around Sully, standing in front of him. "Years ago, Mr. Porter mentioned that he owed you a favor. What was that all about?"

Father's eyes widened and his mouth scrunched. He smacked his lips together and slipped past me, going straight to the riggings on the harness, without looking back. "I have no idea what the man was talking about. He was a vile, temperamental creature, only concerned with himself. It's really a shame Anne ended up with a brute like him. Now that he's gone, she's best rid of him."

Father saw that I was about to speak and he silenced me with a sharp look and a raised voice. "I will talk of this no more, son. I simply wanted to point out to you that although an English girl like Katie Porter may be enticing, you'll find true happiness with a woman from your own culture."

"You mean someone like Miriam Graber?"

"Exactly. Miriam is attractive and sweet-natured. She'll be a good wife and mother. The English world is nothing but trouble. You'll regret it if you go down that path."

As I left the barn to fetch Scout, I wondered why Father had chosen that moment to tell me that he'd had a relationship with an English woman before he'd met Mother. It was a timely revelation, under the circumstances, but how could he possibly know about my feelings for Katie?

The difference between my father and me was that it was the English girl that had captured my heart, not the Amish one.

My eyes dropped closed and I swayed on the bench until Martin elbowed me awake. I glared at him, and he smirked back at me.

He leaned in and whispered. "One more song and we're out of here."

I picked up the hymnal, flipped it to the right page and yawned. I didn't even try to join the others in the singing. Three hours on the hard, wooden bench after a nearly sleepless night had taken its toll on me. The chill in the air didn't help matters any. I lifted my head to glance around the inside of the metal building. It was new construction and the Yoders had it barely finished it when their turn to host church service came up. There was a large space-heater plugged in to the generator on the women's side of the congregation. I certainly didn't begrudge the females getting the only warmth available. What bugged me was that the Yoders hadn't at least put the insulation up before church.

As my gaze passed over the singing women, Miriam's head poked up. She looked directly at me and smiled.

I quickly dropped my gaze, staring at the hymnal in my hands until the words and notes blurred. What a mess I'd made with her. If I could go back in time, I never would have offered to take her home. The damage was done, and now I had to clean up my mess as quickly as possible. Just telling her that I wanted to take it slow wasn't an option anymore. She would only get hurt in the end.

My mind strayed back to Father's incredible

revelation from that morning, although I could barely wrap my mind around it all. I still couldn't picture him with anyone other than Mother. They seemed happy enough together and rarely argued about anything. It seemed Father had made the right decision in the end. But what if he had picked Anne and left the Amish? How very different his life would be now. He would have given up so much to be with an Englisher. His parents and siblings would have been just the beginning. Even as a young man, Father had been popular and well-respected in the community. Like he was doing for me, his own father had deeded him land to farm and raise his family on. Father also read the Bible every night before he turned in, and he never missed a church service. His faith was strong and his belief in our simple ways was very important to him. Until a few days ago, the thought of sacrificing everything, including an entire way of life for an outsider, would never have crossed my mind. I would have accused any man who contemplated such a thing of being insane and probably bewitched. Now, I had an inkling what drove a man to do such a thing. Even Father had fallen prey to the charms of an English woman. And though he'd picked Mother over Anne, I was sure it had been a more difficult choice than he cared to admit.

When Katie was near, I had no doubt that being with her was all that mattered. But on a morning like this, when Father had shared a long-held secret and I was surrounded by a crowd of familiar people and the traditions I'd grown up with, I wondered if I could really give it all up for Katie. Would I grow to resent her because of the great sacrifice I'd made?

The song abruptly ended and in a scurry of movement everyone began handing the hymnals down the line. I rose with the other men and followed the long line out into the waiting sunshine. The bright sky was deceptive. The temperatures had fallen overnight and a heavy frost had covered the ground before the sun came up. The breeze was still crisp but invigorating after the long service.

I would have to work quickly when I got home to put the hay out. I wanted to leave for the ranch as soon as possible. I missed Katie. Our goodbyes had been awkward and quick the night before. I had needed to get Rebecca to bed and Katie had seemed to want to escape from the two of us as fast as she could. I didn't blame her one bit. If it hadn't been for my insane sister, we'd have continued on our night ride, and maybe I'd even have the opportunity to steal a kiss before the night was over.

Instead, Katie had been dragged into a bar fight and to a nasty trailer where a dog had tried to attack us. I rubbed my face, wanting to forget everything. Especially the moment when I'd lowered Rebecca into her bed and her eyes had fluttered open. She looked right at me and said, *"You're not going to win this one, brother. I'm a lost cause."*

I didn't want to believe it was true, but a part of me worried that she was right. Some people were their own worst enemies. You could bend over backwards to help them, but they never listened. They were on a course of self-destruction, no matter what you did – just like Lucinda and Abe. I feared that Rebecca was one of those people.

Martin nudged me, pulling me from my heavy thoughts. "She's coming," he warned.

I quickly straightened. "Hello, Miriam."

She studied me with inquisitive eyes. "You look like you were run over by a train."

"I had a little accident last night."

"Training horses?" she asked in a sweet voice. But I wasn't fooled. Her gaze was guarded and unsympathetic.

Martin cleared his throat. "I'm going to check on the sandwiches. You coming, Rowan?"

"Yep." I tried to get away from Miriam, but she followed me a few steps.

"Can I have a word with you?"

Martin shot me a look of pity but he kept on walking. Smart man. He knew when it was time to abandon ship. He'd been my best buddy since first grade and he was a lot smarter than he looked. He was always there for me but when it came to girls, Martin was as timid as a fieldmouse. On a good day, they scared the tar out of him. The hard-edged tone to Miriam's voice and her dark expression made it clear that she wasn't having a good day.

I reluctantly turned to Miriam, making sure that we stood a dozen inches apart. Courtships kept the gossip mill going. I knew people were watching us.

A few leaves fluttered down from the elm tree above our heads. The loud sound of crunching when kids ran over the dried leaves reached my ears and the sharp smell of hickory wood smoke filled the air. Other than Miriam's glum mood, it was a pleasant autumn afternoon.

"What do you want?" I tried to keep the impatience from my voice, but probably failed.

She licked her lips. "Your mother invited me for dinner tonight."

"She did what?" There had been no mention by her or Father that they would do such a thing.

The conversation with Father popped into my head once again. He was trying to force me and Miriam together so I'd pick her, the same way he'd picked Mother. He must be really worried about the time I was spending with Katie to go to such drastic measures. My parents had never taken it upon themselves to play matchmaker in the past. They knew I took my own sweet time about things, and although Mother had started dropping strong hints about the different girls in the community, she hadn't pushed me to begin a courtship.

I worked to control my surprise. I wouldn't be forced into a relationship with anyone. Father and Mother should know better.

"I have chores when I get home and then I have to—"

Miriam finished my sentence for me. "Go to the ranch to train horses. I figured as much."

The muscles in my gut clenched. "It's not a good time to … begin a friendship, Miriam."

"I thought we were already friends?"

"Yes, of course we are. You know what I mean."

She shook her head. "No, I don't. Can you explain?"

Before I had a chance to answer, her father, the bishop, strolled up. He slapped me on the back. "Rowan, my boy. How are you on this fine Sunday?"

The man was unusually friendly and I cringed inside. "Well enough, sir."

"It will be good to spend time with your family this afternoon. I'm looking forward to it."

He slapped my back again and moved off, talking to the next poor soul he came to. I turned back to Miriam. Her smile reminded me of a satisfied feline.

"I'll see you later," she chirped and then she left me standing alone.

I ran my hand through my hair and groaned quietly. I

wasn't sure how much longer this could go on before the roof came down on my head.

I could almost understand why Father had chosen the easy route and picked Mother.

NINETEEN

Katie

I stretched and yawned. Lady thumped her tail, wriggling closer so I could scratch her belly. I rolled over and wrapped my arm around her furry black body, burying my face in the pillow. The inside of my head burned slightly with tiredness and my lips were chapped. Even though I'd collapsed into bed and fallen immediately asleep the previous night, it had been close to three o'clock in the morning, and not nearly enough sleep time to physically recover from everything that had happened.

There was a knock at the door, followed by the sound of it scraping on the wooden floor.

"Good morning, sleepyhead. I brought you coffee," Momma said in a jolly manner that immediately brought me fully awake.

I sat up, inhaling the wonderful brewed smell. Taking the mug from Momma's hand, I leaned back into my enormous pile of pillows on my bed and took a sip. "What time is it anyway?"

"Nearly one o'clock."

Holy cow, I hadn't slept that late since my junior year of high school. I balanced the mug in my hand and threw my legs over the side of the bed. Lady growled in annoyance at my leaving and I agreed with her wholeheartedly.

"I'm so sorry I overslept."

"No worries at all. I fed the horses and chickens. I even checked on the cows. Everyone is fine and everything is done."

I took a larger gulp of coffee and set the mug down on the nightstand. Wearing my favorite flannel pants and sweatshirt, I brought my legs back up, crossed them, and then folded my hands in my lap. Momma sat down in front of me with a smile on her face.

"What's this all about, Momma? You didn't have to do my chores and why are you grinning?"

Momma's smile deepened. "You've been working so hard, baby girl. Picking up the slack your dad left us and doing a very good job at it. I'm ashamed at how depressed and useless I've been these last couple of weeks." I tried to interrupt her and tell her that it wasn't true, but she shook her head and squeezed my knee to shut me up. "Your daddy's death was a horrible shock, but learning about his infidelity didn't surprise me as much as it probably should have. Charlie always had a roving eye. I should have left him years ago. It sickened me to think of you having to go away every other weekend to stay with him and God knows he'd probably have a different woman each time you visited. By the time you were an adult, I was so used to living here on the farm, it was just easier to stay with him than to uproot and start all over at my age. There was also my MS to consider. When your health isn't the best, it's difficult to make it on your own."

Tears filled my eyes. "You would never have been alone, Momma. I would have taken care of you," I said.

"I know you would have but it's not your place to do so. I didn't want to shackle you with a disabled mom. I wanted you to have the freedom to go live your life any way you saw fit. Anyway, I'm not saying all this to make you feel bad. I want you to understand that although I loved your dad, I didn't like him very much. As awful as it sounds, his death is like a second chance for me."

My heart fluttered in my chest. "What are you planning to do?"

"I'm going to start living again, that's what. I have an appointment with a pain management specialist next week. There's new research and discoveries every day and I want to learn more about my options. I understand you don't want to lose the ranch, and neither do I, but if it comes to pass and we have to sell, we should still have enough equity to walk away with a little money in our pockets. We can always sell some cows and horses and downsize." She reached out and softly wiped the tears from my cheek, just like she'd done when I was a small child. "It hurts, I know, but we have to be ready to move on if necessary."

"I think Rowan's going to do it. He'll get the colts trained up and we'll make enough money to bring the ranch back into the black again, maybe even the green, in time."

"I'm praying for that to happen but it isn't the end of the world if it doesn't. For most of my life I've been too afraid of what was around the corner to live happily. I'm going to stop worrying so much about things I can't control."

I noticed that, for the first time, Momma was wearing a little makeup and had on her favorite blue sweater. I sniffed and wiped my nose. "Are you going somewhere?"

Momma stood up. "As a matter of fact, I am. Since you aren't working today and can take care of things here, I thought it would be a good time to visit my friend Ida. I talked to her on the phone last night and she convinced me that dinner and a glass of wine with my best friend was in order."

"She lives in Nashville, Momma. If you leave right now, you'll barely make it by suppertime."

"That's why I have to be on my way. I'll be back in a few days."

I scrambled off my bed and ran to her before she reached the door. "Out of the blue, you're just up and leaving town? That's not like you at all."

She sighed and grasped my shoulders. "I used to be that person who ran out the door without any warning to visit a friend or play in the sand at the beach. I used to have fun and I'm ready to become that carefree person again."

I was glad Momma had done a one-eighty and was feeling pretty good about everything, but the idea of her suddenly turning into a free-spirited hippy scared the crap out of me.

"I'm sorry I was such a burden," I managed to say.

"Oh, my dear girl, it wasn't you who held me back." She hugged me tightly. "It was your dad."

"I'm happy for you." I sniffed and wiped my nose with the back of my sleeve. "Please be careful, and text me when you get to Ida's."

She pulled away, laughing. "Isn't that funny, you worrying about me for a change."

I always worry about you, Momma, I thought. I didn't say it out loud.

She paused at the doorway and looked back. "Always

follow your heart, dear Katie. It's better to make a mistake than to waste your life being too cautious to actually live it. If you care for Rowan, I say go for it. What's the worst that could happen? Your heart might get broken, but that isn't any worse than it shriveling up, wondering what could have been."

I slumped onto the bed. "How could it ever work out? He's stubbornly Amish and he'll never leave his community."

"You don't know that for sure. Love has a funny way of changing things." She lifted her shoulders. "Or you could try your hand at being an Amish woman."

I let a pillow fly and Momma ducked just in time. I was impressed at her agility.

"Keep all options open, that's all I'm saying."

After the door closed, I fell back on the bed. Lady leaned up against me and I massaged her chest. My head was spinning at what had just transpired with Momma but a dark shadow in the back of my mind darkened my mood. The image of Rebecca lying topless on that dirty couch made me feel like throwing up. How had she fared when she got home? I could only imagine the turmoil she was going through, especially being Amish.

Glancing out the window, the sun was high in a cloudless blue sky. It was the perfect afternoon to go for a horseback ride.

And I knew exactly where I was headed.

I peered around the tree at the white farmhouse on the hill. A few chickens pecked the dirt in the plowed up garden plot and several draft horses grazed in the pen beside the barn. The trees' branches swayed, sprinkling yellow leaves into the breeze. I swallowed down the frantic beating of my heart. All was quiet. I guessed that the Coblentz family were away at Sunday church service.

If I was right, one member of the family wouldn't have gone to church today. She wouldn't have been up for that after last night.

I spotted the hitching rail behind the house and bumped Dusty into a canter. I didn't want anyone driving by to see me riding up the lane. Some of Rowan's paranoia had worn off on me. The last thing I wanted to do was get him or Rebecca into trouble.

Dusty slid to a stop at the railing. I climbed down and tied her up. With a last pat on her neck, I jogged up the stairs and looked through the glass panel in the door. The kitchen was empty. I was contemplating whether to knock when someone tapped my shoulder. I squealed, nearly jumping out of my skin.

When I whirled around, I was face to face with Rebecca. She smiled coyly back at me.

"My, you're a jumpy one," she said smoothly.

Her face was still thin and pale and the dark circles

beneath her eyes were prominent. For all that, her eyes twinkled.

I worked to breathe normally again. "How'd you manage to sneak up on me like that?"

"You of all people should be aware of my sneaking skills. I can be as quiet as a spider when I want to be."

Rebecca would make a perfect Goth girl if she ever did leave the Amish. I could easily picture her smoking a cigarette and wearing black lipstick.

"I came by to check on you. How do you feel today?"

She took a step forward and her mouth thinned. "I'm alive, aren't I? That's probably the best I can ask for under the circumstances."

"What circumstances?"

She spread her arms wide. "All this." Then she dropped her arms and clutched the maroon-colored dress that stuck out below the black coat she had on. "And this." Finally she brought her fingers up to her cap. "This too."

"So you don't like being Amish. I get it."

"It's more than that, Katie. But you wouldn't understand."

She tried to walk past me into the house but I stopped her. "Wait. Try me."

"There isn't enough time," she sighed.

"When will your family be back?" I ventured.

"Not for a couple of hours, I reckon." She shook her

head, brushing me off. "There's not enough time in the day to get everything off my chest."

I'd come here to help Rebecca, and that was what I meant to do, even though she was obviously in a surly mood. "What are you doing here alone?"

She cocked her head. "Enjoying the aloneness. Then you had to show up and ruin it."

I took a deep breath. Rebecca was trying desperately to push me away. If I was a normal person, she would definitely have succeeded. If I wasn't such a sucker for troubled souls, I wouldn't be here in the first place.

"I made a calculation that your family would be at church and that you would have stayed behind, feigning illness."

"I really do feel like shit," she snapped.

"I'm sure you do but you know what I mean. Anyway, I was home alone myself and wondered if you might want to go for a horseback ride with me?"

The idea had just occurred to me when I saw the fat pinto gelding hanging his head over the fence, watching us. Rebecca was Amish. If my memory was right, she used to love riding.

Rebecca's face scrunched up and she glanced over at the same horse I was looking at. Finally, she spoke and her voice was steady. "I haven't gone for a ride in years. I'm always too tired after working and doing the household chores."

"It's a beautiful day. Do you think your parents would mind?"

That last bit was what got her. "I don't care what they think. If I want to ride my horse, I will."

"Then let's go."

Rebecca flashed a white grin and then she was off, running toward the barn.

———

Rebecca peered over her shoulder. "Let's see who has the fastest horse!"

She spurred her gelding into a gallop, getting a sudden head start. The long, grassy field that stretched in front of us was about the length of a football field. I felt like a silly teenager, bumping Dusty to pick up speed. It had been a while since I sat atop a horse running full out. The exhilaration of the pounding hooves beneath me and the cold pummeling wind on my face was a combination of terror and bliss. In the old days, I hadn't worried too much about the horse falling down or tripping, but my grownup mind worked differently. The sling had just come off. I definitely didn't need another one.

Bending low on Dusty's neck, we inched closer and closer to the other horse's rump. Some of Rebecca's hair had come loose from her cap and was streaming out behind her. The cap itself barely moved; it must have been attached to her head with a dozen pins.

Rebecca glanced over. When she saw how close I was, the look of joyous abandon shining on her face disappeared. It was replaced by a look of determination. Her cheeks were beet-red and her dress flapped wildly against her horse. She skillfully sat astride and she'd hiked the dress up to mount the horse. Beneath the maroon material, she wore what looked like black cotton pants.

The poor girl had no idea what a speed demon Dusty really was. A harder bump on the mare's side would propel her straight past the pinto. As much as my competitive side wanted to win, I didn't have the heart to ruin the little bit of happiness Rebecca was experiencing. I had to wrestle the reins tightly to keep Dusty from taking the lead on her own. As the treeline closed in, Rebecca guided her horse onto the dirt path, sitting back up in the saddle.

Her horse immediately slowed, but I had a harder time getting Dusty to calm down. She bumped the pinto hard, and we flew by as I battled with the reins to pull her down. I heard Rebecca shout something from behind, but couldn't understand her words.

Then I realized what she was yelling about. A tree was down across the trail. I didn't have enough time to pull my horse up, so I collected her as best I could with rein pressure and griped with my knees. The trunk was massive and as we closed in on it, I closed my eyes and hoped for the best. Dusty shortened her strides and her muscles coiled tightly beneath me as she left the ground. I grasped her mane as she sailed cleanly over the trunk. Stray branches scraped my legs and I felt one slice my cheek. Once over the obstacle, Dusty began to slow down into a hopping canter and finally a bouncy trot.

Rebecca caught up to me at the next bend. "That was amazing! I thought you were a goner!" she exclaimed breathlessly.

I was breathing pretty hard myself. My heart pulsed madly and my legs and arms felt like jelly. Flexing my bad arm, I winced. "Oh, that's going to hurt tomorrow."

"Were you terrified of crashing?" Rebecca asked as she came alongside. Her cheeks were flushed and her mouth lifted in a lopsided smile.

"More than I care to admit." I reached down and patted Dusty's sweaty neck. She was still trying to prance and her sides heaved between my legs as she snorted. "But I used to do a lot of jumping on this mare. I had faith she would make it over."

"Faith," she muttered, "is something I don't have much of anymore."

Relieved that Rebecca had given me an opening, I asked, "Is it so bad being Amish?"

She let out a big sigh. "Not always. Sometimes it's okay."

Dusty dropped her head finally and I settled into the saddle, swaying back and forth. A barrage of leaves fell on top of us and I looked up through the tree tops at the puffy clouds and blue sky. "When I was eighteen, I went through a bit of a wild patch. I had a boyfriend and I would sometimes break curfew. I partied a little and we'd sneak off and have sex in the hayloft."

"Really? You seem like such a goody-goody girl, though."

I laughed. I didn't understand where she got that impression of me but I let the comment go. This conversation wasn't about me, it was for her.

"Afterwards, I always felt like crap. Like, really stupid and guilty, all rolled up in one horrible feeling. I hated lying to my momma. She's a very perceptive woman and she had suspicions about my behavior." I slanted a look at Rebecca. "The worst part came later, when I looked back and realized that none of my actions had done me any good. I'd wasted my virginity on a guy I wasn't even that into. I wish I'd saved myself for a man I loved."

"Like Rowan?" she asked evenly.

I bit my lower lip, not wanting to discuss Rowan. But seeing her eager curiosity staring back at me, I relented. "Yeah, like Rowan."

"You don't have to tell him. He's never been with a woman; he wouldn't know the difference."

I looked past her, wondering if maybe she was giving me good advice. Rowan may not want me if he knew I'd been with another guy. Because of his culture, he might think I was a slut. It was funny how things changed. A week ago, I never would have even considered the fact that I wasn't a virgin. Now, I worried about it.

The hard truth sank in. Rowan might not even want me.

I shook my head. *No more lies,* I told myself. "I'm not so sure if Rowan and I will ever be together like that, but if we were, I'd be honest with him. It wouldn't be much of a relationship if I deceived him." I shrugged. "I want to be with a man who accepts me for who I am."

"Don't worry about my brother. I don't think it'll matter to him either way." She offered me a knowing smile. "If he loves you, he'll love you very deeply, warts and all."

"Thanks for that." I lifted my gaze. Rebecca was eyeing me. "I told you about my past to show you that we all go through rough times; it's not only an Amish thing."

Rebecca chuckled and her lips curved. We reached a fenceline, and she reined her horse around. I turned with her and we fell silent for a time.

We stepped back into the field when she spoke again.

"I appreciate what you told me, and I see the lesson in it." Rebecca's smile died. "I never did thank you for coming and getting me last night. I'm sorry for causing a scene ... and acting like a bitch. That's not the real me."

"Why were you there?"

"Dressing up English, drinking in bars, and sleeping around, are the least of my problems."

"You also took a controlled substance, Rebecca. You surpassed the usual teenage rebellion thing last night," I pointed out. "You're a smart, beautiful, and talented young woman. Can you make me understand why you're acting out like this? Rowan was devastated. He was so frightened for your safety. All he wants to do is save you from yourself."

A tear trickled down her check and she brushed it away with her hand. "I don't know." Her tears flowed freely. "I'm always unhappy or angry and I don't know why," she sputtered.

"Do you think going English will make it all better?" She had finally cracked. I wasn't a therapist, and I may never get to the bottom of what was really bothering Rebecca, but I could at least be her friend.

She threw her head back. "That's just it. I'm not sure."

"Your friend, Ben, where did you meet him?"

"At the butcher shop. He came in a couple of months ago and started flirting with me. I talked him into picking me up on side of the road a few times and taking me into town. Last night was the first time I went back to his place with him."

I cleared my throat, struggling for the right words. "He said you wanted to stay with him. Is that true?"

She coughed out a snorting laugh. "No. I don't care if I ever see that man again. He was just a way to escape for a few hours. I never meant for it to go that far but so many things have been going on in my head. I wanted to stop the pain of it all for a little while."

"Booze, drugs, and men don't stop the pain, Rebecca. They only make it worse."

She gave a slight nod. "Last night, when I heard Rowan's voice, I thought I was going to die. I wanted to crawl under the couch so bad. He's a good brother to come looking for me. Do you think he'll still help me leave the Amish?"

"Is that what you really want to do? Sounds like you're kind of confused."

"Oh, I am going to leave. I'm not cut out to be an Amish woman. I don't like to cook or clean, and while all the other girls are oohing and ahhing over babies, I don't want any." She fought back a grin. "There are so many things I want to do, like travel and go to college. I've thought about being an artist. All I want to do is paint and read and go to movies." She turned to me. "Is that unreasonable?"

I tried to hold in my smile, shaking my head. "Not at

all. You'll still have to work on the outside. You'll probably want to talk to a professional about how you've been feeling."

"I know it won't be easy but at least I will have opportunities as an English woman. I'll be free." She draped the reins over her saddle horn and stuffed her loose locks up under her cap. "When you asked if being Amish was so bad, I should have just said that it's not my cup of tea. Most of the other girls in the community are perfectly happy, and I've always envied them for it. No matter how I tried, I couldn't stay content. I felt like I was going stir crazy. I've never had a real friend. I was the disgruntled strange girl who talked to herself. No one ever liked me."

"I'm your friend."

She raised her eyebrow at me. "Do you know what you're getting yourself into?"

"I think I have a clue."

"I've changed my mind. I don't want Rowan to help me get out." She raised her head high.

"Why not?"

"If he does, he'll get into serious trouble. I don't want him to have to leave the Amish before he's ready."

"Why would he ever leave the Amish?" It felt like my heart skipped a beat.

"For you, of course."

"I think you're getting ahead of yourself, Rebecca."

"I don't think so, though only time will tell." She pulled her horse up and tilted her head to listen. "Do you hear that?"

I listened to the wind and heard the faint, rhythmic sound of *clip clops* in the distance.

"You better hurry and get back. Your parents might be upset if they see you out riding instead of resting in bed. I'll go through the fields. No one will know I was here."

I reined Dusty around but Rebecca called out, "Wait!"

Tugging Dusty into a reluctant standstill, I looked back.

"This is just what I needed. I feel better than I have in ages. You're a good friend."

"Just like Rowan, I'm here for you, Rebecca. You're not alone."

She lifted her hand and our eyes met for an instant before she reined her horse around and took off toward home. I had mixed feelings as I watched her gallop away. Rebecca appeared to be back on track, but I'd already witnessed her drastic mood swings and manipulative behavior. Deep down, I feared she was just playing me.

I hoped I was wrong – for both Rowan's sake and for hers.

TWENTY

Rowan

I lifted my head from Scout's harness when I saw Rebecca fast approaching. It was the first time in several years I'd seen her ride her horse. Leaning back against Scout's warm side, I waited for my sister.

"Hello, brother. How are you on this beautiful afternoon?" She swung her leg over the saddle and jumped down. Snatching up her reins, she stepped in closer.

"I could be better. You on the other hand, seem to be fully recovered from illness and what not."

Her smile never wavered. "Yes, I am feeling pretty good – just a little headache, but nothing too serious."

"What's brought about this drastic change?" I leveled a hard stare at her. "Last night you were in very different shape."

She whirled the end of her reins, like she used to do when she was a kid. "I owe it all to Katie." She seemed happily smug when my eyes popped wider, and she continued. "She dropped by and convinced me to go for a ride with her. Definitely the best thing I've done in a long time."

I digested what she'd just said. Katie was here? The fact that she'd come to check on Rebecca was admirable, especially after everything that had happened. But Rebecca and Katie hanging around together made me a tad nervous.

"Looks like you did a lot of running," I commented, unsure of what else I should say.

"Katie and I raced. I barely beat her and to be honest, I think she let me win. Then she couldn't stop her horse and they jumped that fallen tree back there on the trail. I thought she was a goner but somehow that little horse cleared it."

I clucked my tongue, rubbing my mouth. I was sure Katie had been riding the rank quarter mare, Dusty. That horse loved to jump. Pride swelled my insides. Katie was an impressive rider.

When I raised my gaze to Rebecca's bloodshot eyes, I sobered. I didn't want to talk to her about last night but it had to be discussed. I looked around and, seeing the coast was clear, I inhaled deeply.

"Rebecca, what were you doing at that man's trailer?"

I splayed my fingers roughly through my hair. "And going to a bar ... what are you thinking?"

She lifted her shoulders in a sullen manner. "Having a little fun."

I took two steps and loomed over her. "This isn't funny. You drank alcohol and took pills. You could have been raped or even died in that trailer."

"But I didn't because you and your English girlfriend came to my rescue." She shifted her weight, cocking one of her hips in a sassy pose. "Yes, I did say *English* girlfriend," she snapped.

"This isn't about me, Rebecca. You're completely out of control."

"Why, because I want to have a good time?"

I shook my head vigorously. "Let me tell you how the evening went for Katie and me. We went out to find you and ended up in a bar fight,"—I pointed to my bruised eye—"then we were chased by the meanest-looking dog I've ever seen and I had the ends of two different guns pointed at my chest. It wasn't much fun for us. As a matter of fact, it was downright scary. How would you feel today if Katie or I had gotten injured, or worse, trying to assist you?"

She looked me in the eye and raised her finger. "Don't try to guilt trip me, Rowan. I'm eighteen years old. I'll do what I want."

"So this is how you're going to behave on the

outside? Hooking up with trailer-trash losers and doing drugs? That's a real good way to improve your life and take a step up from the Amish. Don't you see that if you go out in the world and succeed with your art and live a healthy, wholesome life, you'll show everyone that it wasn't *your* problems – it was theirs."

"That's the difference between you and me, brother. I don't care what anyone thinks. That's going to be your downfall. You really like Katie, maybe even love her, but you're worried about what people will think if they find out."

"I chose to become a member of this church and I take my vows to God and our community seriously. I'm not going to hurt Ma or Da until I know for certain that Katie wants to be with me. We haven't had that much time together and she certainly hasn't given me a lot of hope that she wants to be with me."

"You're stupid," she said mildly and looked past me. "Who's behind Da?"

I followed her gaze. "Dammit," I muttered under my breath.

"Is that the bishop?" When I nodded, a sudden, chilling change came over her. She crossed her arms and shivered. "Why is he here?"

"His family has come for dinner. I just found out about it after the service."

Rebecca's voice turned into a harsh whisper. "This is because of Miriam, isn't it?"

I nodded. "Trust me, I don't want any of them here, either – especially Miriam."

"Talk about me having secrets. You're in way over your head, too."

"It's just one dinner."

"More like one more nail in your coffin." She led her horse into the barn and I got to work on Scout's harness rigging. If God was kind to me, the meal would go quickly and I'd be on my way to Katie's by nightfall.

The bishop bent his head for a silent prayer and everyone followed suit. A moment later, the men lined up at the counter to get their food. The women hung back, waiting until we were seated. Even fourteen-year-old Nathaniel was already sitting at the table with his plate full.

I glanced over at Rebecca. She stood like a cold statue in the corner of the room. Her eyes were downcast and her toe pushed some imaginary object in circles on the floor. Miriam had barely acknowledged her, making me even more resentful of her presence. Elijah's wife, Martha, chatted away with Ma at the kitchen sink. They had probably been the ones to hash out the dinner plans.

When the women finally got their dishes of food and

sat down, Miriam took the seat across from me. She glanced up at me under fluttering eyelashes. I found other things to look at, like Father and Elijah. Even though the bishop was twenty years my father's senior, they were fast friends. They were all rooting for Miriam and me to officially begin courting, and then to marry.

My food was a heavy knot in my stomach at the thought of marrying Miriam. For a short moment, I'd considered her when I thought Katie wouldn't have me. I realized my stupidity now. I would never be happy with Miriam. She might be the perfect young woman for me in my parents' eyes, but the only thing we had in common was that we were both Amish. That wasn't enough to build a lifelong family foundation on. Even though Katie was English, we shared many interests, like our love of horses, riding, and dogs. We also had the same cynical sense of humor, and our passion for each other was undeniable. Her father had kept us apart for years and yet we still had an unshakable connection. It was as if we were meant to be together, even though we were from different worlds.

I straightened in my seat. "What was that?" My eyes darted around the table.

"I asked how the horse training was coming along." The bishop twisted a piece of his beard between his fingers. "Your father told me you've taken on a side job."

I gathered my wits quickly. "It's going well, but will

only last until December when the string of horses will be sold at the McGovern horse sale."

"How is the family holding up after Charlie's death?"

"As well as can be expected. They really need those colts sold for top dollar, and that's why I signed on." My brows drew together. "Did you know Mr. Porter?" I asked Elijah.

"I bought a few horses off him in years past." He glanced sideways at my father and the knowing look caught my attention. "Not an easy man to deal with, I'd say, but fair enough when it came to doing business."

The conversation turned quickly to the new fencing Elijah was putting up. Nathaniel asked to be excused once he'd cleaned his plate, and the women discussed the success of their benefit quilt, and their plans for the next one. Miriam chirped suggestions to the older women while Rebecca sat sullenly, pushing her food around with her fork. All the excitement she'd displayed earlier from the horseback ride was gone. Replacing the spirited, argumentative girl, was a joyless, pale shell. I wished she'd at least eat. Her dress hung loose on her, exposing a boney shoulder. My gaze shifted back to Ma. She wasn't paying Rebecca any mind at all.

I knew if Katie had been there, she'd have tried to include my sister in the conversation. There was no denying that Rebecca was difficult and disturbed but in that instant, I wondered if she would be that way if the others were friendlier.

The sun was setting in a brilliant display of reds, yellows, and oranges beyond the kitchen window. My shirt felt sticky in the stuffy room. With her parents so close by, Miriam was careful not to speak to me or to be caught looking too much at me. I was glad for the respite and rose from the table. Unlike Nathaniel, I scraped my plate into the swine bucket and placed it into the sink. Downing the water in my glass, I grabbed my coat off the peg by the door.

"I'll feed the horses and calves, Father. I'd like to get a few hours with Mrs. Porter's colts this evening." I was careful not to use Katie's name. I waited as Father's brow shot up and he contemplated my intentions.

My gamble paid off when he said, "Go on then." He didn't want it to look like anything was amiss in front of the bishop and he did exactly what I figured he would do.

Poor Rebecca would be stuck inside until the table and kitchen were cleaned up. At least that meant so was Miriam. The blast of cooler air was welcome as I stepped out into the dull light of dusk. Scout whinnied at me from the other side of the fence but I didn't stop, going straight to the Bobcat. I loaded up four bales of hay and drove out into the side field, where the calves were waiting. They ran and bucked around the Bobcat while I threw flakes of hay out for them. When I was back in the barn, placing more bales onto the lift for the horses, a voice suddenly came from behind me.

"Rowan, may I have a word with you?"

I turned to find the bishop standing there, hands on hips. His sharp eyes never left me as I took my gloves off and joined him.

"Sure. Of course."

"Letting you take my daughter home the other night wasn't something I took lightly. I thought I made that very clear to you."

I had rehearsed what I was going to say in my head, but facing the serious, bushy face of the bishop, the words didn't come so easily. I was resigned to get it over with, though.

"Yes, you did. I appreciate your trust in me and I enjoyed spending time with Miriam. I never asked for her hand in courtship though, and I hope you haven't misread my intentions."

"What are your intentions?" he asked in the straightforward manner I had become accustomed to.

"I like Miriam a lot but I fear that friendship is as far as it goes. I had hoped I would feel differently, but after the other evening I'm more convinced that we're not right for each other."

The bishop's face showed no emotion. I tried to keep my breathing even and remained as collected as he was.

When he spoke, there was heat in his voice. "It's good that you know what you want. Few young men can say so much and many live with regret later in life. You should take care that you're not making decisions because of a silly infatuation. You can learn by your father's example."

The sweat on my skin chilled. Straightforward was one thing, but his deliberate frankness was unsettling. It appeared he knew about my father's romance with Katie's mother. I was careful not to say too much.

"I'm not sure what you mean," I lied.

He smiled and the expression was indulgent. "Before your father settled on your mother, he became enchanted with an English girl. I was a minister back then, and the only reason I know of his affair is because an English boy came to me and told me what was going on. The boy was in love with the English girl and he was quite cocky about it. He thought if he could get rid of his competition, the girl would be his."

I braced my hand on the ledge on the wall, listening carefully to each word flowing from the bishop's mouth. "Charlie," I stated.

The bishop licked his lips and nodded.

"It came to pass that I met with your father and confronted him with what I'd learned. At first he denied it and then he grew arrogant, saying that he was leaving the Amish to be with this English girl. At the time, I was young enough to understand his desires. I advised him to wait a while and see if a change of season might put him in a different state of mind. He wouldn't have it. In the end, I agreed that I wouldn't go to our bishop until we had talked to his father. A week later, we did just that. You already know that your father was his father's only son. The news rattled the old man so much, he begged your father to reconsider. Your father refused. Later that same night, your grandfather was taken by our Lord into heaven."

I caught my breath. Grandfather died of a heart attack before I was born. The timing of it might be just about right to coincide with my father's rebellion that Elijah was speaking of. As faithful as Father was, he would have considered Grandfather's passing as a sign that leaving the Amish and a union with an outsider was not what God intended for him.

Coldness gripped my heart as I thought back to Father's telling of the story. He'd left out the part about his serious intention to leave the Amish, his discussion with a young Elijah, who was only a minister at that time, and how the news of his decision might have caused Grandfather to go home to Christ earlier than expected.

There wasn't any reason for the bishop to lie about the matter – it didn't really serve him a purpose, except maybe to warn me that there could be unforeseen consequences if I chose an English girl over my family and community. It would be hard on my parents, I knew, especially since Rebecca would also leave in due course.

Something else had occurred to me during the bishop's telling of the story – a side to it that hadn't come to mind when Father had spoken of it. Did Father regret his decision to remain Amish and let Anne Porter go? He certainly didn't like Katie's father one bit. If he'd really been at peace with the outcome, he wouldn't be so bitter talking about him now. Thinking back on my parents' relationship over the years, they got along well enough, but they never seemed to be in love. It was more like a business arrangement to me.

I pursed my lips and met the bishop's stony stare. "There is something that is confusing." The bishop's brows arched but he remained silent. "Mr. Porter hired me on to work on his ranch seven years ago. He spoke of a favor he was doing for my father. Do you know what that was about?"

The bishop smoothed down his bushy beard the best he could in a gesture of discomfort. Then he stepped up to the nearest horse and began rubbing its head. When he finally spoke, his tone was quiet and reserved. "Charlie Porter believed that by revealing what your father had done with the English girl to me, he had gotten James into a lot of trouble. Charlie was grateful, though, that your father ended the relationship and in jest, and perhaps even feeling some guilt, he told your father that he owed him a favor."

I ran my hand through my hair and exhaled. What a wicked web Father had wrapped himself in. But I wasn't him, and Katie wasn't her mother. I could only hope that Father's feelings for Mrs. Porter weren't as strong as I felt for her daughter.

"Why have you told me all of this?" I asked.

The bishop came back to stand before me. His expression was thoughtful. "We all go through a time when we question our Amish ways, and the lives we've chosen to live. I've seen some of our people leave and it's been my observation that those who stay and truly embrace our beliefs are content with the Plain life. The ones that leave are discontented for different reasons, and if they'd stayed, their presence would only have weakened our community. A girl like your sister is deeply troubled. I'm not sure if she'll fit in anywhere. She has a self-destructive nature and might actually be better served to remain in our culture where temptations don't run rampant. Then again, she might corrupt others, like a future husband or children. My hope is to instruct her the best I can and have the other women in my community step up to make her feel more at peace among us. If Rebecca chooses to leave, that's up to her. I will not allow her decision, in either direction, to disrupt our way of life. You, on the other hand, do not have a troubled spirit.

I can easily see you settling down on a farm of your own, with a wife and raising a large family. Amish ways suit you well, Rowan. I fear though, that if you've been drawn by an outsider, your heart will forever be restless. In that case, I'd pity any woman in our community that you may call wife. Since my daughter has favored you with keen interest, I'm especially worried about the outcome. You're at a turning point and are old enough to choose your own path. I advise you to think carefully before you take action, but know that I am not concerned with your wellbeing, only that of my community and the future survival of our way of life."

With that, the bishop tipped his hat and left in a hurry. I watched him go through the doorway into the house without turning back. The sky was darkening with every minute and I drew in a quick breath and went straight to work. The bishop was right. It was my path to choose, and I wouldn't make the same mistakes as my father.

TWENTY-ONE

Katie

I stepped from the shower and, after drying myself off, I used the end of the towel to wipe the fog from the mirror. I hardly recognized my reflection. The same blue eyes stared back at me and the familiar smattering of freckles still covered my nose. My cheeks were flushed from heat but otherwise were the same shape as before. I patted and scrunched my red locks to a wavy damp dryness that hung past my shoulders. Something was very different, though, and when I paused and considered, I realized it wasn't my looks that had changed but my soul.

A lot had happened over the past couple of weeks. Even though he'd been a stern, temperamental man and it had come to light that Daddy had been cheating on Momma, he was still my dad. I'd barely had time to dwell on the fact that he was really gone – until the ride back from the Coblentzes's farm. It was probably the very first time in many days that I'd been alone with my thoughts and the reality that Daddy was dead had sunk in hard and fast. Until now, I'd been too focused on taking care of Momma and trying to raise the money to save the ranch to think about anything else.

Except Rowan – and his younger sister.

They'd been occupying a lot of my time lately.

Even if Rowan managed to get the horses trained and they brought high prices, Momma and I would still have to make a lot of adjustments in our lives to make up for the lack of Daddy being there. He was the one who fixed the tractor when it broke down or worked with the really rank colts like Remington. It had suddenly occurred to me, when I'd been unsaddling Dusty, that when Rowan finished his job there would still be a heck of a lot of work to do on the ranch, and that I would struggle with it all by myself. Now that Momma seemed to have caught her second wind and was planning to live the life she'd missed out on for all these years, I wondered how much she'd be around to help me out.

Then there was Rowan Coblentz. The instant attraction I'd felt when we were reunited days ago was at first thrilling but now my head thrummed with the absurdity of it all. He was an Amish man; what the hell was I thinking? The weight of the entire situation made me move slowly around the bathroom. I brushed my teeth without hardly tasting the strong peppermint flavor. I hated feeling like my entire life was spiraling out of control. I was angry and depressed at the same time. Daddy had let us down, but maybe I should have been investing more of my own time into running the business. I couldn't go back in time, so the only way was forward. I had to get ahold of things – and not just keeping the ranch going. Rowan was a distraction that was only going to bury me in heartache. He would come around for a while, driving me crazy with uncomfortable desire, and then one day he'd realize he was making a mistake – just like his good ol' daddy had. He'd break it off with me and that would be that. It was better to invest my time and emotions into a guy like Dillon. He knew exactly what he wanted in life and we lived in the same world. No one would be shunned or forced to change their way of life for the other. With the chaos my life was already in, Dillon was sounding better and better. I had to think with my brain and not my heart when it came to Rowan.

Lady's excited barking downstairs caught my attention. I went to the small window and looked out, thinking that perhaps Momma had changed her mind and come home early. Darkness had fallen while I showered. I couldn't see a car, but Lady's barking grew louder and more incessant. Blowing out an agitated sigh,

I grabbed my blue fluffy robe off the peg and quickly put it on, tying the strap. I didn't bother with slippers and jogged barefoot down the steps into the dark kitchen. Only a dull spray of moonlight came through the windows from moonlight, but my eyes adjusted quickly and I navigated the table and chairs until I reached Lady and the door. With my hand on the top of her head, I lifted the curtain and peeked outside.

I couldn't help gasping. It was Rowan. His hands were in his pockets but he stood alertly, glancing around. The black knit hat he wore allowed a fair amount of his dark hair to show. The plain black coat looked warm and reminded me of what he was: an Amish man.

My first thought was that he might be having a problem with one of the horses and that made my heartrate soar. I cracked the door open. "What's going on?" I asked sharply.

Rowan's eyes passed over my face, lingering on the robe and my exposed cleavage. I tugged the material together and his gaze lifted ... but not as fast as it should have. I saw him swallow.

"Can we talk?" he asked in a controlled yet rough voice. "I see your mother's car is gone."

"She's away for the night," I replied, still holding the door open only a few inches. I felt a little stupid acting so leery of him, but dammit, I knew if I let him in, we wouldn't be talking for long. Goosebumps rose all over my skin and I wasn't sure if it was the cold air pressing in or Rowan's hot gaze that had me shivering.

"You're alone tonight?" His tone was startled and worried at the same time.

"Yeah, it's no biggie. I'm a grown woman and have spent many nights on the ranch by myself."

"Are you going to invite me in?" He dug his hands deeper into his pockets. "It's cold out here."

His expression suddenly relaxed. There was a challenge in his eyes that hadn't been there an instant before. Lady pushed her furry head through the door opening and sniffed Rowan's pant leg. When he brought his hand out of the pocket and lowered it, she began licking his fingertips. I sighed and held open the door for him to enter. He wasted no time and I closed the door behind him, slumping back against it.

The pounding of my heart gained momentum and my face flushed. I was very aware that I was completely naked beneath the robe. I suspected Rowan was aware of it too.

Rowan sauntered across the room like a lion surveying the territory. It was hard to take normal breaths but I willed my respiratory system to work properly. Inside my head I kept repeating, *he's Amish; it can't work. He's Amish; it can't work.*

"What do you want to talk about?" I forced out.

He finally turned around. His gaze swept over me

from feet to head before it rested on my face. "You really have to ask?" He took a step closer.

My mouth went dry and I pressed my lips together. "Did Rebecca mention we rode together this afternoon?"

He took another step. I was backed up against the door and had nowhere to go. I wanted to bolt. The way my dog was at his side, thumping her tail happily, made me question my reaction to this man who I'd determined was only going to be my friend.

Judging by his intense expression, he wasn't viewing me in the *friend* category. My insides trembled when he stopped a couple of feet away.

"Yes, she did. Thank you for doing that. It meant a lot to her – and to me."

"She's a good rider," I commented, fumbling for words.

"She was impressed with you too, saying that you went over a good-sized fallen tree that most riders wouldn't have cleared."

I shrugged, thinking back to the moment I'd known Dusty wasn't going to stop. I'd lowered my head, squeezed my eyes shut, and hoped for the best.

"You know how Dusty likes to jump. It was easy for her."

Rowan's gaze traveled around my face and then paused on my mouth. "Do you really want to talk about horses?"

The hushed voice he'd used caused my belly to constrict tightly. Tingles raced up my spine.

I should have told him to go away but I couldn't. He was close enough that I caught his scent – horses, leather, and cool wind. He loomed over me, appearing to wait patiently. The set of his jaw and the tenseness of his wide shoulders belied his emotions. He was just as nervous as I was. I remembered what Rebecca had mentioned earlier. This sexy creature was a virgin. My breathing slowed and my heart drummed in my chest.

I inhaled, grasping for any thread of control I had left. "You should probably leave," I muttered, probably not sounding too convincing.

Rowan's eyes widened and then returned to normal. He braced his arm on the door by placing his hand next to my head. Butterflies took flight in my stomach and I held my breath as he leaned in. His mouth was only inches from mine and his warm breath tickled my nose.

With the lift of a brow, he asked, "Do you want me to leave, Katie?"

He was dangerously close. The tension between us was so thick, I could have strummed it with my finger. His gaze dropped, watching the rise and fall of the swell of my breasts. Then his nose flared and I knew he was inhaling my scent.

I can only describe the look on his face as need. I felt the same way, so I understood perfectly. After our long separation from teenagers to young adults, it wasn't surprising that we wanted each other as badly as we did.

The nagging voice inside my head that told me to say yes was silenced by the chills racing through me. I was lost in a tide of awakening feelings. All inner warnings to be reasonable or cautious were swept aside.

Shaking my head, unable to say a word, I lifted my hands and cupped his face, bringing his mouth to mine. When our lips touched, my mind went blank. I swayed into him, loving the prickles from his stubble on my cheek. Our kiss deepened as I slid my tongue into his mouth. He sighed into me and hugged me close. Kissing Rowan was the most natural thing in the world. I closed my eyes and his fingers brushed my face as he nuzzled my neck, inhaling deeply. In a sudden movement, he scooped me up into his arms and crossed the kitchen to the staircase. As if my weight was nothing to him, he took the steps two at a time until he reached the upstairs foyer.

I wiggled my arm from his embrace and pointed at the door that led into my bedroom. He didn't hesitate, crossing the space and pushing the door open with his booted toe. His hand pressed to my racing heart as he lowered me onto the bed. He paused just long enough to kiss the tip of my nose and then he stepped back. With slow, deliberate movements, he unbuttoned his shirt.

My breath came out in a hoarse noise when he

dropped the shirt onto the floor. His chest was chiseled like a Greek statue. The muscles bulged and his stomach was firm and toned. The room was bathed in soft moonlight but I still noticed how pale his chest was, reminding me that, as an Amish man, he never took off his shirt unless bathing or ... making love.

When his fingers moved to his pants, a shiver sliced through me. He still wasn't hurrying and a breathy groan erupted from my throat. The skin beneath my robe pricked with cool tingles and frustration bubbled up that he was taking his sweet time stepping out of his pants. When I finally gazed at Rowan in all of his naked glory, hot blood coursed through my veins.

The bed creaked as he climbed slowly over me, pinning me to the mattress. My pulse fluttered when he paused, looking down with a hungry passion that nearly took my breath away. It scared me a little, too. I'd tried so hard to talk myself out of getting sucked in by any strong feelings toward this man, but here I was, almost lost to them.

"I'm in love with you, Katie. I have been since that moment we kissed in the barn all those years ago," he admitted in a low, raspy voice.

His body was long, lean, and strong, and just out of reach as he hovered there, his arms supporting him above me. Reaching out, I felt the pounding of his heart beneath my palms. He wanted to hear me say the same words, but I couldn't. That little quivering voice of reason at the back of my mind wouldn't let me tell him how deep my feelings were for him.

Instead, I swallowed the knot that had formed in my throat and wished my eyes weren't wet with tears. I said softly, "Please, I want you to make love to me."

Rowan scrunched his brows and pulled back a little. "Are you sure?"

"Oh, yes."

He hesitated. "I can't do this if you don't feel love for me. I won't do that to either of us."

Desperate chills washed over me and I arched against him. Reaching up, I traced the defined lines of his shoulder then down his arm. He shivered beneath my touch.

I can still stop this from happening. I stared up at his passion-filled eyes. There was a glint there and I saw the tear. In that instant, all of my stubbornness vanished. Rowan needed me, and I needed him. We could work the Amish thing out later. I couldn't deny my feelings for this man any longer.

"I do love you. I do," I whispered, wrapping my arms around his neck and pulling him down. His hands tugged at the tie at my waist until it came loose. Without breaking off the kiss, his fingers played over my breasts until my nipples became hard, delicious buds. I moaned into his mouth, digging my fingers into his back. He trailed soft kisses along my jawline and down my neck. When his mouth closed over my nipple and sucked, a jolt I'd never experienced before rocked my core. I felt his hard bulge pressing into my thigh and I writhed against him with a desperation I'd never known before. Rowan might have been a virgin, but his body knew what to do. He shifted his weight and, positioning his knee, he spread my legs apart before settling in between them. I wrapped my legs up over his hips and he grasped my waist. His mouth returned to mine and his hand traveled over the curve of my hip. Cupping my butt, he rubbed himself against me. Just when I thought I might die from the pulsing between my legs, I guided Rowan inside of me. He grunted, resting his forehead against mine, and then he began to move in a controlled rhythm. He was holding back. I laced my fingers behind his head, almost losing my mind.

"Are you sure?" he asked again.

"Don't stop," I begged, not recognizing the rough voice that escaped my own lips.

His pace quickened and I grasped him tightly. Our heavy breaths mingled and sweat trickled in between the exquisite friction of our rubbing skin. A roaring filled my head, like a storm crashing over a forest. The sweet sensations rocking through me were new and incredible. I ached for Rowan, with a pulsing need so great I couldn't contain it. His body locked around mine and he groaned, coming just an instant before I did in an explosion of hot flames.

We stayed locked together as lingering waves of pleasure shuddered through me. After a few quiet moments, our breathing returned to normal. My mind was still thick in a blissful haze when he buried his face in the crook of my neck, kissing me lovingly there.

So this was what I had been missing out on with Dillon? I smiled into the pillow and enjoyed the heavy feeling of our warm limbs tangled together.

I was feeling sleepy when Rowan rose up on his elbow and looked down at me.

"Are you all right?" he asked.

I touched his lips, tracing them with my finger. "I've never experienced anything like that before."

He tilted his head, his eyes dark pools of passion. Absently, it seemed, his hand roamed the curve of my waist. Then he smiled too. "I didn't hurt you?"

I raised an eyebrow at him. "Definitely not. It was the most amazing experience of my life."

"Really?" he teased. His hand found my breast. Incredibly, little puffs of pleasure spread out from my nipple.

I tried to ignore the fresh stirrings, but it was difficult. "How do you feel?"

I shivered from the new rush of tingles and Rowan must have mistaken the movement for me being cold. He reached down and grasped the comforter, pulling it up over us. He didn't disengage his body at all, only arranging my head to rest on the bulge of his arm.

He took a long, deep breath. "It was beautiful ... and frightening."

"Why frightening?" I asked.

He scrunched his mouth, lost for words. I waited, twirling my fingers over his taut stomach.

"I don't want to ever let you go, Katie. You belong to me now, but I worry that you don't feel the same way."

My belly lurched at his tentative words. I felt the same way; he was mine now ... and it scared the crap out of me.

"What can we do? You're Amish and I'm not. It's a problem, you know?"

Rowan lifted his head, suddenly very awake and serious. "That doesn't matter, Katie. If we love each other, we can make it work."

"But how?"

"I'll go English, if I must. We'll get married. We can have our own horse farm, or perhaps we can stay on here to help your mother, if that's what you want."

Queasiness stirred in my belly at the thought of marriage. I definitely wasn't ready for that.

"Don't you think talking about marriage is kind of rushing it? We've known each other for a long time, but we've only been back together for a few days."

"You could be pregnant," Rowan stated with no hint of humor.

I sat up, pulling the covers with me. Thudding my head back on the bedboard, I sighed loudly. I was hoping to avoid this conversation for a while. Nope. I couldn't be so lucky.

"I'm not going to get pregnant."

"How can you know that?" He scowled.

I took a calming breath. "Because I'm on birth control pills."

His face registered first understanding, and then shock. "I see."

Seeing the immediate hurt flare across his features, I touched his hand. "I've been on the pill since I was nineteen. I used to have really bad menstrual cramps. My doctor gave me a prescription, saying it would help, and it did." His face relaxed and I knew I had to be completely honest with him. He was talking about marriage, after all. I didn't want to be with a man that I had to lie to or be made to feel ashamed. "Rowan." It felt like I had a stone in my gut. "You aren't the first guy I've been with. There was one other; we only dated a few months when I was eighteen. It was a stupid teenage thing. I didn't even like him that much."

Rowan swallowed and looked straight ahead. "Why would you give yourself to him, then?"

I crossed my arms. "I don't know." I shrugged. "I

guess it was peer pressure, in a way. I waited until I was eighteen, while all my friends had already lost their virginities. I never thought I'd experience love, so I just wanted to get it over with."

He turned back and relaxed his features. "Why would you think such a thing?" he demanded.

This was the really hard part. My lips trembled and I sucked in a wet breath. Rowan clasped his hands around mine, pulling me closer. *Be brave*, I told myself. *Be honest.*

"When you left that day, after Daddy told you to, I thought you'd contact me somehow. I waited for a long time, just hoping to see you again." My voice rose higher, even though I tried to keep it steady. "You lived right up the road and yet I never heard from you again."

Stupid tears streaked down my cheeks and I quickly tried to wipe them away, but Rowan caught my hand and held it. He bent forward and kissed the tears, pressing his cheek to mine.

"I'm so sorry, sweet Katie. I never meant to hurt you. I took what your father said seriously and I couldn't disobey his wishes. I want you to know that every single day since then, I've thought about you. You were always on my mind and it drove me crazy sometimes."

"Why didn't you at least call, then?" I pulled back just enough to see the pain in his eyes.

"It was more complicated than that." He rubbed his thumb into my shoulder and continued to hold my hand firmly with his other one. "I was young and what I felt for you that day when we first kissed scared me. I thought it was a sin to experience the rush of passion that happened when I held you in my arms."

I sniffed. "Because I'm English?"

He let out a big sigh. "That was most of it, sure."

"Then what's changed?" I dared to ask.

"Everything. I'm a grown man now. I always figured that eventually all the crazy daydreams about you would end and I'd find an Amish woman to spend my life with." When I tensed, he brought my hand to his lips and kissed it. "That never happened and then you came along again and all those feelings flared back to life, only stronger than ever. I realize what I want now."

"You don't care if I was with someone else, before you?"

He gave a light shake of his head. His eyes were locked on mine. "It's my fault. If I'd only disobeyed your father and come back for you, it never would have happened. Can you ever forgive me?"

The light shining in Rowan's eyes made a hiccup of breath surge into my lungs. Was he really asking for my forgiveness?

I stared, dumbfounded. "You don't have to apologize. My father kept us apart."

Rowan wrapped me in a bear hug. I clung to him. He was strong and solid against me and I marveled at the feeling of rightness that washed over me. When his mouth drifted back to mine, I kissed him back. There wasn't the same urgency from before. It was a low boil that made my toes tingle. With the quickness of a diving hawk, he swooshed in and lifted me onto his lap, facing him. I straddled his waist, sinking against him. The primitive grunt that erupted from his throat made my pulse race.

"I want you all over again," he mumbled into my hair. "How is that possible?"

I was almost lost to the throbbing sensations in my core, when I pulled back, causing him to growl at my sudden departure.

"There's something else I need to tell you." Rowan's brows shot up and his features tightened. "It's nothing bad – at least not awful." He settled back into the pillows. He still looked worried, but he continued to squeeze my hips, kneading them with his fingers as he listened. "It's about my mom and your dad." I hesitated and his spine snapped straighter. "They knew each other when they were young ... like, teenagers."

My words didn't have the impact I was expecting. Rowan nodded and gave me a small smile.

"I know. Just the other day, Father told me about it, but it was the bishop who filled in the important details that Father had left out."

"Details?"

"Believe it or not, my father was in love with your mother—"

My eyes bulged and I interrupted, "No, he broke up with her. He told her it was because she was English."

He shook his head, clasping his hands behind my back. "That was probably what he told your mother, but it wasn't how he really felt. Your father found out about the two of them and he sought out Elijah Graber. He's the bishop now but at the time he was just a minister." I waved my hand, encouraging him to get on with what he had to say. "Father told Elijah he was leaving the Amish to be with your mother, and he went so far as to tell my grandfather, too. Of course, my grandfather was upset by the news." He paused and caught his breath. "He died later that night from a heart attack."

"Are you kidding?" It wasn't really a question, more of an oh-my-God moment.

"My father was eaten up with guilt about it, thinking his decision to leave the Amish to be with your mother was the cause of his father's death."

"He really was going to leave the Amish?" My jaw dropped.

He nodded solemnly. "After his father died, being the only son, he felt it was his place to stay with the Amish, and carry on our family name in the community. Apparently, he went to your father, letting him know he wouldn't be seeking your mother's hand any longer.

That's why your father felt he owed mine a favor and hired me on at the ranch."

Everything swirled around in my head, like a car wreck, as the pieces of the puzzle dropped into place. It sure did explain a lot.

"Poor Momma had no idea your father was ever even considering leaving the Amish to be with her. She hoped something like that would happen, but he was mean to her about it, making her feel that their entire relationship meant nothing to him."

"Oh, it meant a lot. I think he's never forgotten about her, either, but he's been a good husband to my mother, trying to go on without looking back."

"That's so tragic. They were in love but they couldn't be together."

"They chose not to be together, just like we're choosing to *be* together. Your father and mother were meant to marry and have you—"

"And your parents were destined to have a family with you and Rebecca and your little brother."

"There's something you should know, while we're telling all of our secrets." He held my attention in a sympathetic gaze. "Do you remember when I told you that I saw your father at the Willoby horse sale a few months ago?" He waited until I nodded. "He had his arm around another woman. She was fairly young and they even kissed."

I took a steadying breath and closed my eyes for a second. "I know all about her. That's why the mortgage and back taxes hadn't been paid. Daddy was spending all his money on her. She was in his truck with him when the accident occurred. She was seriously injured, but survived. That's how we found out all about his cheating ways."

Rowan bent forward and rested his forehead on mine. "I don't want to talk about our folks anymore."

Neither did I. I wouldn't dwell on the past or dredge up what Daddy had done in my mind. Right now, I would think only about Rowan and his glorious muscled arms, holding me tightly. I couldn't stop my lips from curling up as anticipation rushed blood through my veins. "Do you really think it's our choice ... about having a relationship?"

"You might not want to rush things, and that's all right, but you belong to me. There's no turning back now."

I breathed happily into his mouth. At that moment, I knew it was true.

Rowan and I were meant to be together. Always.

TWENTY-TWO

Rowan

"I have to feed the horses," Katie reminded me, trying to push the shower curtain aside.

I gently pulled her back against my chest. She didn't struggle at all so I figured she was fine with another kiss and her lips parted, responding eagerly. Each kiss seemed to mean more than the last. The long, low sigh into my mouth urged me on. My hands roamed over her back and bottom, still wet from the shower. I kissed my way down her neck and breasts, squeezing her tight, pink nipple between my fingertips. She cried out when my tongue found the nipple and began to suck. It was impossible to imagine that I felt the hot ache in my groin again, but I did.

"Rowan, honey, please," she begged in a rushed voice, scratchy with passion.

The need burning inside of me grew quickly. She raised her leg, wrapping it around my waist. I knelt a little and thrust inside of her a few seconds later, filling her. I tried to stay in control, but when she groaned, I came undone. Coherent thoughts disappeared. There was only me and Katie, locked together in wondrous lovemaking. Her muscles clamped over my hard length. I stroked deeper and faster until she gasped loudly, and a powerful wave of feeling surged through me. I shuddered inside of her, hugging her close. Never had I felt so bound to a person.

"You're spoiling me, Rowan," she said in a trembling whisper. "I'm sure going to miss you tomorrow morning."

Her words shook me. I leaned back and looked at my love. Her skin was flushed pink and her nipples were still raised. My gaze traveled the curve of her hip and over her flat stomach, then down her slender legs to her small feet. When I looked back up, she was watching me with those bright blue eyes. Up until a few hours ago, I'd never seen a naked woman and now it seemed I knew every lovely bend, nook, and turn of her body. Never once had I felt uncomfortable or unsure. With Katie, it all came naturally. Looking at her now, naked and still dripping wet, she seemed so vulnerable. The drumming of my heart quieted, and an overwhelming sense of wanting to protect her rushed through me. The fact that I wouldn't be with her the following morning dampened the exhilaration of a moment before and heavy wariness returned.

I grabbed the oversized blue towel and wrapped her in it. She smiled up playfully at me. "Are you finished then?"

Slanting a sideways look her way, I wrapped another towel around my waist. "Don't do that, Katie. I'll be forced to pick you up and carry you right back to bed."

Her eyes widened and she dodged my arm, sprinting out of the bathroom and straight up to her chest of drawers. I fought my grin as I settled onto the edge of the bed and watched her dress. Somehow, she managed to pull her panties up under the towel without revealing anything to me. I became mildly disgruntled when she turned her back and clipped on her bra in the same way.

"It'll have to be bacon and scrambled eggs for breakfast. I don't think I have anything in the cupboard to make pancakes," she mused, tugging on her jeans.

I glanced at my clothes in a heap on the floor and winced. I wanted to share breakfast time with Katie, more than anything – but in all truth, it would be impossible. I shook my head and reached for my pants and followed Katie's example.

"I wish I could stay, I really do, but I have to go home. My folks are probably worried sick that I didn't sleep in my own bed last night. By now, they'll surely be aware that I never returned home."

Katie pulled a warm-looking tan sweater over a tan top and paused her fidgeting fingers on the belt buckle at her waist. She frowned, her eyes troubled. "They'll be angry, won't they?"

"I imagine they will be," I said, buttoning up my shirt.

She lowered her head. "Are you afraid to go back there?" She gestured at herself with both hands and added, "Under the circumstances?"

My heart filled with love for the feisty little redhead staring back at me with a seductive yet still wary expression. I sat on the bed again, spread my legs, and lifted my arms. Swelling my heart even more, she lurched forward into my embrace. I held her tightly, stroking her damp hair and rubbing my cheek against hers.

"I'm not afraid at all. The only fear I have right now is that you won't marry me when the time comes."

She pursed her lips. "I told you last night that I love you and I want to spend the rest of my life with you. Will you be content with that for a little while? Just until I get used to the whole marriage idea?"

Smiling faintly, I nodded. "I'll wait forever for you, Katie."

"What about your parents, though. Will they kick you out?"

I inhaled deeply and blew out slowly. "It's on my mind. Honestly, I don't know what they'll do. I'm praying they'll understand and give us their blessing. It would be nice if I could live on with them for a little while longer." I couldn't resist raising my brows expectantly. "At least until you officially say yes and we can begin our lives together," I baited her.

She found her smile again. "It won't be long, and if the worst happens you know you can always stay here."

I looked down at her hands that I was rubbing between mine. "It might come to that, I dare say. But after our discussion last night, you know how I feel about us living together before we're married." I raised my gaze. "It's not fair to you or your mother."

I had to hide my grin at her pouting face.

"What difference does it make if we're having all this sex?" she asked.

She had a point and I realized that because she hadn't been raised Amish or in a strict, religious home, she'd never really understand my feelings on the matter. So I tried to come up with something that she would get. "I have to hold back a little, Katie. Otherwise, you'll never want to become my wife."

She laughed and then quickly became serious, nestling deeper into my arms. "I want that more than anything. I do. We have to take a little time to figure it out. I would feel very irresponsible if we rushed into it. Wouldn't you?"

"No, Katie. I'd marry you this afternoon if you'd say yes. I'm dreading being away from you tonight."

She peppered my face with quick kisses and then found my mouth. Just when our kiss became passionate, she broke it off.

"Depending on what your parents do, you might be back here sooner than you think," she teased.

I groaned. Katie was only joking, not fully appreciating the impact of what I was doing on my family. "We'll see." I stood up, still holding on to her. "Regardless of what happens, I'll come by tonight to see you and work with the horses."

"Maybe I'll whip something up in the kitchen for our dinner. No promises, and I can't guarantee it will be edible."

I grunted out my laughter. "I'm sure anything you create will be wonderful." I pulled her against my chest and we stood there in a long, silent embrace. Neither one of us wanted to say goodbye. "I have been known to do some cooking, so when we're properly married you won't have to worry about always preparing the meals. I'll do my share."

She squeezed me harder. "An Amish guy who cooks. Could I get any luckier?"

Letting go of Katie and swinging my leg into the saddle was the hardest thing I'd ever done. As difficult as it was to part ways, I had to be strong for her. We'd face many challenges in the coming days.

With Katie looking up at me with hope brightening her eyes, I knew one thing for certain: No matter what my parents said, she belonged to me, and I'd never let her go.

The scents of breakfast still hung in the air when I entered the kitchen. Father and Mother sat at the table, steam rising from the mugs of coffee in front of each of them. I shut the door behind me and turned to face them. Dark splotches and puffiness greeted me when Mother finally looked up. Father continued to stare at his coffee mug.

"I apologize for being gone all night," I said with haste, wanting to get the damn conversation over with as quickly as possible.

"Where were you?" Mother asked in a hushed voice.

I swallowed, said a prayer in my head for God to give me strength, and strode across the room. I sat in the nearest chair. "I was with Katie Porter. She's my girl now. We're going to get married someday."

Mother's hand went to her neck and she gasped. Father grunted, shaking his head with wary movements.

Father snorted and finally looked at me. "At least you're honest about it. I guess our little talk didn't help at all."

"Maybe not in the way you intended, Da. But it did help." I breathed deeply. "I love Katie. I have since we were teenagers. I know it sounds irrational. We're going to court properly for a time, and not rush into anything."

Mother's head dropped and Father's eyes closed. It would have been better if they'd reacted with yelling and screaming than this almost indifference.

"What is it about our way of life that doesn't suit you, son?" Mother asked quietly.

"That's not the reason I'm leaving. I love Katie and I'll do anything to be with her – even leave the Amish. You both must understand that, even a little." My gaze settled on Father. He, of all people, should know how I felt. He was stubbornly silent. "This is very difficult for me, too," I assured them. "It's terrifying to leave my family and friends, and the only life I've ever known."

"Why is it our children must go English instead of the other way around?" Mother turned to me. Her eyes were wet with tears, and my stomach clenched.

I answered her softly. "It's just easier this way. If I go English, I won't be losing any freedoms, I'll be gaining them. It would be much harder on Katie to become

Amish. A person not born into our ways, especially a woman, would be miserable. It wouldn't be fair to her."

"What about us? What about your job?" Mother's voice rose to a sharper pitch.

"I hope you'll allow me to visit and even if I can't work on the same building crew, there are many other foremen who would appreciate my skills and hire me. My passion is training horses and perhaps, with Katie by my side, we can build a horse business."

"So you have it all worked out, eh?" Father said with barely controlled sarcasm.

"It's a start." I rose from the table. "I'm twenty-two years old. I've never been a problem to either of you and have always worked hard, whether it was here on the farm, or on the crew." My eyes settled on Mother. "You began pestering me about finding a good woman and settling down. I wish you'd be happy that I've found that woman and wish me well."

Mother looked away, shaking her head.

"You know it doesn't work that way, son," Father said. "You will be shunned. It's inevitable. How much contact we have with you will depend on many things and that will be decided in the future. You can stay for a few weeks until you get your plans in order but I won't have you influencing your younger brother. I forbid you to mention any of this to him or anyone else. Until the day you leave, we will not speak of it again."

Father's words pierced my head and my vision fogged. It was all very reasonable – even generous – under the circumstances. He'd given up without a fight or even an intervention with the bishop to change my mind. It felt unreal.

My vision cleared. Why hadn't he mentioned Rebecca, only Nathaniel?

I swallowed an uncomfortable knot down. "Where's Rebecca?"

It was Mother who answered me. "She's gone."

She held out a piece of neatly folded paper and I took it.

Dear Ma & Da,

For some of us, it's not an easy thing to be Amish. I've tried for a long time to fit into the community and make you proud. I'm sorry I failed so miserably. I can't stay here any longer. I have dreams of my own and if I don't chase after them, I'll go crazy. I hope in time you can forgive me.

I love you.

Rebecca

I'd barely looked up when Mother handed me a sealed envelope. I searched her tear-filled eyes.

"Go on. Open it," Mother urged.

I broke the seal and began reading.

Rowan,

Today, for the first time in ages, I felt like my old self. The freedom of horseback riding with Katie awakened my spirit, and I know what I have to do to find the peace and happiness I've longed for. I hope you'll be brave enough to go out on your own too – Katie is definitely worth it. It will be hard, as you already know. Our parents raised us to only feel whole if we're a part of the community, but I think we'll both find our own way on the outside.

I leave here today with the quiet thrill that anything is possible, and surely it is now. Don't worry, I won't fall into the same trap as Lucinda. I'll be smarter than that.

Someday, when you least expect it, I'll return. Until then, stay strong and don't let anyone talk you out of following your heart.

Your loving sister,

Rebecca

"Rebecca is gone, Rowan. She left sometime in the night," Father confirmed.

I dropped my head back and closed my eyes, trying to remember everything she said when we'd last talked the day before.

"She didn't say anything to me about running away," I said – to myself or them, I wasn't sure. It was a partial lie. A few days ago, I had been planning to help her do just that. "Are you going after her?"

Mother wiped her eyes dry with her handkerchief, swallowed the last of coffee, and pushed her chair back. Her face was all stony resolve. "No, son. We'll let her be. That's what she wants, and it's best for Nathaniel. If our prayers are answered, at least one of our children will remain Amish. He'll inherit this farm and the vegetable business. He's already shown interest in young Sarah Yoder. We'll give him our blessing to begin courting her when he turns sixteen." Her voice shook a little and she paused, collecting herself. She searched Father's eyes and he gave her curt nod. "At least you came to us, and didn't leave us with a note and our tears. For that, I'll forgive you for your choice. We'll follow the rules of shunning. You won't be allowed to take meals with us any longer but we won't cut you from our lives completely." She stepped forward and gave me a quick hug and a pat on the back. "I'll pray that you find happiness with this English girl."

She left without another word, and the kitchen felt suddenly lonely and cold.

Father was preparing to leave and I stopped him. "Wait. Will you completely shut me out?"

He cocked his head and his eyes gleamed. "I'm disappointed in you, son. I don't think you realize the pain you're causing your mother. I won't counsel you on this." He let out a heavy sigh and lowered his voice. He looked over his shoulder to make sure Mother wasn't near before he spoke. "I wasn't completely honest with you the other night. When I faced the same choice, I picked the safest, easiest path. Partly from guilt and in part because I didn't have the courage to take a leap of faith. I made peace with my decision years ago, but sometimes"—his mouth thinned into a tight line—"I wonder what might have been. I suppose it's best for you to experience it firsthand and then decide whether you have regrets."

"So you're all right with me leaving the Amish to be with Katie?"

Father's smile was sad. "No, son. I'll never be all right with it. It's something you must do. You're a man and can choose your own path."

When I was alone in the kitchen, I sank into the chair, dropping my face into my hands. I couldn't stop the tears from falling and my body rocked softly with my weeping. Rebecca was gone and I'd taken the first step of leaving my family.

My tears weren't only for the sadness of everything lost. They were also for the joy of my sweet Katie, and the life we'd soon share together.

TWENTY-THREE

Katie

December 2020

McGovern horse sale, Indiana

I climbed over the fence into the pen where Rowan and Remington were. The palomino colt's golden coat gleamed richly and his mane and tale were as white as snow. The horse's muscles bulged beneath the saddle. He was tense and alert, watching the other horses in the sale barn with keen interest.

"How's he doing?" I asked, barely able to control my rising excitement.

"So far, so good," Rowan said from Remington's back.

He reached down and offered his hand, and I squeezed it. "The other horses sold higher than I could have wished for." I patted Remington's taut neck. "Momma and I don't have to worry about selling the ranch. There's already enough profit to pay the back taxes and mortgage payments. You did a wonderful job with the horses, Rowan. Without you, none of this would have been possible."

His mouth lifted into a wicked smile, making my cheeks grow warm. "I aim to please. You know that."

I recognized the husky growl in his voice. It promised kisses and other things, later on in the dark.

Seven weeks had passed since Rowan had come back to work at the ranch, training the horses. Our romance had been a whirlwind of horseback rides, dinner dates, and movies since then. Once Rowan had told his parents that he was going English, he'd fully embraced his choice, and the first thing he'd wanted to do was see a movie at the theatre. He'd also grown quite fond of streaming services on the smart TV and we'd binge-watched several shows into the wee hours of the mornings. He'd even gotten his driver's permit and once I had finally replaced my crushed pickup truck with a new one, the driving lessons had begun.

Sometimes, I'd catch him staring off into space and I feared that maybe he was having second thoughts or missed being Amish. Then he'd turn to me, as if he'd read my mind, and tell me how much he loved me. I still fretted that he'd regret it someday, but until then I'd enjoy every minute with this handsome man.

"You know what I'm doing with my cut of the profits?" Rowan lifted an eyebrow and grinned.

"I think I have a clue," I muttered, resting my chin on his knee.

He'd already told me several times that he'd spend some of the money on buying his own used truck and the rest on a ring. The Amish didn't do rings, either engagement or wedding, so buying one seemed to be a huge thrill for him. I'd made the decision, quietly in my own mind, that when he presented the ring and popped the question, I'd say yes. There never was any real doubt in my mind, but I wanted to take a little time before I agreed, for Rowan's sake as much as mine. He was the one giving up his entire culture and way of life for me. He needed time to make sure he really wanted to go through with it. After weeks of spending all our free time together, he'd done the unimaginable and moved in with me. I'd been shocked when he went to Momma and asked her how she felt about it. Of course she'd been very supportive of the idea. I wasn't a girl anymore and she was well aware of how often Rowan was already sneaking into my room at night. I wasn't naïve about her intentions, either. Momma loved the idea of having Rowan being a part of the family ranch business. She had been almost giddy with plans to improve the facility if we managed to make enough profit from the horse sales to pay off our debts.

Falling asleep each night with Rowan's arms wrapped tightly around me and waking to his loving kisses in the mornings had sealed the deal for me. I never felt as alive as I did when I was with him and I was ready to fully commit. I could have kicked myself for being so stubborn and cautious, but those days were over.

"I'm going to miss this ornery beast." He rubbed the top of Remington's rump, and the colt pinned his ears back, making Rowan chuckle.

"We have three palomino foals at their momma's sides. One of them can be yours if you want," I offered. A lump formed in my throat. I hated selling any of the horses but it was a part of the business I'd become used to.

"Are you giving me a horse as a wedding gift?" He flashed a brilliant smile.

I slapped his calf, hearing Remington's number called out over the speaker system. "Time to go," I said.

Rowan caught my hand and pulled me back against his leg. He bent down, close to my face. "I love you, Katie Porter."

I smiled up at him. "I love you, Rowan Coblentz."

His lips touched mine, ever so softly, and then he sat

up and winked at me. My legs were reduced to jelly at his touch and he knew it.

I climbed back over the fence and jogged along the corridor into the sales arena. I saw Momma's hand shoot up from the railing where she was holding a spot for me. Squeezing in between her and a barrel-chested cowboy, I hugged Momma's arm.

"We've had a good day, Katie," Momma said.

"Yes, it's a miracle how high the colts have sold for."

"It's all because of Rowan's hard work." She winked. "You picked a good one."

I jabbed her side with my elbow. Momma was feeling good, both physically and emotionally, and that made my heart sing.

I'd come to terms with what Daddy had done and now that Momma was on the mend, I found I could forgive him. Holding on to a grudge like that wasn't the way I wanted to begin the rest of my life, anyway.

"Katie!"

The arena was standing room only and when I heard my name shouted out, it took me a few long seconds to search the crowded seats. When I spotted Tessa, I waved back. She was sandwiched between Peggy and Jessica on her left and Dillon on her right. Things hadn't worked out with her and Jimmy, and a few weeks ago, I'd suggested Tessa give Dillon a try. It was a little weird for her at first and she had initially refused, but my masterful matchmaking skills paid off when she reluctantly agreed to date my ex. Sparks had flown on day one and, unlike the bad-boy type of guys she usually went out with, Dillon was ready for an intense relationship from day one. They'd been inseparable ever since.

I caught a glimpse of someone further up in the stands that made me do a double take and I craned my neck to see into the crowd better. I had to wait for several large men wearing cowboy hats and carrying bags of popcorn to cross my line of vision before I found what I was looking for.

An exuberant smile spread across Rebecca's face. She lifted her hand and I returned the gesture, taking a good look at her. Her long hair was pulled back into a ponytail and she wore a shiny tan coat with blue jeans. Her pink boots stuck out, resting on the guardrail in front of her. She looked healthier than before. Her cheeks were filled out and the hollows beneath her eyes were gone. She appeared to be sitting with a group of young women. She leaned over and whispered something into one of their ears. Rebecca laughed and pointed at me. I rolled my eyes, wondering what she'd said and then dismissed the thought. It didn't matter. Rebecca was here and she looked really good, but most of all, she appeared to be happy. I wasn't really surprised. I guessed it could have gone either way with Rebecca. She was either going to crash and burn or soar to the highest mountain peak. That girl would never do anything in a small or insignificant way.

I couldn't wait to tell Rowan. Perhaps the little bit of homesickness for the Amish I'd sensed in him lately could be alleviated if he got his sister back. I could only hope so, anyway.

The trilling voice of the auctioneer brought my attention back to the sale's pen. Hands shot up and the price soared. Rowan took Remington into a smooth canter, stopped the horse, and backed him up several strides at high speed. Then he was off again in the opposite direction. Remington moved willingly for Rowan. After weeks of hard work, the horse finally trusted the man.

As the numbers rattled off and the bids went even higher, I felt a pang of regret about selling the beautiful golden horse. If he hadn't thrown me, injuring my arm, I would never have had to hire Rowan to train him and the other colts. The picture of Rowan, leaning casually against Remington's stall door, his hand on the horse's face while he appraised me with those wolfish eyes on that very first day flashed before my eyes. I sniffed and let the vision go.

"Going once ... going twice..."

Momma's hand shot up and I nearly fainted dead away.

"What are you doing?" I hissed.

Momma didn't look at me. She was too intent on the auctioneer and making sure she got the last bid.

The auctioneer awarded the sale to Momma and I stared dumbfounded at her.

"That horse is too fine to let go. We'll show him for a couple of years and then put him up for stud. After the day we've had, we can easily afford to pay the auction commission on Remington. It's good business, Katie," she said.

"We could have used his sale price to give us a cushion on the farm's expenses going forward." I made a weak attempt to argue what Momma had just shockingly done.

She shook her head, resting her hand on my shoulder. "When I went to Nashville to visit Ida back in October, she insisted on helping us get our feet back on the ground. Her aunt died and left her a sizeable inheritance so it wasn't a hardship on her. Her generosity, combined with the sale proceeds from the other horses, puts us over what we need to stay in business and keep our ranch."

"But you're still going to have to pay the sale's commission on him."

She shrugged and waved her hand like she was swatting away a pesky nat. "It's an insignificant amount for getting to keep that horse." She raised her chin at

Rowan, who was leaving the sale ring, but stared wide-eyed over his shoulder. "That one will be mighty happy to still have Remy in the family, don't you think?"

I put my arm around Momma. What a perfect day it had turned out to be.

TWENTY-FOUR

Katie

"Like I already told you when I looked up, she was
gone." I stared at Rowan.

He ran his hand through his hair and his brows drew
together. We had just unloaded Remington from the
trailer and led him out to his paddock. Rowan's obvious
relief at being able to keep his favorite palomino had
quickly turned to wariness when I'd informed him that
I'd seen Rebecca at the sale. He'd immediately returned
to the sale ring and searched the seating area for his
sister. She hadn't been anywhere in sight, though.

The sun was setting on the horizon and a spattering
of clouds shone orange. The temperature had risen
during the day but now that dusk was near, a chilly wind
brushed my face. I zipped up my jacket and put my

hands in my pockets, watching Remington take a good long roll before he jumped up and galloped across the field.

Rowan's boots crunched in the fallen leaves as he paced back and forth. I leaned back against the fence and frowned at him.

He stopped. "Why wouldn't she want to see me?"

Out of the corner of my eye, I spotted the glimmering streak of a shooting star. I silently wished that Rowan would find peace about Rebecca.

"Are you really that surprised? Rebecca likes to play mind games. I haven't known her very long but that was one of the first things I noticed about her. She enjoys making everyone around her unhinged. Maybe it's her way of dealing with her own insecurities. I don't know."

"How did she look? Do you think she's all right?" he asked in rapid succession.

I rolled my eyes, digging the toe of my boot deeper into the leaves. I had already gone over every detail of her appearance, and even the women that were with her. Because I loved him so much and pitied what his crazy sister was doing to him, I indulged his questions – again. "She was in great shape. She's gained some weight, which she desperately needed. She was dressed normally and smiling and laughing. Wherever she's been, it's done her a world of good for her."

He rubbed his palms together. "Do you think she'll ever come back?"

I tilted my head. Rowan loved his sister, of course, but there was a lot more going on in his head. His need to see her was heightened because of his own separation from the rest of the family. Rebecca was English now, like him. They could actually have a normal relationship, but for whatever reason, she was still avoiding him.

"I'm sure she will. At a time of her choosing, she'll flutter back into your life and probably bring chaos along with her," I said.

"You said she seemed to being doing well—" Rowan began.

I silenced him with my finger pressed to his lips. "It's just the way she is, Rowan. She might change and settle down happily for a while, but she has a restless spirit." I grunted. "Her life will never be dull anyway."

Rowan's cellphone rang and he looked at me with wide eyes, probably thinking that it was Rebecca calling. Then he recognized the number and his face paled.

"Answer it," I urged.

He brought the phone to his ear. "Hello," he said carefully. "Yes, that works. We'll be over in a few minutes." He hung up and raised his gaze. "It was Father. He wants us to come over right away."

"Us?" My voice wavered and my heart banged in my chest.

"Yes, he mentioned you by name."

"Are you ready for this?" I asked, more worried that I was the one who couldn't handle meeting his parents.

He nodded and a slight smile spread on his lips. "I am."

TWENTY-FIVE

Rowan

O nce we were seated at the kitchen table, the awkwardness of the situation settled over me. I wore denim jeans and a gray sweatshirt. I hadn't considered how wearing English clothes around my folks would feel so completely wrong. Having Katie sitting close beside me, her hand clasped in mine, only made things stranger. I couldn't help twirling my thumb against her palm, trying to absorb some of her calmness.

The ticking of the mantel clock was the only sound until Father's voice cut the air. "Samuel Miller was at the sale today. He said the Porters's horses sold well, bringing high prices all around."

I nodded, loosening up a tad. "They sure did. The market for well-trained, good-looking quarter horses is excellent right now."

Mother cleared her throat and my gaze drifted to her. "You haven't introduced your girlfriend, son. Let's not be rude."

Her scolding tone made me sit up. A shot of adrenaline coursed through my veins and I tried not to smile. "I'm sorry. Forgive me." I turned to Katie. She sat quietly and, if I had to guess, she was trying not to be noticed. "This is Katie Porter. Katie, these are my folks, my mother, Rachel, and my father, James."

Mother extended her hand over the tabletop. "It's nice to meet you," she said.

Katie shook her hand, smiling. The relieved look on her beautiful face nearly took my breath away. Then she shook Father's hand, too.

"Would you all like some iced tea? I made it fresh this morning," Mother asked, standing up and heading to the refrigerator.

"Yes, please," Katie chirped.

A moment later Mother had deposited a plate of freshly baked cookies in front of Katie and was pouring her tea into the glass in front of her.

The tension had eased, and I was finally able to breathe normally again. I took one of the snickerdoodle cookies and bit into it. Mother could be a difficult woman at times but I had no complaints about her baking skills.

"Have you heard from your sister?" Father asked.

Mother paused, the pitcher of tea frozen in her hands.

"I haven't talked to her, but Katie saw her today at the sale," I answered truthfully.

All eyes turned to Katie. She appeared to have a difficult time swallowing a bite of cookie. After taking a sip of her tea, she said, "It was from a distance, but it was definitely her. She looked happy."

Mother nodded and set the pitcher down, returning to her seat.

"I'm glad to hear it. I was worried about her," Mother admitted. "I pray every night that she'll find her way back to us."

I spoke up. "I don't think Rebecca will return to the Amish, Ma."

She looked up at me. Her eyes were glassy. "Oh, I know that. My hope is that she will come for a visit now and then ... so that we can sleep at night, knowing she's safe."

It was then that I noticed the puffy lines beneath her eyes. I reached over and she quickly took my hand, squeezing it.

"This will be the first holiday season without my daughter and my oldest son," she said quietly.

"It's not the time, Rachel," Father said briskly.

"We'd love to come over for a visit on Christmas, if you'll have us?" Katie piped up cheerfully.

Mother rested her gaze on my girlfriend. "Child, it's not our way. Hasn't Rowan explained things to you?"

Katie licked her lips and glanced over at me. I dropped my gaze. Katie would never truly understand, but I did. I knew what it meant to be Amish, and the lengths my parents would go to in order to ensure the survival of that way of life.

When Katie folded her hands on the table and leaned forward, I bit my lip, sucking in a quiet, quick breath. I knew that determined look on her face very well.

"You might think that it's okay to treat Rowan this way because it's how you've always done things but it's not acceptable." I didn't try to silence her. She was an English woman, after all. She would speak her mind. "Rowan is your son. He loves you both so very much – and his little brother. It's not fair for you to cut him out of your lives, just because of some agreement you have with the other members of your community."

Father leaned back, sighing loudly, and Mother just stared at Katie, a shadow of hurt crossing her face. This wasn't a new argument for them to hear. It came up almost every year with one family or another. They didn't like it, but in their minds it was the only way to preserve the community.

"Katie, it's fine with me," I assured her. "I knew what would happen when I left, and I have no regrets in doing so."

"But—"

Father cut Katie off. "We invited you here to

introduce ourselves and make peace with our new relationship with our son." Father swiveled in his chair, looking at me. "Rowan, when Nathaniel comes of age, I'll be giving him the bottom acres I'd promised to you. You worked hard over the years toward that goal and I thought it only fitting that your mother and I should pay you back for your contribution." He reached inside his coat pocket and pulled out an envelope. I believe it's a fair amount of compensation."

"Father, you don't have to do this—"

"Yes, I do. You will need your own money to bring into a marriage and you earned it." He pushed the envelope across the table.

I reluctantly took it. It was thick and heavier than I thought it would be but I didn't open it. "Thank you. I really appreciate it." I avoided looking at Katie when I added, "We'll send you an invitation to the wedding."

Mother patted my hand and rose from her seat. "You know the rules, son. I wish you and Katie a happy union, with many children."

I chanced a look at Katie and saw her become noticeably pinker at Mother's words.

"I have some laundry to fold." Mother gave me a quick hug, forced a smile for Katie, and then left the room.

"Stay in touch, son." Father tipped his hat to Katie and followed in Mother's footsteps.

Katie let out a long breath, picked up a few cookies from the plate, and grinned at me, shrugging. I held out my arm. She came to me without hesitation and nuzzled against me.

"That went well, I guess," she said with a soft snort.

I clutched her tightly to my side. Giving up being Amish and distancing myself from my family was hard but it was all worth it when I looked into Katie's eyes. She was the most precious thing in the world to me and I thanked God every day for answering my prayers and bringing her back into my life.

"At least they're talking to me. That's a start."

We were about to climb into Katie's truck when Nathaniel called out.

"Hold on!"

He ran full speed from the barn, stopping in front of us with a heaving chest. He shoved his hand at Katie. "I'm Nat, Rowan's brother. We haven't met yet."

Katie burst forward and grabbed Nathaniel into a bear hug. My little brother's eyes bulged in alarm. When Katie released him, he quickly took a few steps backwards. "You're awfully friendly," he said.

I threw my arm around Katie's shoulder. "You have no idea," I teased Nathaniel. Katie popped me in the ribs with a jab and I grunted. She was stronger than she looked.

"I get it that there are rules and all but I want you to

know, you're always welcome to come over to the ranch," Katie told Nathaniel. "I'd like to get to know you."

Father's voice boomed from the back doorway of the house. "Nathaniel, you're needed in the house."

Nathaniel rolled his eyes. "I got to go."

"I know. Be good," I said.

He began to turn and then pivoted back, giving me a quick half-hug, before he spun away.

As we drove down the driveway, I glanced back over my shoulder at the white farmhouse on the hill. It was a bittersweet moment and Katie must have read my mind. She leaned over and planted a kiss on my cheek, and I knew everything would be all right.

TWENTY-SIX

Katie

S now fell gently, blanketing the field in a soft, white glow. I pulled my knit beanie down lower to cover my cold ears and breathed in the icy air. Dusty pranced beneath me, steam shooting from her nostrils every time she snorted.

It was Christmas Eve and the countryside was appropriately silent; creaking leather and the crunching of horses' hooves in the packed snow were the only sounds. Dull light filtered through the gray clouds, making it seem much later in the day than it actually was.

"Race you," Rowan breathed out in a puff of steam.

Remington's muscles gathered as he danced in place. His neck bowed so tightly, I could see dozens of veins popping out from his golden fur. I flashed Rowan a sideways smile and bumped Dusty into action.

The horses took off with a spray of snow. My heavy coat and layered clothing made me feel uncoordinated in the saddle. Squeezing with my thighs the best I could, I leaned over, using Dusty's neck to block some of the frozen air that was striking my face. Tears pooled in my eyes and it was difficult to see clearly as we swept by the skeletal trees along the hedgerow.

Remington pounded through the snow with the force of a tank, but with Rowan's extra weight, he wasn't able to pull away. We were neck and neck when we reached the wooded trail and our knees bumped together hard when we closed the distance to fit side by side. Rowan glanced over, not slowing, and I caught the look of admiration in his eyes. In the deep place in my belly, heat spread, warming my insides. I was in real trouble if a mere glance from him could reduce me to liquid jelly. Maybe he was using that against me to win the damn race.

I struggled to inhale a full breath, settled even lower in the saddle, and bumped Dusty hard with my heels. She responded, shooting forward. She passed by Remington and I shouted out an indistinguishable whoop when we crossed into the big field. Sitting straight up, I gripped the reins and tugged back, trying to get the exuberant mare back under control. Looking over my shoulder, I saw that Rowan was already slowing down, Remington responding perfectly to his trained hands.

Of course, one of the reasons Dusty always won our races was because she was a bit mad. I felt like I was streaking along on the back of the wild wind when I opened her up. She wasn't completely tame, and we both knew it. All of a sudden, she swerved hard to the right and threw a buck. The combined movements were too much for me to adjust to. My butt rose from the saddle and when I came back down, she jerked sideways, leaving only empty air beneath me. The ground came crashing up at a speed I wasn't expecting. I sank into the snow as it flew everywhere.

When I opened my eyes, I found myself buried in snow and staring up at the quickly moving clouds. My face burned from the wet cold and I could feel the icy tentacles seeping through my pants.

In the distance, I heard my name shouted out. I didn't move a muscle. I'd hit the ground enough in my life to know that the wobbly feeling of my limbs and the heavy pressure on my chest would soon pass. Then would come the sharp pain.

Because I'd tunneled into the snow when I'd fallen into it, there was an icy tomb surrounding me. I couldn't see anything except snow and sky but I heard the approaching hooves. I closed my eyes, taking deeper breaths to settle my pounding heart. Warm moisture touched my face and I popped them open again. Dusty sniffed and then snorted on me. I pushed her muzzle away and wiped my face with the back of my glove.

"Sure, now you feel bad, huh?" I muttered, struggling into a sitting position.

Rowan jumped from Remington's back and slid up against me. "Are you okay?" He cupped my face with his hands and pressed his warm cheek against my freezing one.

"I think I'll live. I feel like I'm a cat when I ride Dusty. One of these days I'm going to run out of lives," I joked, pressing even closer to Rowan after I noticed how warm his skin felt.

"Don't kid like that. You had me scared half to death. When you surged ahead like that, I was afraid this might happen."

"You're the one who wanted to race."

"You couldn't just let me win for a change, could you?" His words were harsh, but his tone was light.

I shook my head. I didn't like to lose – especially to Rowan.

The clouds parted and a spray of sunlight rained down on us. I tilted my head back and basked in the warmth of the rays on my face.

Rowan went to work, squeezing my legs and bending my knees. "Any pain yet?"

"Mostly my butt." I laughed from relief that nothing seemed to be broken and from happiness that I had indeed beaten Rowan once again.

Rowan sat back and joined me. We lounged in the snow for several minutes, rocking with laughter. The two horses stood idly nearby, watching us with pricked ears as if we were nuts.

Rowan suddenly became serious, glancing around. "I think this is the exact same spot you came off all those years ago during the storm."

I was hoping he wouldn't have noticed. "Yep, this is my special place," I snorted, grinning back at him.

"Really?" He took a deep breath and reached into his inside coat pocket, pulling something out that he kept hidden in his hand. "Then it's the perfect place for this."

My heart went crazy and I had a difficult time catching a breath. *Is he about to do what I think?*

"My dear, sweet Katie. I know I told you I'd wait, but it's Christmas Eve and I can't put this off any longer." He swallowed and a tear glistened in the corner of his eye as he opened the small black box and held it out to me. "I love you more than I can properly describe. There can be no other woman at my side, only you. Will you spend the rest of your life with me, Katie? Will you be my wife?"

My heart lurched and I choked back tears. It was appropriate that we would find ourselves here, in the same spot that he'd come to my rescue so many years ago. Because it was at that moment, back when we were teenagers in the pouring rain, that I'd first felt the twinge of love for this handsome horseman. Sure, he was Amish back then but he'd left that world to be with me. Deep down, he'd always be Amish at heart and that was okay. All the doubts of rushing things slipped away as I gazed into his dark hope-filled eyes.

I nodded excitedly. "I love you ... and yes, I'll be your wife."

Rowan pulled my mitten off and quickly slipped the ring onto my finger. The diamond was huge and sparkling.

"Rowan, how did you afford this?" I looked up in shock.

His lips curled up. "My parents gave me twenty thousand dollars in that envelope. I was waiting for the right time to tell you."

My jaw dropped. "Your dad was serious about paying you back, wasn't he?"

Rowan still knelt beside me, balancing on the balls of his feet. "I believe he felt bad about how things turned out. That bottom land is worth a hell of a lot more than the money and he wanted to make things as right as he possibly could." His smile wavered and he stared past me. "He might have felt guilty too about what he did to your mother. Either way, I was able to buy this ring and have enough extra to put a down payment on building our own home."

"At the ranch?" I asked, staring at him with wide eyes.

"If your mother is all right with it, of course," he agreed.

"She'll be so happy," I mumbled, sinking closer to Rowan. "We're going to have so much fun."

His brilliant smile took my breath away. "Every day, for the rest of our lives."

When Rowan's mouth closed over mine, I forgot all about the cold snow and my sore backside. It was just him and me, like it was always meant to be.

Acknowledgments

A big thank you to my amazing agent, Sarah Hershman, who sees endless possibilities in everything and is always willing to listen to and act on my crazy ideas.

Many thanks go out to Heather Miller for her stellar proofreading skills and willingness to read anything I send her way.

I want to give a huge shout out of thanks to Charlotte Ledger and One More Chapter for taking a chance on an Amish romance. I'm thrilled to work with their team in creating this heartwarming forbidden love story.

As always, much appreciation and love to my husband, Jay, and my five wonderful children; Luke, Cole, Lily, Owen, and Cora, for all their continued support and encouragement.

Special thanks to Lindsey Michels, my future

daughter-in-law, for taking some fabulous author pictures.

The seasons in the sleepy Amish community I live in are measured by the planting and harvesting of crops, the spring and autumn schoolhouse benefit dinners, and the smell of wood smoke in the air during wintertime. I'm forever thankful that I found this place of buggies, open fields and honest, hardworking people, and for the inspiration it gives me for my writing.

ONE MORE CHAPTER

One More Chapter is an
award-winning global
division of HarperCollins.

Sign up to our newsletter to get our
latest eBook deals and stay up to date
with our weekly Book Club!
<u>Subscribe here.</u>

Meet the team at
<u>www.onemorechapter.com</u>

Follow us!
 <u>@OneMoreChapter_</u>
 <u>@OneMoreChapter</u>
 <u>@onemorechapterhc</u>

Do you write unputdownable fiction?
We love to hear from new voices.
Find out how to submit your novel at
<u>www.onemorechapter.com/submissions</u>